Just Like Old Times

Amastasia,
Keep it spicy!
~ Chi Chi

Just Like Old Times

Chichima Cherry

Write and Vibe Publishing
Cleveland

Published 2022
Printed in the United States of America
ISBN: 978-1-953430-10-6 (pbk)
ISBN: 978-1-953430-11-3 (ebook)

For information, address:
Write and Vibe Publishing
3675 Warrensville Center Road
P.O. Box 201372
Cleveland, OH 44120
cori@writeandvibe.com

This book is dedicated to my family and all the readers who journeyed with me through these last ten years.

AUTHOR'S NOTE

Hey Readers!

I can't begin to explain what this book means to me. In 2011, I self-published my first fictional novel, *The Red in Her EYES*. Now, just slightly over 10 years later, I'm releasing the rewrite of it, *Just Like Old Times.*

I chose the title, *Just Like Old Times,* because it encapsulates the return of Tristyn and Trey's story, their return to a relationship, and the return of me writing fiction. I thank all of you for hanging in there as I journeyed through how to be an author, what to write, and how to do it to the best of my abilities.

If you read *The Red in Her EYES,* I hope you enjoy Tristyn and Trey's story even more than before. You'll also meet the rest of The Daltons, Chelsea, Derrick, Onyx, Phoenix, and Xavier. Each of them will have their own book and their own unique love story so watch out for their releases.

Cheers to the next 10 years! I wish you peace, prosperity, and joy.

~ChiChi
Writing real life with a scoop of spice.

PLAYLIST

Music is such an integral part of our lives and if you remember, I connect all my fiction titles to music. Each chapter's title is the name of a song that helps establish a deeper connection to what I've written. Listen to the *Just Like Old Times* Playlist once, all the time, while reading, or during a long drive. Enjoy!

Scan Below for Apple Music Playlist or go directly to
https://music.apple.com/us/playlist/just-like-old-times/pl.u-PDb40J4uepP19gY

Scan Below for Spotify Playlist or go directly to
https://open.spotify.com/playlist/0wHiiQxK6A0pZwp-N6oTjkX?si=deb7cf5dd35c466d

Scan Below for YouTube Playlist or go directly to
https://youtube.com/playlist?list=PLuikT_5-mlbwbT3l42myrd-n96O-H-JnRI

PROLOGUE

HEARTBREAK ANNIVERSARY

5 YEARS AGO

They were in an intense game of one-on-one. First brother to eleven won bragging rights and fifty bucks. Trey, the oldest by four years, won the first game, and Derrick won the second. The small hoop hanging off the front of the garage taunted Trey to shoot the shot and Derrick, leading by two points with nine on the board, was talking crap by the mile. Where Trey had the advantage in weight and experience, Derrick was an inch taller and had quickly learned to resort to other tactics, such as tricks, to win. As far as Trey was concerned, they were on equal footing.

They'd grown up challenging each other in the driveway of their Mama's house, an older two-level home in Cleveland that sat close to the border of the inner city. With as many games as they had played over the years, Trey should've been used to Derrick's trash talking but he was off his game, and it wasn't because of the sweat clouding his vision.

Derrick stole the basketball and did an easy layup. "This nigga weak!"

Trey punched his palm. He was getting too old to play midday summer games.

"Watch it," Mama warned from her seat in the backyard next to their baby sister, Chelsea, who officially, was no longer a baby at eighteen years of age. The slot of grass they sat on was about three times bigger than the one car garage next to it. Over the years it had served a million purposes. From senior photo backdrops to campout sessions, the backyard had housed it all.

"Sorry, Mama," Derrick called out, a wide smirk on his face pointed toward Trey.

Trey mouthed, shut the hell up, causing Derrick to laugh aloud. Mama sat far enough away for him to say it with his chest, but he didn't want the same kind of problems that Derrick loved to bring out.

Derrick bounced the ball to Trey and prepared for the next play. "What you thinking about big bro?"

Per his usual, Derrick was being a jerk. He was well aware that every year, Trey's mood negatively shifted on this date. It was clockwork and Trey hated it. He debated throwing the ball at Derrick's face but didn't want to spark Mama's wrath.

Derrick taunted, "Can't focus? Someone on your mind? Got you playing like an eight-year-old."

Trey continued bouncing the ball, waiting for the moment to cross Derrick. He saw an opening to the hoop, but Derrick stopped him in his tracks by bumping him.

Unable to help himself, Derrick laughed. "I see you still can't shake your ex just like you can't shake me."

Trey's nostrils flared. Yeah, he needed to throw the ball into Derrick's nose. Instead, he stepped back and shot the ball in. When Derrick turned from watching the ball go into the net, Trey said, "Shake that."

Derrick bounced the ball, positioning himself for the win. "I ain't had trouble shaking you the whole game, old man." He crossed the ball in between his legs, giving Trey the opportunity to steal it and make a shot. Tie game.

"Oooo," Derrick howled and caught the ball as it fell. "I see you're back, but you got me fucked up if you think I'm 'bout to let you win."

"Keep talking and showing off and you'll lose again. That's how I took your last shot. Come on." Trey motioned for Derrick to come closer, patting his hands on his thighs.

Derrick's back went ramrod straight. Still dribbling, he stared down the driveway. "No way. How did Tristyn know you were in town?"

Trey just about tripped over his feet to turn around and look. Derrick laughed all the way to the hoop and made the winning shot. When Trey slow turned his head toward him, Derrick shook his head and tapped his forehead with his finger. "Gotta stay focused.

Can't believe you fell for that." When he walked past, he patted Trey's chest and said, "I hope you heal from this sickness."

Had it been any other day, Trey wouldn't have fallen into Derrick's trap. But it wasn't any other day. This day served as a reminder of the life he'd left behind. A life of what ifs that had plagued him ever since. "What sickness?"

"You're lovesick. Get over it and find a new girl. It's been five years, right?"

"I don't know, man." Trey rested his tired hands on his hips, breathing heavily. "And I have a girl. Tristyn. Remember?"

"Tristyn, huh?"

Trey squeezed the bridge of his nose and grimaced. Any. Other. Day. "Eve! I meant Eve, you know that." He'd only slipped up because they were talking about Tristyn. He hoped. He prayed. His lovely girlfriend's name was Eve and thank God she wasn't there to hear him call her by his ex's name. He would never hear the end of that.

"Whatever you say. Where is Eve, by the way? Didn't bring her home with you, huh? Per usual. You would've brought Tristyn."

Trey watched as Derrick jogged to put the basketball back into the garage. He loved his brother but every time he brought up Tristyn, Trey wanted to wrap his hands around his neck a little bit tighter. "Let it go. It was a long time ago," Trey yelled after him.

"You do the same." Derrick yelled back before play squeezing sweat from his basketball shorts onto Chelsea and Mama.

Trey followed behind to join his family. Derrick noticed him approaching and tapped their mama on her shoulder. "Mama, you saw who won?"

Eyes closed but shielded by sunglasses, she replied, "I'm assuming it was you based on your question."

"You already know," Derrick gloated. He beat his chest like a gorilla. At six-foot-three and twenty years old, Derrick's body still hadn't filled into his frame. Often teased by family and friends about his weight, or lack thereof, he grew up with an enhanced sense of humor, usually teasing others before they could tease him. Mama assured him that what he lacked in weight, he made up for in looks.

His even skin tone, a copper color in the summer, was what women always complimented him on first, right before they asked about his hair. Mama swore there was Indian on their late father's side, but they had yet to confirm it. Their only indication was the dark black wavy hair that grew from their scalp. Currently, Trey chose to keep his short, but Derrick's was longer. He much preferred sitting between his female friend's legs while they braided it.

"You distracted me," Trey pointed at Derrick. "We can go another three rounds right now and I bet I'll beat your ass."

"You two have one more time to curse at my house before I kick you out." Mama turned toward Chelsea. "I'm so happy you're not competitive like these two."

"Me too." Chelsea hushed her brothers. "We only have ten more minutes left in our meditation. Go away and let us have our moment." She took a deep breath and tossed her locs over her shoulder, straightening her back.

Derrick's head snapped toward her. "Go away? My dear, little sister, you should know that we don't go away. Who do you think you're talking to?"

"Yeah, she trippin' bruh," Trey smirked. Behind Chelsea, he saw Derrick grab the hose. He cleared his throat. "I think you should take back what you said."

Chelsea opened one eye, looked at Trey, and shushed him before closing it again.

"Don't say I didn't warn you." He laughed a well needed laugh before jogging across the yard.

Chelsea and Mama's high-pitched screams lit up the backyard as they scrambled to their feet with Derrick chasing behind.

1

Must Be

CURRENT DAY
Tristyn paused mid stride and rolled her eyes. Her four-inch red pump in her hand waved frantically in the air. "Let it go? You want me to let it go?"

Georgia's monotone came through the speakerphone louder than the words that followed. "Yes, you are losing your mind. And honestly, I don't care to hear about your dream anymore."

Tristyn sat down in her office chair to continue the motion of replacing her heels with her sneakers. Not wanting to disturb her coworkers outside of her office, she harshly whispered, "Maybe I could let it go if I didn't see his sexy face in my dreams every night. Every night. Do you know what that's doing to me? It's like I can literally hear his voice and feel his breath on my neck."

Georgia's voice remained unchanged. "Deep breaths, girl. This too, shall pass."

Tristyn's head dropped to her hands atop her desk. "I know, I know. I mean, but do I even want it to pass? Maybe this is a sign. I do kind of mi..."

Interrupting, Georgia bluntly reminded her, "Don't even say you miss him. Did you forget about all the nights you spent crying on my shoulder? He abruptly left you and your relationship without so much as a goodbye."

Tristyn's shoulders sagged and air whisked from her mouth. "I haven't. Back then I swore if I ever saw him again, I'd kill him. Now, here I am pining away all because of a stupid dream. And may I add, he looked good as hell in it."

Without missing a beat, Georgia spoke an unsubtle reminder. "He was an ass then and he's probably still one. And you have a boyfriend."

Responding with a deep breath, Tristyn spun around in her chair to gaze out her twentieth-floor window that overlooked downtown Cleveland and Lake Erie. Looking at the lake had calmed her nerves on many stressful days when quarterly reports and customers were blowing up her email. She wished for more of that inner peace now. "You're right. It was just a dream. It meant nothing."

"Umm hmm, make sure you remember that. I'm not tryna lose another thirty minutes of my life listening to you talk about ex-lover man, Trey."

"I really can't stand you." The two shared a laugh as they'd been doing since they wore pigtails. As youngsters, their mothers had gone into business together to open a local floral shop that grew to be a staple in their community. Opening a business as a double minority had been difficult but the long hours spent building their business was all the time Tristyn and Georgia needed to become best friends.

"All right sis, I gotta go. I was off five minutes ago and if I don't hurry, I'll miss my train."

"Train? I thought you said, and I quote, "Public transportation? Tristyn does not do commoner things." End quote."

A smirk arose in the corner of Tristyn's mouth. "First of all, I was joking, kind of. Second, I don't know, I needed a change of pace."

"Third, you're a liar. What are you saving for?"

Excitement sent goosebumps up Tristyn's arms. "Well, I'm eyeing this white leather Prada backpack. It is sooo beautiful. It has this really thin strap that runs down the middle and it's the perfect size for my laptop, lunch, and the rest of my work stuff." Her eyes scanned her office to make sure she wasn't leaving anything behind and stopped at the clock on her desk. "Shoot, I gotta go. Talk to you later." Without waiting for a response, she disconnected the call, grabbed her backpack, and jogged out of her office.

Seconds later a text from Georgia came in. *Prada bag on train with commoners. 10 out of 10 would not recommend*

"We gotta go, like, now."

"I know." Aiyanna, work bestie and fellow train rider, slammed her laptop shut and stuffed it in her bag when she noticed Tristyn walking toward her. "We really need to stop cutting it so close. Think we'll miss it?"

Years prior, as the only black woman holding a role in upper management at their accounting and finance firm, Tristyn sat on the hiring panel with greying white men, trying to convince them that Aiyanna, the more qualified black woman, was the best fit. Tristyn had advocated for Aiyanna until she was blue in the face. Whether the men gave in because they were tired of Tristyn protesting, or because they finally noticed Aiyanna's qualities, the bottom line was that they finally agreed. Since then, the two had been inseparable. From her frustrations with her boyfriend, Jacob, to her dreams of Trey, Aiyanna knew of it all.

Tristyn chuckled as they rode the elevator to ground level. "I'm pretty sure we will. I don't know why we always rush to catch it anyway when the next one comes fifteen minutes later."

Aiyanna's face lit up. "The rush is exhilarating. Who wants to waste time waiting anyway? Time is precious and limited. We could die tomorrow."

"That's very morbid."

Aiyanna shrugged. "It's true."

"So, you're saying we should run to catch our train because we could die tomorrow? That makes plenty of sense." Tristyn raised one eyebrow.

Aiyanna's petite finger pointed at Tristyn. "Don't start with me. All I'm saying is that we need to seize the day."

They rushed across the street and half-ran, half-walked to their train stop, dodging other commuters on their way home, with Tristyn doing her best to keep up with Aiyanna's miniature strides. Once their ears perked up on the last call to board, they ran the rest of the way, making it right before the doors closed. Struggling to catch her breath, she slid into the seat next to Aiyanna. "I can't keep running to this train. How much longer until retirement?"

Aiyanna adjusted her backpack on her lap. "Too long."

"We need rich boyfriends."

"One of us already has one."

Tristyn conveniently ignored Aiyanna's comment. Her boyfriend of...her fingers touched the soft patch of skin underneath her earlobe. How could she not know how long they had been dating? Had it been a year yet? Well, it was at least six months. A very long six months of unclimactic dating. Unclimactic kisses. Unclimactic looks across the room. The relationship wasn't bad, but it certainly wasn't great.

Jacob made millions from investing in start-up businesses. She didn't know how many companies he co-owned, but she assumed it was at least fifteen. As a silent owner in most of them, he spent his days travelling the world and scouting out other potential investments. While away, he often sent her authentic gifts from places like Dubai or Paris. Recently, he requested she accompany him to New Zealand but she avoided by saying she had forgotten to apply for her passport. To her calculations, he should be home any day.

Any other woman would have run her over to have a man like Jacob, but something was missing. That spark, that connection—where the hell was it? Only one man, ever, made her feel cozy on the outside and alive on the inside. Although he shattered her heart, her mind had the audacity to keep reminding her that good times also existed in those days.

"Stop thinking about Trey." Aiyanna had a special skill on reading people's minds exactly when they didn't want to be read.

Tristyn's mouth dropped open. "Get out of my head."

Aiyanna chuckled and stuffed her phone back in her bag. "You make it so easy."

"Ugh!" Tristyn dropped her head onto her backpack sitting on her lap. "I'll be back to not thinking about him by the time we come back to work on Monday. I just need a weekend to clear my head." She lifted her head and scrunched her eyebrows. "Think it's too late for me to be an Instagram model?"

Aiyanna laughed out loud. "Your mind be all over the place. While I'm glad you're gonna get your shit together over the weekend, you're too good to limit yourself to modeling on IG. But with your body, you could be an IG model at any age and get flewed out by all the professional sports players."

A deep chuckle stood out amongst the crowd, causing Tristyn to turn her head. "Speaking of sports players, that man surely played sports back in the day and he'd be perfect for you."

Aiyanna turned toward where Tristyn's gaze had landed. The man's clean-shaven face with a hint of a mustache clung to his cell phone just as his dark blue suit clung to his body. Ebony skin paired nicely with his neat locs that hung in a ponytail down to the middle of his back.

"He is all of my type," Aiyanna licked her lips. As if he felt her watching, he turned, and they locked eyes.

"He definitely is. Why is it that the littlest people like the biggest ones?"

"Should I go over?" Aiyanna's fingers twiddled in the air and she answered her own question. "Yes, I should. You know I wanna get married."

"It'll happen, just be patient."

The most meticulous of her friends, Aiyanna had a plan for everything and always executed to perfection, which was why she was the best at keeping and executing the budget at work. The only goal that hadn't panned out as expected was her plan to be married with kids by age twenty-seven. Now she was approaching thirty and becoming more anxious by the day.

"Do you want me to go over and introduce you?"

"No, no," Aiyanna hushed Tristyn. "I'm not ready. Or maybe I am."

Aiyanna laughed and then looked back to where the man had stood. "Too late now anyway, he's gone."

"Damn," Aiyanna slumped in her seat.

"Gotta be quicker than that." Tristyn's ears piped up to the train conductor's announcement. "And your stop is next. I'll see you next week."

Aiyanna jumped up with her backpack. "See you Monday. And you better be back to normal."

"I will be." Five stops later, Tristyn swung her backpack onto her shoulder and prepared to exit. A light breeze lifted her naturally long, thick, and straight, dark brown hair as she shielded her eyes with her favorite pair of Dolce and Gabbana sunglasses. Shoulders back, stomach in, head high, just as she had learned in etiquette school, she glided over to her ice blue convertible, allowing her hips to sway.

Yes, a little sunshine and a ride in her convertible were all she needed to get her mind right. Anticipation of revving her engine coursed through her body. There was no comparable thrill to the g-force she encountered when the light turned green and she sped away.

She sat with her door open while waiting for the top to completely retract. Her foot dangled out the door keeping beat to the music already thumping through her speakers. On her driver side, a matte black luxury pickup truck with tinted windows pulled into the parking spot next to her. She tried to ignore it, quickly feeling irritated that the truck pulled directly next to her instead of any of the other empty spaces.

"Tristyn Miller."

No! She froze. That voice. She knew that voice and she would always know that voice. Her dreams had played that voice repeatedly. Either it was truly him or her brain was insisting on making her feel like she had utterly lost her mind. She turned toward the truck slowly, preparing herself for the mirage of a moment.

Trey sat in the driver's seat of the truck and Derrick, on the passenger side. Yeah, she wouldn't be clearing her mind this weekend. Her throat threatened to close as the only person to ever render her speechless stared back at her with a wide smile.

When she realized they were climbing out the truck, she mustered a throaty, "Hi," and retrieved her composure.

Derrick was the first to emerge, running the few steps to give her a hug that left her feet hanging in the air.

"Wow! How's that for a hello?" She giggled when he put her down. "Hey Derrick! How have you been?" He replied but for the life of her she couldn't recall what he'd said. Out the corner of her eye she noticed Trey licking his lips, his bright grey eyes roaming seductively over her body, causing her heart to ache for him. Damn that dream. Damn trying to save up money to buy a purse she didn't need.

Trey walked over and wrapped his arms around her, his hands lingering dangerously near her lower back. Before she could pull away, he kissed her cheek. Holding her waist, he smiled. "It's so good to see you, Tristyn. You look good."

Tristyn felt her cheeks flush at the compliment. "Thank you and same to you." Both men had always been good looking, but age had been good to them. Trey, looking eerily similar to how he looked in her dream, wore olive-green chino shorts, a navy blue and white horizontal striped shirt, and plain untied white sneakers. His hair, more black than brown, lay perfectly against his head, his wide shoulders showed he lifted weights on a regular basis, and his light golden skin now held a couple freckles around his nose. Derrick took a more casual approach. His grey sweat shorts with a hanging drawstring that made his grey eyes stand out, accompanied a loose-fitting white shirt that stretched taut across his biceps.

She turned her attention toward Derrick to end the moment Trey seemed intent on developing. This could not happen. She needed to focus on something else. Anything else. "You look good too, Derrick. Looks like you finally put on some muscle."

"What!" Derrick laughed loudly and clapped his hands. "I haven't seen you in how many years and you're still teasing me about my weight?"

"It's a compliment, now. What'd you do, double your weight in muscle?"

"Something like that," he replied and then flexed his biceps, causing her to laugh and Trey to roll his eyes.

"No need for jealousy, big bro."

Trey shook his head but still smiled.

Tristyn tried keeping her voice steady but the struggle was real. Trey still hadn't taken his eyes off of her and her body was beginning to warm under his intense stare. "So umm, what else have you been up to?"

"Nothing much," Derrick answered. "Working as usual. Gotta make that money."

"What do you do now?"

A large smile took over his face. "I own a landscaping company and business is good. Really good."

She couldn't help but to return his contagious smile. "That's incredible, Derrick. Congratulations!"

"Thank you." A beat passed while Derrick scratched his nose, casually motioning for Trey to jump in.

"I'm good, too." Trey raised an eyebrow when Tristyn finally looked at him.

"I was going to ask but you didn't give me a chance."

He nodded and his eyes roamed her body once more. Suddenly, she felt self-conscious about her plain Jane work attire of a fitted black suit, white dress shirt, and her walking sneakers. Normally, she allowed her colorful personality to shine through her clothing but today, she had presented at a meeting and then had an interview.

"What about you? How have you been?" Trey stuffed his hands in his pockets and Tristyn was on her best behavior to keep her eyes from wandering south.

"No complaints," she responded after a deep breath. "I have a good job that I don't love but I also don't dislike. It pays the bills, you know? Umm, my family is healthy."

Trey's spine straightened and his voice rose an octave. "You have kids?"

"No, no kids. I'm single. I mean, I'm not single. I have a boyfriend but we don't have any kids. What I meant was that my parents are well. And I'm good, too. I wasn't saying that I have kids but I do want them...at some point."

Across from her, Derrick slow nodded and then raised his eyebrows.

Eager to change the subject she asked, "Did you move back to Cleveland?" but instantly regretted it, hoping she didn't seem too eager to know more about him even though she was. Had it gotten hotter outside?

Trey held her gaze. "No, I'm here for my family reunion."

Tristyn nodded.

"It's actually funny we're running into each other. I wasn't even supposed to be in town yet, but my mom asked me to come home early to help with the prep. Now, I'm really glad I did."

Derrick glanced at his brother and back to Tristyn. "You should come to the reunion. We could catch up. It's been too long since we all hung out."

Tristyn cocked her head and before she could stop herself, she said, "Through no fault of my own." A smirk crossed her face when Trey's hand flew to his chest.

"Ouch! I guess I deserved that."

They all laughed and Tristyn looked over to the side, stalling as another train went by. "When is it?"

Taking an unnecessary step closer, Trey responded. "It's Saturday, umm tomorrow, at one, and I'd really love for you to be there. Plus, Mama's been asking about you since I got here."

"I really doubt that."

"I swear, Princess." The endearment slipped right off his tongue, but he never bothered to correct it.

"He ain't lying," Derrick vouched. "That's the first thing Mama asked when Trey walked in. We were sitting on the sofa at her place and soon as Trey put his keys down, she asked how you were."

"Doesn't she know we haven't talked for years?" Tristyn asked, wondering how much Trey had told his mother about their breakup.

"Yeah, must be that motherly sense. Maybe she knew we'd run into each other."

"Maybe so." Tristyn's foot scooted around on the pavement. "I think I already have something planned but I'll check my calendar when I get home." Truthfully, she was free, all day, but she needed time to figure out her life. Their breakup had been hard, forcing her into counseling after too many rounds of Jack Daniels and key lime ice cream. She thought she was over him but after her dream she hadn't been able to stop daydreaming about what a second chance with him would be like. Not only was his mom intuiting things, but she seemed to be as well.

Trey put on his best pout. "You're turning us down?"

Derrick played along. "She said she doesn't like us, Trey."

"I did not say that." Tristyn laughed and crossed her arms. Before she could stop her betraying mouth, she offered her number. "Look, call or text me tomorrow. If I'm not busy I'll stop through for a bit."

While Tristyn and Trey exchanged numbers, Derrick turned his attention to her convertible. "Is this yours, Tristyn?"

Tristyn's face gleamed with pride. "Yeah, this is my baby."

"I've never been a fan of BMWs but this one is nice." He continued to ask questions about the year and how it drove.

As she spoke, she felt Trey's eyes burning a hole in her body. It wasn't long before he ventured close enough for her to smell his cologne. She eased away, not so subtly checking her watch.

"Before you go," Derrick held up his pointer finger. "Are you still friends with Georgia?"

"I am."

His face lit up. "You should bring her with you tomorrow."

"If I come," she corrected.

"If you come," he nodded.

Tristyn continued, "She'd also need to bring her husband. She's married now and they have eight-month-old twins. A boy and a girl."

Derrick's shoulders slumped, ever so slightly. He'd always loved Georgia, but she could never bring herself to see him as anything more than Trey's younger brother. He was always too skinny. Too young. Too little melanin. Too little money. If she could see him now, she would kick herself for not snagging him back then.

"They can all come," Trey suggested.

Derrick nodded but he mouthed to Tristyn, *Only Georgia*.

Tristyn giggled under her breath. "I'll let her know. I need to get going. And if I don't see you tomorrow, it was nice seeing you both."

On shaky legs, she stepped into Trey's outstretched arms to hug him goodbye. Like a gentleman, he kept it short but caught her hand when she pulled away. "I'd really enjoy seeing you again before I have to go back home. It would be nice to catch up." He winked at her and then returned to the driver side of his truck.

They watched as she jumped over the door and into her car, as she always did. Far enough away, she pulled into a grocery store parking lot and pulled out her cell.

"Hello."

"Georgia, you won't believe who I just ran into!" Tristyn practically screamed as she slammed her door shut, then apologetically rubbed the door handle. She needed to walk off the nervous energy.

"Trey."

Tristyn stopped pacing and looked at her phone. "How did you know?"

Coughing on her drink, Georgia cleared her throat. "I was just playing. You really just saw Trey?"

"Yes!"

"You gotta be kidding me. See, you done talked up that man. Is he back in Cleveland?"

"Nope. He's in town for a family reunion, which he invited me to."

"Shut the hell up. Are you going?"

"Haven't decided. But girl, the way Trey was looking. Just-oh my God. He looked so good."

"Sexy?" Georgia prodded.

"Scrumptious." Tristyn and Georgia laughed. "And his brother was looking fine too. Derrick's still in love with you and invited you to the cookout."

"Did you tell him I'm married with twins?"

"Yeah, Trey said they can come but Derrick said not to bring 'em." Tristyn slapped her thigh as she laughed.

"He is still crazy. I really can't believe you ran into Trey. I guess there was something to your dream. Maybe you should let bygones be bygones, see where fate is leading you. Enough time has passed for some major change to happen. Growing up. Maturing."

"Definitely."

Georgia moved the conversation along. "When is the reunion? Tomorrow?"

"Yeah. Maybe I'll swing by the mall to get an outfit before going home. Something simple. Some shorts. Some cute sandals."

"As if you don't have enough clothes already."

"Not for this kinda event. Me and my outfit will need to make him ask for forgiveness eight times before he pulls down my Fenty lace panties and sticks out his tongue."

"I swear you're always so damn horny. That's probably the only reason you wanna go to the reunion tomorrow."

"It's not the only reason, Georgia. It's one of the reasons. And there's nothing wrong with sex. Sex is relaxing and gives off plenty of feel-good hormones."

"That it is, but you don't need to go back down that road with Trey. Leave that part in the past."

"I'll think about it. Can you come with me to the reunion?"

"You know I can't."

"The twins."

"Exactly."

"Why can't Aaron watch them? It's the weekend and you haven't had one hour to yourself since they were born."

"Because I'm a mother now, Tristyn."

Before she made Georgia madder she stopped pushing and leaned against the door of her car, eyes grazing the parking lot. "Fuck!"

"What?"

"Trey just pulled in. Maybe he won't see me." Tristyn scrambled to jump back in her car but dropped her phone on the ground. "Damn it."

"What's happening? Did he see you?"

"No." In a haste, Tristyn picked her phone back up.

"Why does it matter if he sees you anyway? You literally just talked to him."

"He makes me nervous." Tristyn turned around just in time to see him exiting his truck. "He looks so good. Makes my legs shake." She casually looked over her shoulder. "Anndd he's coming over. Again. We saw each other five minutes ago. Why does he need to come over to talk again? I gotta go."

"Leave me on the line. I wanna hear it all."

"Fine," Tristyn hushed Georgia and held the phone next to her leg.

Time froze as Trey approached in slow motion. His long gait carrying him across the lot and his smile hardening her nipples.

"This is too much," she crossed her arms over her chest.

"Everything okay?" His smile reached her before his body.

Her legs quivered unapologetically, forcing her to take one long, deep breath. "Yeah, I just, my phone, I needed to call a make really quick, so I pulled over."

"Call a make?"

"Make a call. I meant to say I needed to make a call." Trey stood with his hands in his pockets staring at her, not saying a word. Tristyn shifted her weight to her other leg, praying for their awkward moment to end. "I was talking to Georgia."

"Had to tell her you saw me, huh?" The cocky smile she'd been used to seeing when they dated brightened his face.

A familiar level of comfort settled into Tristyn's body, but she kept quiet.

"I, uh," Trey's prominent Adam's Apple bobbed. "It was really good seeing you, Tristyn, and I hope to see you tomorrow."

"Yeah."

"Yeah," he drew his last word out as if he didn't want to walk away, but knew he had nothing more to add to the conversation. He cleared his throat. "I'm gonna run in and get this food for my mama. See you."

"Bye, Trey."

He waved as he briskly walked to join Derrick, waiting in front of the store.

Tristyn picked her phone back up. "Okay, he's gone."

"That couldn't have been more awkward. I felt the damn tension through the phone. You don't need to go to the reunion tomorrow because y'all gonna end up in bed and you'll be back in love with that man. You don't know how to separate anything."

"Whatever." Needing to change the subject, Tristyn said, "So I had my interview today." On a whim, she had applied for a new job after being matched with the position through an online hiring site. Things had moved fast and after interviewing earlier, a job offer was emailed almost immediately. Now, she was torn. Accepting the position meant leaving everything familiar for the unknown.

"That's right, you did have the interview today. With Northrup, right? How did it go?"

"They loved me and it seems to be an almost perfect fit. I don't know if I wanna take it though. I lived in Cleveland my whole life. I know Columbus is only two hours away, but I don't know anything about it."

"The key is that it's only two hours away. They're practically the same city so I doubt it would be a huge adjustment. It's not like you're moving to New York or Houston."

"You're right. I guess I just need to think it over more. It's such a good company and I could climb even faster there. They invited me to tour the company and meet the team I'd be over so I'm gonna do that. I told them I'd be there on Tuesday, and I plan to spend Monday touring Columbus. Just to see if I like it."

"That's a good idea."

"To top it off it comes with a pay increase. We're talking six figures."

"Six figures? Girl, you are blessed. Other than the location, what is your hesitation? Is it because of Jacob?"

"I don't know what's stopping me at this point. For sure, it isn't Jacob and I feel like that's what's bothering me. Like, why don't I care if I see him less often?"

"He's not the one, Tristyn. Stop trying to make him fit the position."

"But what if he is and I'm being too picky?"

"When your gut tells you to do or to not do something, listen to it."

Tristyn released a deep breath and then heard Trey's laugh. She turned to it and her heart skipped. With a paper bag in his grasp, he waved, but didn't stop.

"Look," Georgia continued, unaware of the pull Tristyn was receiving. "Do what's best for you without thinking of others. It's all about you. That's it and that's okay." Her twins started crying in the background. "Let me get off the phone before my titties start leaking."

Tristyn stared at the ground. "You're right. Thanks for the advice."

"As always. Bye."

She hung up and dialed Aiyanna's number. "Please tell me you're free tomorrow."

"I'm free tomorrow. What are we doing?"

"Going to Trey's family reunion."

"Come again? Run that back because I need an explanation. We just left each other."

"I know right. I saw him when I was getting off the train."

"Oh my God! This is fate. I knew you two were always going to end up together especially when you told me about your dreams."

"Slow down Disney Princess, this does not mean we're getting back together. It's just a reunion and I don't wanna go by myself."

"Of course, I'll be there. Does Trey have a brother?"

"He does but Derrick is madly in love with Georgia."

"Georgia is married."

"I know that and so does he."

"What about uncles or cousins?"

"Umm, he has a few cousins-Xavier, Onyx, and Phoenix, but I don't know if they'll be there and I don't know what they look like, I never met them."

"Works for me. Maybe I'll get lucky and all three will be there and I'll get my pick."

Tristyn bit the corner of her lip hoping she'd also get lucky. "Maybe."

2
ROUTINE

CURRENT DAY

Tristyn swung open the door to her condo, her robe showing ample amount of thigh. "You're late."

Aiyanna waltzed in, addressing Tristyn's lack of outfit. "Apparently not late enough. Why aren't you dressed?"

Tristyn's condo balanced nicely between high maintenance and cozy. The furniture, all white with brass accents, included mustard yellow pillows that spanned every piece of furniture that you could've sat on, had there not been so many pillows. The sectional she didn't spend enough time on, perfectly aligned underneath the deep blue accent wall filled with photos of exotic countries she wanted to travel to in the future.

Tristyn padded over her fluffy white carpet back to her bedroom to get dressed, Aiyanna following. "I need you to help me pick an outfit."

Aiyanna snorted. "Ain't no way I'm falling into that trap. Just pick something."

Tristyn placed her robe back in her closet and stood in front of her bed in her nightgown. Two outfits stared back at her crossed arms. The first, ripped white high waisted jeans and a multicolored camisole. The second, a red sleeveless bodysuit with white high waisted shorts and a white duster.

Aiyanna took a closer look at Tristyn's choices. "If it helps, it could get breezy tonight so the duster would be the better option."

"You're right," Tristyn agreed. "I'll go change and we can get outta here." The outfit, tight enough to proudly display her curves and make Trey salivate, but modest enough to avoid offending his mama, was perfect.

All she had to do was find her other Gucci sandal and they'd be ready to go. She flung discarded clothes from the floor to her hamper, huffing harder the longer it took to find it. After not finding it in her bedroom, she stomped to the living room and repeated the same task until she found it under the couch. She flew into the bathroom to put the finishing touches on her makeup and hair, smiling triumphantly as she passed Aiyanna.

"Tristyn," Aiyanna called through the bathroom door, "your condo is kinda disgusting. What's going on? I've never seen it like this." Clothes lay on the back of the couch, dishes filled the sink, and mismatched shoes were strewn all over.

Tristyn emerged from the attached bathroom. "I know," she shook her head. "It's *never* been like this. Work is taking up too much of my time. And when I'm not working, I'm either with you, Georgia and the babies, or cruising in my car, soaking up all the sun I can get. It won't be long before there's snow on the ground. You know how it is."

Aiyanna nodded. "Just making sure you're good. I'm gonna tidy up a bit while you finish getting ready."

Tristyn chuckled as Aiyanna went to work discarding junk mail and straightening pillows. "I forgot you hate dirt."

"As should everyone."

"I'll help as soon as I put on my lashes." Tristyn waved the lash in the air to dry the lash glue quicker. Once on, she stepped back, eyeing her face from various angles. Yes, Trey would beg for forgiveness as long as she held her ground. She leaned into the mirror and whispered, "You got this. Don't be nervous."

While loading the last plate into the dishwasher Tristyn's phone rang. She tapped her earbud to answer, half expecting Georgia to be on the other line. "Hello."

Loud music and laughter came through before the reply. "Hey, it's Trey. I wanted to see if you're coming. You told me to give you a call to make sure."

"Yep, I'm coming."

"Great. I'll be here waiting."

"Is it okay for my friend to come with me?"

Trey paused but then asked, "Is your friend a man?"

"No."

"Then that's cool."

"Great, her name is Aiyanna."

"The more the merrier. We have tons of food that Mama will make me and Derrick eat and/or take home with us. Don't get me wrong, I love barbeque, but a man can only eat so much of it."

Her fingers paused over the start button on the dishwasher. "We'll be there in about twenty minutes. I just need to finish loading the dishwasher."

"Now I'm offended. You chose dirty dishes over me?"

Tristyn laughed. "I plead the fifth."

"All right. See you soon."

Laughter and the smell of sweet and spicy barbecue greeted them as they walked up the driveway. Aiyanna's nose pointed to the sky and her hand circled her belly. "I am gonna tear that food up."

Derrick, the first to spot them through the kids playing tag in the driveway, waved them over to the backyard. Even more casual than yesterday, he managed to make a pair of basketball shorts and Puma slides look good.

Aiyanna nudged Tristyn in her side. "Please tell me that's not Derrick."

"That is Derrick," Tristyn confirmed.

"Too bad he's hung up on Georgia because that man is fine." A permanent tan from working outside with his employees, the golden undertone caused his eyes to stand out even more. Like Trey, he'd inherited his eye color from their late grandfather.

Derrick walked over and lightly wrapped his arm around Tristyn's shoulders and introduced her to the people sitting at the table. "Everyone, this is Tristyn. Tristyn, this is everyone."

Tristyn tilted her head playfully. "Great introduction, Derrick."

"Thanks." He turned his attention to Aiyanna. "Trey said you were bringing a friend. This must be Aiyanna."

"Nice to meet you all," Aiyanna waved.

"Likewise." He released Tristyn and pointed to the side of the garage. The food spanned five table lengths and somebody's uncle was still on the grill. "Help yourself. It's like, four types of chicken, ribs, steaks, burgers, hot dogs, salad, fruit, you name it-it's over there. And if you wanna start with dessert, it's in the house." He winked and grabbed two unoccupied chairs from the next table and placed them next to his, patting the seat before he turned back to the table.

Tristyn nodded and headed to the buffet with Aiyanna at her side.

"I know how you love your sweets. You sure you don't wanna start with dessert?" Aiyanna smirked.

"I'll pass. I'm not here for that."

Aiyanna placed her hand on her hip. "Then just what are you here for?"

Not having an appropriate answer, she cut her eyes at Aiyanna.

"Oh wow!" Aiyanna continued with her rouse. "Look at all this dessert here on this table. I wonder what kind of *dessert* Derrick was referring to since it seems that all this *dessert* is outside." She leaned in closer, speaking normally again. "Honestly, if Trey is as fine as Derrick, you definitely need to start with dessert."

Tristyn's eyes darted toward the house, causing a wave of heat to creep up the back of her neck. Just the thought of seeing Trey again left her stomach uneasy. Her hand shook as she poured a cup of sweet tea from the pitcher, and she started to wonder if she'd made a mistake in coming. Her hormones had led her right back to Trey as soon as he had asked. Meanwhile, Jacob hadn't a clue that she was hanging out with her ex and his family, just like old times.

Aiyanna put down her plate and smacked her lips. "Trey must be fine. He got your hands shaking and you ain't even in his bed. I need a man like that. Are you sure Derrick is in love with Georgia? If he's single maybe I could persuade him to look my way."

"Girl, shut up. Even if Derrick is single, it wouldn't matter because he's loved Georgia since the day he met her when we were in college and he was still in high school."

"Figures. He ain't my type anyway. I like my men big."

"I know."

"And wood toned."

"Wood toned?" Tristyn took another calming sip of her tea.

"Yes. Keep up, sis. I need a man who is either ebony, mahogany, walnut..."

"I see."

"And when I say big, I mean I need him to look like he just bench pressed a whole football team while running for a touchdown."

Tristyn's eyebrows raised quickly in the air. "That is totally opposite of what I like. I like them long and lean. It doesn't matter what color, I like them all. White, light, chocolate, midnight...give them all to me."

*   *   *   *   *   *   *

Trey watched Tristyn sip her drink from the kitchen window inside the house. How was it she was more beautiful than yesterday? And that outfit was doing things to him. Just looking at her almost made him forget his name.

"Did you invite her?" Trey's mom noticed him staring out the window instead of adding the cut potatoes into the bowl for the potato salad.

"Yeah. Don't act like you don't know her now."

Mama took a second look at Tristyn and slowly shook her head as if trying to place where she had seen her before.

"We dated when we were in college." When Mama still seemed to be in thought Trey added, "Come on Mama, you just asked about her."

"That is not Tristyn! You didn't tell me she was coming. She looks wonderful. How did you find her?"

Trey recapped their chance run in that he felt was caused by a mixture of fate and Mama's prayers. By the end, he couldn't keep the boyish grin off his face. Since seeing her, his mind had gone through all the moments they shared in their younger days and he'd dreamt about the moments he hoped to share with her in the future.

Trey was brought out of his reverie by a strong slap against the back of his head. His hand flew to where the stinging from Mama's slap was the strongest. "Ow. Shit!" Another whack to his head. "Mama! Why are you hitting me?"

"Stop cussing in my house." She pointed to the backyard. "I tried to tell you to make better decisions when you were younger. Now look at you. Go on out there and talk to her. I can finish this myself."

He leaned down and kissed her temple before wiping his hands on the dish towel. "Thanks, Mama."

"And tell her I said hi. I'll be out soon to catch up with her."

The only thing he heard was the screen door slamming shut on his way out. He was sure Mama would get the back of his head for that too but right now, his focus was on Tristyn.

3

I Don't Wanna

Tristyn finally started making her plate when goosebumps appeared on her arms.

"I don't even have to ask, this gotta be Trey walking over here. I see why you're stuck on him. And is he walking in slow motion?"

Tristyn turned around. Just as Aiyanna suggested, Trey's stride appeared to be in slow motion. He waved to guests he hadn't yet said hello to, smiled to cousins, and locked eyes with her. Like the second hand had slowed to a creep, he slowly made his way over.

"What is this sorcery?" Aiyanna joked.

Tristyn hushed Aiyanna. "Hey, Trey."

He gently kissed her cheek. "Miss me?"

Miss him? How could she not? She'd missed him since he disappeared seven years ago. She'd missed him in the time between yesterday and now. Every day she longed to be in his presence, and she hated that. The hold he had on her was as unbearable as it was necessary. "Nope."

"I'm kidding," he grinned out the side of his mouth. "You must be Aiyanna."

"I am," she shook his hand. "Nice to meet you. I've heard a lot about you."

"Really?" Trey searched Tristyn for a response that she avoided.

"She didn't say she heard good things," Tristyn joked.

"I'm not worried. That's all she'll hear soon."

"Yes, honey," Aiyanna's eyes closed and she hugged her body. "That's what I'm talking about. Tristyn says your brother is somewhat off the market but tell me about your cousins. She said you have three."

A look of understanding passed between the two. "Oh yes, my cousins."

Tristyn tried focusing on their interaction instead of staring at Trey but was failing miserably. His cologne proved he wasn't afraid to spend more than necessary to make a statement even when dressed in all black, as he was today. His black short sleeved shirt looked on the verge of being a size too small due to his muscles and fit right into his straight cut black jeans. At his height of six-foot-two, and Aiyanna's petite stature of only five-foot-two, Trey had to crane his neck to hear her over the music.

Aiyanna bounced on her tiptoes and clapped. "Yes! I wanna know all about them. Are they single?"

"As far as I know."

"Tell me more."

"There's Onyx, Phoenix, and Xavier. Onyx and Phoenix are identical twins and X is their younger brother. They all have good jobs and no kids. Onyx is a detective, Phoenix is a personal trainer, and Xavier owns a cigar bar or something like that. They don't look anything like me and Derrick though. They're bigger and darker than us."

"Say no more. Are either of them coming? Better yet, are they here now?" Aiyanna glanced around the backyard.

"They should be here at some point so when I see them, I'll introduce you."

"You're a godsend. Tristyn is lucky to have you."

Tristyn narrowed her eyes at Aiyanna.

"I'll be the lucky one if she haves me. Let's eat, shall we?"

Seated at the table, Tristyn leaned over to Aiyanna and harshly whispered, "Tristyn is already lucky to have Jacob."

Aiyanna shrugged and whispered back. "Again, then what is Tristyn doing here?"

"No whispering at the table," Derrick called out. "You either eat, talk to everyone, or play Spades."

From that point on, Aiyanna wolfed down her food, looking up occasionally to see if any of Trey's cousins had arrived. Tristyn, on the other hand, picked at her food until she heard a story Derrick told about one of his customers and she couldn't stop laughing. Derrick was known for making sure guests were comfortable. Whether that be through a joke or an offer of hospitality, he was sure to make you feel at home, wherever you were.

In her back pocket, her phone buzzed lightly. Jacob wanted to know what time she would be home this evening. As she had guessed he must be back in town. She tapped out a response saying she was having a girl's night with Aiyanna and wouldn't be home until late.

She hated liars. Had always hated them. Hated that she was becoming one. In the end she decided, this was for the best. There was nothing wrong with hanging out. Trey had said they needed to talk and that's what she intended to make sure happened.

With the sun now casting a golden mix of colors across the backyard, the temperature had dropped to a much more comfortable feel. Most of the guests, including Aiyanna, had gotten drunker and louder as time ticked by. Tristyn enjoyed their antics and had fully assimilated into the familial environment. The only thing she was becoming concerned about was Trey's bedroom eyes. The more he drank, the more he stared at her over his bottle of beer.

Aiyanna turned to Tristyn and pouted. "I can't believe Trey's cousins didn't show up. I really wanted to meet them."

"Maybe they're running late. There's still time."

One of Trey's uncles, teetering on the edge of wasted, walked over, his beer belly leading the way and his Jesus sandals flopping behind. "Nephew, if you ain't gonna dance with this woman I'm gonna dance with her for you." He pointed to Aiyanna. "And you're next."

Trey chuckled and looked for Tristyn's quiet approval or denial. She uncrossed her legs and sat up in her chair. She would've taken anything that got her away from Trey's intense vibes. "You better have some moves," Tristyn kidded.

"I have moves that my nephew would kill me for if I put them on you." He burst into laughter.

Trey practically spit out his beer before issuing a warning. "Best behavior, Uncle Wayne."

Wayne waved him off before pulling Tristyn onto the makeshift square concrete dance floor.

Derrick looked up briefly from his spades game. "Trey, you know Uncle Wayne drunk as hell. He probably gonna fall and take Tristyn with him. If you don't go and save her, I will."

"I ain't 'bout to fall," he called behind him. "Stay outta grown folk business."

Having spent the day behind the grill, Uncle Wayne smelled of pure smoke and his eyes had turned red. One hand held onto hers and the other guided her through the melody. "How do you know my nephews?"

"I met Trey back in college. We drifted apart and ran into each other yesterday, so he invited me. And of course, I know Derrick because he's Trey's brother."

He grunted. "Ain't that somethin.'"

"Why do you say that?"

"No reason. My nephews are good men. I'm glad you two reconnected. And I got something for you gal!" He spun her around and her long hair graced the ground as he dipped her over his arm, eliciting a fit of laughter from them both.

Derrick's eyes cut to the corner to look at his brother, who was focused on Uncle Wayne and Tristyn. "Man, go get your girl. Quit playing."

Trey nodded in response. Uncle Wayne noticed Trey walking toward them and whispered in Tristyn's ear, making her look over and giggle. He twirled her around and Tristyn twirled a couple more spins for good measure, her duster and hair spinning through the air.

"May I cut in?" Trey cleared his throat.

Uncle Wayne looked at him. "Nope." He danced Tristyn to the corner of the driveway, chuckling the whole way. The smile wiped from Trey's face. "Just kidding, Nephew," he yelled out to him and danced Tristyn back over. He turned his attention back to Tristyn. "It was an utter pleasure," and clapped Trey on his shoulder as he made his way back to Aiyanna. "Your turn sweet thang!"

The music that had been upbeat all night turned to a slow song. Trey looked to his teenage cousin who was cuing music from his phone to the speaker, who nodded approvingly. "I didn't ask him to do that," Trey's teeth moved from side to side.

"It's fine, Trey," Tristyn reached up and wrapped her arms around his neck.

Trey involuntarily licked his lips and stepped close enough to snugly wrap his arms around her waist. With just the sight of him, she wanted to snuggle into his embrace all night.

"Are you having fun?" he asked.

She sighed. "I am. Uncle Wayne was the icing on the cake. I don't remember meeting or hearing about him when we dated, though."

Trey nodded. "That's because we didn't spend too much time together. He's actually Onyx, Phoenix, and Xavier's dad. We didn't get close until my grandmother passed."

"That explains it. And I'm sorry to hear about your grandmother." The look in his eyes was almost her undoing. It would be her lucky day if this song never ended.

"Thanks, Tristyn." His fingers rubbed up and down the small of her back.

"You're welcome." A pull urged her closer. She wanted nothing more than for him to kiss her right then. Right on the dance floor. Right in front of all the people...all the people. What was she doing? She snapped out of it and took a small step back. She needed to clear her head. "Where's the bathroom?"

He removed his hands and stepped away. "It's umm, I'll show you."

"No," she said, startling them both. She tried to recover. "You don't have to do that. I can find it on my own if you just point me in the right direction. I somewhat remember the layout of the house."

His left eyebrow raised. "Is something wrong? Did I make you uncomfortable?"

"No, you're fine, you didn't do anything wrong. I just have to use the bathroom and it just hit me."

"You sure?"

"Positive."

"Cool. I'll still show you where it is."

On the way in, Aiyanna caught Tristyn's attention and she faked like she was sipping tea before twirling back around in her seat to continue chatting with Derrick.

Trey led her into the house and to the bathroom located near the kitchen but found it occupied. "You can wait, or I can show you to the other one. It's upstairs in my old bedroom."

Tristyn and Trey in a bedroom...together...yes, that was a wonderful idea. She could handle whatever happened. It's not like they were teenagers. They were adults and honestly, she just needed a minute to herself. She didn't care if she had to lock herself in a closet. "I'll use the other one."

Trey grabbed her hand and they walked up the stairs just as they had done countless times when he brought her home from college with him.

When inside, she released the breath she hadn't realized she was holding. Even if Trey didn't have feelings for her, she was having the worst time keeping hers in check. She leaned over the sink and took five deep breaths then fanned her face with the towel from over the toilet.

She pulled out her cell and texted Georgia. Aiyanna, a lover of romantic endings, had fallen in love with Trey's charm and was of no help. *SOS I'm at Trey's!*

While waiting for her response she ran some water and poured it into the toilet. "I'll just be a minute longer," she called out.

Her phone vibrated. *I can't believe you really went*

Tristyn rolled her eyes. *Me neither. No time for lectures. Need an excuse to leave. HELP!!!!*

Trey's voice drifted through the closed door. "We haven't had a chance to talk yet but with everyone around there hasn't really been an opportunity."

Tristyn looked to the door and back to her phone, only partially paying attention to Trey. Why hadn't Georgia texted her back yet? "No worries, we'll talk when we talk."

"When we were in college I, it's crazy but I don't even know where to start." He released an awkward chuckle that left him shrugging. "I guess I could start by saying I'm sorry for leaving you like that. You meant a lot to me and I left you on some immature shit. I didn't realize what a mistake it was until it was too late."

Tristyn's heartrate increased. She'd prayed for the day where Trey apologized and they followed it up with passionate makeup sex. Now it was here and instead of hot sex she had wet panties, sweaty palms, and was frozen in a bathroom.

GEORGIA!! HELP! Now he's apologizing for breaking up with me and I don't have a thing to say back. Where are you? Call me and get me tf outta here!

"Yeah, umm, well thank you for apologizing but it was a long time ago." She flushed the toilet and continued talking as she washed her hands. "You know, everything happens for a reason. Maybe it wasn't meant for us to be." When she opened the door Trey was standing directly on the other side, blocking her exit, his shimmering eyes drilling into hers.

"Maybe it wasn't meant for us to be back then, Tristyn, but maybe this is our second chance. I have never missed anyone as much as I've missed you. I swear, seeing you was kismet."

"Excuse me?" Tristyn's weight shifted to her other leg.

"Kismet. It means fate."

She chuckled nervously. "Oh, I thought you said kiss me."

Trey chuckled along with her, his eyes suddenly appearing a shade darker. "What if I did say that?"

Swallowing, she looked up and found it hard to think. Why hadn't Georgia called her yet? Trey had always affected her and years later, she still found it difficult to overcome. She licked her lips and turned away from his face that was now inches from hers. "I'd say you're crazy."

She managed to avert his gaze for a mere few seconds before his index finger reached out and turned her head back toward him. In a low voice he asked, "Why would I be crazy for wanting to kiss you? Or for wanting you to kiss me?"

Thoughts swirled in her head. "Because we only just ran back into each other yesterday after what feels like forever. Can we get to know each other again? I've changed. You've changed. The world has changed. And do we honestly want to go back down that road again?"

"Absolutely."

"You can't be sure of something like that. We tried before and it didn't work. Let's just do each other." Trey smiled at her slip of words. Flustered, she self-corrected. "Jesus! I can't believe I said that." She spoke slower to avoid misspeaking again. "I meant let's just *not* do that. Let's not go back down that road."

"You had the right idea the first time." His hand cupped her chin. Her brain screamed out *abort, abort, abort!*

Space, she needed space to think because she certainly couldn't do that with him acting all sensual and putting her right back in the relationship like it never ended. She slipped around him and started for the bedroom door. "I gotta get outta here."

"Tristyn." Hot on her heels, Trey used his long reach to grab her wrist. "Hey, I'm sorry. Please don't go yet." His rough hands rubbed up and down her arms. "Can we just sit and talk? I'm not ready for you to leave yet. Call me selfish."

"Now that, I remember. You are selfish."

Trey fake gasped. "I am not selfish."

"Do you still not share your apple juice?"

"Why can't people buy their own apple juice? It's only costs a few bucks."

They shared a laugh, effectively bringing the physical tension to an end. Trey sat on the edge of the bed and reached out, pulling her in between his legs. And just like that, the sexual tension returned just as quickly as it had left. "It's hard for me to not pick back up where we left off, Tristyn, but I won't apologize for that."

Words stopped at Tristyn's lips. The pressure of his hands against her skin tempted her to forget about waiting on Georgia's return call. Tempted her to forget about Jacob.

His entire body invaded her personal space. She chanted *be strong* repeatedly but then she did it. She looked into his eyes again and in the flick of a wrist his mouth was over hers and she did not stop it. He tasted so damn good, and her body responded to his instantly. To resist stripping off her clothes, she pulled him in closer by wrapping her arms tighter around his neck. His erection pressed against her, and she moaned in response.

"Fuck," he moaned under his breath. Before she knew it his strong arms pulled her onto the bed with him. He shifted so she was underneath him and like always, her legs opened for him like it was the most natural thing to do. When their lips parted it was only so he could run his down her neck. She moaned softly and he pulled her bodysuit down to get a full taste of what he'd been missing.

Her phone rang.

Trey briefly lifted his mouth from her skin. "Need to get that?"

"No." She pulled his mouth back down and he continued his fiery assault against her skin.

Again, her phone rang.

"Maybe you should get that." Trey pulled away but kept her within arm's reach. "Whoever it is must need to talk to you since they're calling back."

Tristyn simultaneously cursed and thanked herself for getting Georgia involved in her dilemma just minutes prior. "You're probably right." She moved to rise off the bed, so Trey stepped out the way.

Pulling her shirt back over her bra, she grabbed her phone to look at the caller ID.

"Was that your boyfriend?" Trey crossed his arms.

Tristyn quickly stashed her phone back in her back pocket. It was, and for a split second, she worried that somehow, Jacob knew she was being unfaithful. "No." A silent moment passed. "I should get going."

"You don't have to do that. Don't worry, I won't maul you again. I'll be a perfect gentleman." He looked her up and down and gritted his teeth.

"I think it's best. We need to cool our hormones before we do something we regret."

"Trust me, ain't no regrets coming from this side of the room."

Derrick burst in the room and stalled when he saw them. "Oh, I ain't know y'all was in here." A cheesy grin crossed his face. "Oooo y'all was 'bout to do the nasty, huh? Next time lock the door." He crossed the room and closed the door to the bathroom.

Trey shook his head. "I can't stand him."

"I need to get home, Trey."

Trey nodded and begrudgingly, walked her and Aiyanna out.

When Trey could no longer be seen in the distance, Tristyn's head hit the back of the headrest.

"Ain't love something else," Aiyanna smiled widely.

4

DON'T WISH ME WELL

7 YEARS AGO
Mama's hands quivered as she removed the chain from the door. Unable to get her shaky fingers to grasp the lock, she took a full breath, then tried again. "Hey, baby." She stepped aside to let in Trey.

"You okay, Mama?" Gloria never bothered with the chain, reasoning her boys couldn't come and go if they couldn't get in. "Why is the chain on?"

"I don't know, it just is."

Trey watched as she relocked the door behind him and wiped her hands on her skirt before wringing them.

"I made some food for you and Derrick."

Trey glanced at the clock on the wall, seeing it was just about time for Derrick to get home from school. "You cooked? What's going on? Are you sick?"

A small smile came over Mama's face before fading back into worry lines. Even if she wasn't sick, something had her worried, and it was big. The last time she cooked a large meal in the middle of the week was when she broke the news of her breast cancer diagnosis. Thankfully, the doctors found it early and she had been cancer free ever since.

His swallow got stuck in his throat. "Mama, you can tell me. Is the cancer back?"

"Trey, I am not sick. My health is just fine."

"Promise me, Mama."

She stopped on her way to the kitchen. Her voice was still low, but her fire was back. "Boy! I don't need to make no promises to my son to prove I'm not lying. Now get in here and set this table. Your brother will be here any minute."

Relief settled in Trey's gut. It was just like his normal, cancer free mama, to snap at him like that. She was still hiding something, but he'd have to wait until Derrick arrived to find out what it was. For now, he focused on placing the antique gold rimmed plates on the table that she insisted on using for every family dinner. The plates couldn't go in the microwave. They couldn't go in the dishwasher. They couldn't be set on the table too hard or else they'd crack. Worthless was what they were. The one time he'd told her as much he'd been slapped on the backside of his head. With as many slaps as she loved to give, he was glad his brain still functioned adequately.

"How's college classes going?" Mama broke the silence.

"It's good."

"That doesn't tell me how it's going. What's it like? Are your classes hard? Any girls caught your eye?"

Trey couldn't help the smile that popped up on his face and it had nothing to do with his classes at the state school a couple hours away. The classes were what they were, a means to an end to start making money so he could send some home to Mama. No, his smile was due to the girl in his class that he couldn't keep his eyes off of. She continued to not pay any attention to him, but he'd found out her name and that she was single. He planned to finally talk to her, once he got up the nerve.

Mama turned to him with her hand on her hip. "I guess that smile means you met somebody. I don't care what you do but remember why you're there. You've come too far to be distracted by a pretty face. They're a dime a dozen. You better not let your grades slip and you better not make me a grandma. Wear your condoms."

"Mama!"

"I'm serious, Trey."

"Come on, Mama. As if that conversation wasn't awkward enough the first time." The birds and the bees conversation at age thirteen hadn't been like the ones his friends described. No, his mama had walked into his room during an intense session of a basketball video game and she'd dropped three boxes of condoms on his bed saying she didn't know which ones would fit him, nor which ones felt the best. All she knew is that he had better act like he knew how to use them when the time came. His fingers hadn't moved fast enough to end the game and disconnect from his friends on the other end. She'd then opened a packet and showed him how to place the condom on a dildo. The worst had been when he, then, had to do the same to prove he knew how to put one on. He had yet to recover. When Derrick came of age, Trey volunteered to talk to him just so he wouldn't have to endure the same terror.

"I don't care how awkward it was as long as it did what it was supposed to do. You know how to put one on don't you?"

Trey's head dropped to his chest. "Yes, Mama. I know how to put one on."

"Good. Make sure you remember that as you're running through these girls."

"Mama, I'm not running through any girls."

"Keep it that way then." She went back to adding the finishing touches to her famous greens and Trey counted his blessings.

"Aye, yo, the favorite son is here." Derrick walked in and threw his keys and backpack down. Mama cast a side glance in his direction. A sly smile lifted the corner of his mouth. He retrieved his things from the sofa. "Sorry. I'll go put this in my room."

On his way, he noticed all the food and stopped in his tracks. His mouth dropped open. "Who died? Mama, are you sick?"

"See," Trey's arms flew out to his side. "I'm not crazy."

Mama placed her hands on her hips. "I beg to differ. I can cook meals even when nothing is wrong. I don't know why you boys think I don't cook."

A look passed between Trey and Derrick.

"And I'm not blind, I saw that. Derrick go put your stuff in your room so we can sit down and eat a meal as a family."

Frozen in place, Derrick's face had dramatically dropped. Mama could claim to cook dinners all she wanted but that was far from the norm. Working two jobs to keep up with the tuition at Derrick's private high school kept her busy enough to only cook on holidays and special occasions.

Derrick asked, "Then we'll talk about what's going on?"

She huffed, but then looked at her sons and sighed. "Yes."

Derrick stayed a bit longer and then walked out.

Trey stared at his mama. She said she wasn't sick, and he prayed she hadn't lied. As the oldest, he'd had to bear the brunt of reality for his brother and be strong for Mama while she went through treatment. They said that what didn't kill you made you stronger. With all they had gone through, he hadn't gained any muscles, but he swore that at twenty-one, his hairline was already receding.

"Thank you for setting the table baby."

Trey collapsed in his seat. Mama didn't believe in thanking them for doing chores they were expected to do as part of a functioning family unit, such as setting the table. They were about to get the worst news of their lives.

Mama set her son's plates in front of them, her own seat wobbling as she took her place at the head of the table. Grace was said in a round-the-table kind of style. Gloria started, Trey added his piece, and Derrick closed it out. As much as Trey wanted to dig in, he'd already lost his appetite.

"Mama, you know I can't eat until you tell us what's going on."

Mama stuffed her mouth with a forkful of sweet potato pie before placing her fork back on her plate. Since the boys were little, whenever she made dessert, she preferred starting there. She picked up the paper towel and wiped her mouth. Derrick also sat, not touching his food.

"You boys will eat first. I don't care if you have to stuff it down your throats but I'm not talking until you are going back for seconds."

"Damn, Mama," the curse word slipped out before Derrick could stop it. "Oops. I ain't mean to say that." Mama dropped her fork and crossed her arms. His eyes darted from his food and then back up to see if she was still watching. She was. He didn't want any problems especially when his goal was to wait around long enough to see what secret she held.

Trey knew what was best for him. Despite not having an appetite, he popped a mouthful of curried chicken in his mouth. As much as he hated having to eat it right now, he loved the food even more. Forkful by the forkful entered his jaws. He tried to come home often enough but even when he did, there was no guarantee that Mama would cook. College cafeteria food just wasn't the same.

Satisfied, Mama asked, "So what girl have you set your eyes on?"

Trey dipped his fork in the greens and macaroni and cheese, then paused. "Her name is Tristyn. We don't have the same major, but we have the same English Lit class and I've seen her in the cafeteria a couple times."

"What's she look like?" Derrick nodded his head.

"Man, she has a big..." his hand brushed over top of his head and a large grin forced its way out before he saw Mama had leaned forward with a disapproving look on her face. "She's really pretty. Maybe about five foot five. She's light skinned, has long, dark hair that kinda looks like she might be mixed with Greek or something. And she's really smart. She's always answering the questions in class and she's always right."

"What's her major?" Mama's head leaned to the side as it always did. The simple act had a way of making it seem like she was disinterested in whatever conversation was going on, but she'd made it clear early on that every word they said would always hold her interest.

"I don't know yet, but I think it's something to do with money, or numbers."

"Yes, definitely a smart young lady. Does she know you're interested?"

"Probably not. I swear she don't even see me." Trey chuckled and stretched his legs under the table.

"Well, when she does see you, remember what I told you. But also, don't wait too long to say something to her. If there's anything I've learned in the last couple of days is that time passes so fast and before you know it, tomorrow was years ago."

"That's deep Mama," Derrick looked up from his plate where only the greens remained.

"Are you being smart?"

"No, ma'am." The smirk on his face that disappeared before he took another bite of the roll in his hand suggested otherwise, but Mama let it go.

"All right then. Your turn smartass." She nodded toward Derrick.

"Nothing to report over here since you put me in an all-boys school."

Trey snickered and Derrick kicked his leg. "Ain't nothing funny about that."

Mama spoke up. "Your grades have already improved, and you're focused. Stick to those points and you'll be fine. And get into that entrepreneur program like I told you. The last day to sign up is next Friday. Did you make the basketball team?"

A broad smile slowly developed on Derrick's face and he sat back in his chair. "I don't wanna brag but," he popped the invisible collar on his shirt. "I made it! And I'm on varsity. They said they don't normally put new students on varsity so I'm like, the first one they ever made an exception for."

Trey pushed away from the table so hard that his chair fell over. "That's what I'm talkin' 'bout!" The hug they shared was the longest they'd had, ever. "I'm so proud of you, man."

"Thanks bro." Derrick couldn't keep the light out of his eyes.

Tears caused Mama's eyes to glisten. "I'm proud of you, Derrick. All that ball bouncing in my driveway between you and your brother paid off. Great job."

"Thanks Mama." He noticed the tears in her eyes. "You all right?"

She licked her lips and pushed away from the table. Her foot tapped the floor until she decided to stand.

Derrick watched Mama pace. "I guess this is where you tell us what's going on. Whatever it is, we're grown and can handle it."

Mama didn't bother correcting him. A typical baby of the family, he held that place proudly, requiring the most care. She balanced herself on the edge of the kitchen countertop, gathering strength.

"Your affinity for basketball, both of you, is just like your father. He loved basketball so it's no surprise that you two took after him in that way."

Trey and Derrick remained quiet. There weren't many times when Mama mentioned their dad. Whenever they asked about him, she became short, providing quick responses to redirect the conversation. Rarely, if ever, had she brought him up on her own.

"When you two were little, Trey, you started asking questions about him, which prompted Derrick to start asking as well. It was a lot to deal with and I didn't have the answers you two wanted. The answers I did have, well, I tried answering what I could, but talking about him was too unbearable.

"He'd always wanted to be a father and loved you boys to death, but when it came to being a husband, I don't think he knew how, and I feel like that made him act out in ways that I'd still rather not discuss. We argued all the time. One night, we got into it really bad. I'd had enough and I kicked him out. I even threatened him. Told him if he ever came back I'd slit his throat."

Trey reared back in his chair. "Damn, Mama."

"We fought all the time and to be honest, it wasn't the first time he'd left or even the first time I threatened him. That was just how our relationship was. He always came back home, until one day, he didn't." Mama swallowed tears. "I looked for him. I called every day until his phone was disconnected. At first, I couldn't believe he actually disappeared, but after a few months I started to worry that something happened to him. I went as far as to hire a private investigator but by that time, I was broke from having to take care of two growing boys, and I couldn't hire the best that money could buy. The investigator, Tony, or he went by that, said he couldn't find him and after paying him for months, I had to trust that he'd done a good job and didn't just take my money."

Mama finally faced them. Trey remained slumped in his seat with his arms crossed across his chest. Derrick, quite the opposite, looked like he was ready to bolt from the room. "I don't know how to tell you this but your father..."

Trey's head snapped up. "Mama, are you trying to tell us our dad is alive?"

Derrick, his spine straight, both hands balled into fists, blurted out, "You told us he was dead."

Mama nodded. Her head nodding so slowly the untrained eye wouldn't have noticed.

Derrick fell back into his chair, squeezing his eyes shut.

"Why are you telling us this now? We would've been fine not knowing." Trey's hand briefly popped up from his crossed arms before falling back down.

Mama looked out the kitchen window overlooking her backyard. "I got a call earlier this week from a girl named Chelsea. She is your father's daughter. You have a sister."

Derrick's eyes narrowed. "We have a sister?"

"I couldn't believe it myself." Suddenly feeling weak, Mama sat. "Your sister, Chelsea," she palmed her forehead. "Lord help me. As much as I tried to find your father, it never dawned on me that he might've stayed close. I always assumed he was long gone but he's living just a couple towns over in Lorain, about forty-five minutes from here. He's widowed now, and Chelsea is only a couple years younger than you, Derrick.

"Her mom died when she was little so your father raised her, but Chelsea says David is sick now. I guess his last dying wish is to see you boys, so that's why Chelsea reached out. I'm sure it wasn't too hard to find us since we never moved. Your father could've done this years ago instead of waiting until now." Mama rolled her eyes and waved off the thought. "If either of you are up to it, Chelsea would like to meet you."

"What about dad?" Derrick asked.

"He wants to see you as well. The sooner, the better."

5

ME AND YOU

Tristyn lie in bed unable to stop replaying the chain of events that led to Trey in between her legs trailing kisses from her lips to her breasts. She needed to break free. Being around him sent all common sense out the door and that was the only thing she had left.

Though he apologized, she still hadn't a clue as to why he had left when she had, supposedly, aside from his mother and brother, been the most important person in life. The memory of her heart being picked apart still held her in bondage and she wondered if she even wanted to know why he'd left. Had it been another woman? Had they moved too fast? Only counseling had helped her believe that regardless of his reason for leaving, she wasn't to blame for such an abrupt departure.

On her side table, her phone alerted of a text message. She scooted across her bed to grab her phone. Her heart leapt immediately.

Roses are red violets are blue. I'm sorry for earlier but I can't help it. I like u

Tristyn chuckled aloud but then her face sobered. No, no, no. She could not just fall right back into his trap. She hit the reply button, sending only the thinking emoji.

Trey replied. *Roses are red violets are blue. I wanna know if you like me too*

A smile that she couldn't stop, spread across her face. She despised her traitorous heart for still holding feelings for him. Trey didn't wait for another response.

Doing her best to disguise the joy, she bade hello to Trey.

"I was laying on this couch and realized I couldn't fall asleep if I wanted to because every time I closed my eyes I saw your beautiful face."

"So, I'm the one keeping you awake?"

"Somewhat. I wanted to apologize for earlier. I didn't mean for things to go that far."

"Yeah, umm, me neither. I was just as involved as you were so I'm sorry, too."

"We're good?"

"Yeah."

He released a sigh. "You left so fast I thought I'd scared you off and that's the last thing I wanted to do. I'm heading back home tomorrow around four and wanted to see you before I leave. Can I take you to lunch?"

Tristyn pulled the corner of her lip into her mouth. Once again, all the reasons to not attend lunch with Trey were forefront but she was like a bull charging forward with no cares about hurting anyone, even if it was herself. "Umm, yeah, I'm free. Lunch sounds good. Did you already have a place in mind?"

"How about Soul Plates? That still open?"

Her heart dropped into the pit of her stomach. Soul Plates was the restaurant they had gone to when she introduced him to her parents and she hadn't been back since they broke up. "Yeah, it's open. I'd love to go there."

"Great. What's your address? I'll pick you up."

Concerned about Jacob dropping by unannounced, she decided it'd be best if he didn't. "I'll meet you there. Don't you have a long drive back?"

"Nah, the drive is only about two hours and that's if you go the speed limit."

Two hours? Tristyn's face scrunched up. "Where do you live now, I never asked."

"I moved to Columbus about a year ago to be closer to my family. It's close enough for me to get home to see my family, but far enough away for them to not drop by unannounced. So far it's working out." Trey laughed.

Tristyn's heart sped up. "You live in Columbus now?" The same Columbus she was headed to tomorrow.

"Yeah. The traffic is awful during rush hour, but I work from home sometimes so it's easy to deal with. And the people are cool, so it works."

Trey's voice rang in her ear. *Kismet.* Her feet wore a path into her carpet as she paced with her robe tied around her waist, wondering if she should tell him about Northrup. When she paused, she blurted out, "You are not going to believe this, but I am actually headed to Columbus to see about a job opportunity."

"What? When?"

"Tomorrow evening, actually. I have a meeting on Tuesday morning with a company called Northrup." She could practically hear the gears turning in his brain and had to remind herself that she had gotten herself into this predicament. She could've headed to Columbus and Trey would've been none the wiser.

"This is unbelievable. I'm familiar with Northrup. The firm I work at designed their building. I was the lead on the initial design. Their new building is only about fifteen minutes from my house. This is one hell of a coincidence. So, you're heading to Columbus for a job interview?"

Tristyn raked her mind for the details she received from Bob, the balding white man who had virtually interviewed her and offered the position. "Well, it's more like I'm interviewing them. I was randomly searching for jobs and I ran across the position. It's similar to what I do now but pays more and I'd be in charge of my own team. I wasn't expecting to get the position so when they offered it, I wanted to think about whether that was the best move career wise, and also, if I wanted to uproot my home. In conversations with the owner, he suggested I meet the team in person and also explore the area, so I took him up on the invite."

"So basically, you already have the job?"

"I guess you could say that. Everything would still have to be official after I either say yay or nay. I need to talk to them about workload, hours, and there's so much to think about."

"What I hear you saying is that we're going to be living together soon," he chuckled.

Tristyn started pacing again. "What I'm saying is that we could soon be neighbors."

Trey laughed harder and Tristyn joined in. "We'll see about that. I have an idea."

"Should I be nervous?"

"Only if you're scared of me. But since I live near Northrup, how about you crash with me?"

Tristyn swallowed the lump in her throat.

"Tristyn? Are you still there?"

"Yeah," she scrambled for more time. "I'm here."

"What do you think?"

"I don't think so, Trey. Considering what happened earlier I'm not sure that's a good idea. And I already booked my hotel, Northrup is paying for it."

"Some hotels only require a twenty-four-hour cancellation notice. If you cancel early in the morning, or now, I bet you'll make the cutoff time." When the silence continued, he pressed, "I know we got a little out of control earlier but I promise I don't have any ill intentions. You can sleep in my guest room and I will be on my best behavior. I really just want to spend time with you and re-get to know you."

Tristyn frowned at his choice of words. "Re-get to know me? Is that even a word?"

"Hell yeah," Trey defended himself.

"Give me the definition," she challenged.

"I don't know it off the top of my head," he chuckled.

"Umm hmm," Tristyn laughed.

"If you stay with me, you will have no regrets. I'll treat you like a queen."

Tristyn pondered his words. No regrets. "Let me see if I can cancel my reservation. If I can, then I'll stay with you. If I can't, we can still hang out while I'm there and you can show me around. But I'll let you know at lunch tomorrow. Well, should we still have lunch if we'll, at the very least, be hanging out while I'm in Columbus?"

"Of course we should." Trey tried to keep his enthusiasm in check. "I'll let you get back to sleep and I'll meet you at the restaurant around noon?"

"That works, see you then." Tristyn pulled out her suitcase and adjusted her undergarment wardrobe. Just in case.

6

SHAWTY

Tristyn grabbed her keys and then placed them back on their designated holder on the wall. Things had moved so fast that she hadn't thought anything through. Now she was considering taking the job at Northrup just because it was closer to Trey. She nervously ran her fingers through her hair and took a deep breath. What she needed was for the sun to whip through her hair before the world woke up and crowded the roads. To smell the freshly polluted air. To rev her engine. Because the longer she stayed in the house the more panic threatened to boil over.

"This is familiar ground. I know Trey. I know what to expect. I know how he is and how he isn't. Well, no, I know how he was, not who he is now." She glanced around her living room and cried out in frustration. "Ugh! He has me talking to myself."

Absentmindedly, she turned off the TV and went to search for her cell. Her fingers immediately scrolled to Trey's contact and dialed him. Once his number appeared on the screen, she realized her error and rushed to hit the end button before the call connected. She breathed deeply and scrolled to Jacob's name. She still hadn't told him she was heading to Columbus for a few days.

"Hey you." His deep voice seemed to ricochet off her living room walls as if he was standing next to her. Then his face appeared and Tristyn remembered why she'd been so smitten with him. Every feature from his cropped, light brown hair, to his olive-colored skin and contagious laugh, had stood out. From the moment they met, Jacob had been in pursuit. He'd thrown in all the stops from roses and chocolates to poems and concerts. Nothing had been too good or expensive for her.

Tristyn sighed. "Hey Jacob."

"What's wrong, baby?"

"Nothing actually. I just wanted to tell you I'm going out of town. My boss called and I need to be in Columbus in the morning. Our top customer got notified that they're being audited so I need to go and start a preliminary review."

"When will you be back?"

"I'm not sure." Tristyn bit her lip. She was horrible at lying. "I'm guessing it shouldn't take too long. Maybe a couple of days."

Jacob blew out a small breath of air. "Will I get to see you before you leave?"

"You're in town?"

"Yeah," Tristyn could hear his smile through the phone. "I got back in late last night, so I was taking a nap before I made my way over to you."

Tristyn raised her eyebrows and blew out a deep breath. Immense relief flowed through her veins. Now, knowing Jacob wasn't coming over, she could allow Trey to pick her up. "Unfortunately, not. I need to pack and get on the road."

Jacob waited a beat before responding. "I understand."

"I should only be gone for a couple of days, sweetie." Tristyn tried reassuring him.

"Yeah but I had wanted to see you since I'd been gone for two weeks. I miss you."

Tristyn cringed. "I miss you too, sweetie-poopoo."

With laughter in his voice he said, "Woman, I told you to stop calling me that."

She laughed also. "Okay, okay."

He took on a more serious tone. "Be safe driving there. You know I worry about you."

"I know," Tristyn smiled.

"And call me when you get there. I love you."

"I will. You too." Tristyn hung up the phone. That had gone more smoothly than expected and now she felt completely awful. Still, she sent a text to Trey. *Still able to pick me up?*

He replied immediately. *Yes*

She text her address. *See you soon*

Right after she finished dressing for her lunch with Trey, Georgia popped up at her condo without the twins and had yet to say a word.

Tristyn sat next to her and handed her a bottle of water. "You're making me nervous. What's wrong?"

Pretending not to hear, Georgia continued to file her nails and watch TV.

"Come on Georgia. What's going on? Do I need to treat you like a kid and threaten to turn off the TV?"

Georgia rolled her eyes. "You could do that, but I'll just turn it right back on."

"Georgia, we need to talk, and I know you didn't come over here to watch reruns. Talk to me. And where are the twins? How dare you come over here without them."

It worked. A smile finally appeared before Georgia's face transformed and she started crying. Tristyn pulled her into a hug. "What's going on?"

"I got into it with Aaron last night. Really bad. I'd put the twins to sleep. Junior wouldn't sleep so by the time I put him down it was around midnight, which sucked because I had planned to do something sexy for Aaron. But I sucked it up and decided to do it anyway. I showered, put on this cute black negligee that I hated but thought he would like." Georgia started crying again, so Tristyn went to grab a box of tissues.

"He wasn't in the basement like he always is, but I heard talking and knew he was still up. I found him in our driveway with another woman."

Tristyn gasped. "Did you say something to him?"

"I confronted him and it led to us arguing outside. It was so bad. We've never argued like that."

"Did you suspect there was someone else?"

"I've suspected there was someone else almost our entire marriage."

Tristyn's mouth dropped open and she fell back against the sofa. She had never thought Georgia and Aaron were the perfect couple, but she never would've thought he would treat her like this. She was at a loss for words.

"I know Aaron can be an asshole. I'm trying my best to do the right thing by sticking by my husband and he doesn't even appreciate it," she said in a relaxed tone.

"Well, it seems as if he doesn't appreciate you."

At twenty-eight, Georgia could have any man she wanted. Her honey brown skin and full chest were everything a man was physically attracted to, but her unmatched devotion appeared to be her downfall.

Georgia looked at the floor and spoke. "This morning we talked and I think I got through to him. He's watching the twins and you know he never does that. He said he realized it's been tough on me and felt like I could use a break, but I'm still nervous and don't know if I can trust him again now that I have proof." She bit the corner of her lip. "What would you do if you were in my situation?"

Tristyn was still shellshocked. "I would have kicked him to the curb the first time he stepped out on me. I'm too valuable to lower my standards for someone that doesn't respect me and you are too. I can't say what you should or shouldn't do, but I can say that the Georgia I've known almost my entire life would never let anyone treat her like this. She would've cheated on him, flaunted the affair all up in his face, and then left. But ever since you met him you've been different."

Every feature on Georgia's face dropped. "That's my husband."

"I know that and so do you, but I don't know if he does."

After Georgia thought for a minute she said, "This gotta be karma from a past life or something. Maybe I deserve this."

"My best friend does not deserve this kind of treatment." Tristyn pulled her in for a hug but paused. "Georgia?"

A devious smile appeared on Georgia's face. "You're right, the old Georgia wouldn't take this." Georgia grabbed her purse and stood up. "I gotta go."

A knock on the door diverted Tristyn's attention. "Don't move," Tristyn warned.

Trey stepped through the door and greeted them but stopped short when he noticed the frown lines on their faces. "Am I interrupting something?"

"Nope, come on in." Tristyn held the door open.

"Look who the devil brought back from the dead." Georgia popped the gum in her mouth and crossed her arms. "You didn't tell me Trey was coming over."

"I see the old Georgia decided to make an appearance earlier than expected." Tristyn talked out the side of her mouth. "Things moved fast."

Trey looked at the plastered smiles on their faces.

Georgia waved on her way out. "Fill me in later. Bye, Trey,"

"See ya, Georgia. Nice seeing you again, too." Trey waved back.

Tristyn mouthed *be right back* to Trey and closed the door behind her. "Georgia, what are you about to do?"

Georgia laughed. "I don't have a plan yet. All I know is I have to do something."

Backing down, Tristyn said, "Don't do anything stupid."

Georgia leaned against the wall. "You know me better than anyone. Stupid is not in my vocabulary but crazy is. I'm tired, Tristyn. This has gone on too long." She turned around and started down the steps. "I'll keep you posted."

"Please do," Tristyn yelled after Georgia who was already out the main door of her building. She said a silent prayer for Aaron's safety before walking back inside her condo.

Trey's smile greeted her as she walked inside. He leaned against the counter as he closed his social media feed. Today, he wore another simple white t-shirt and his shorts showed off perfectly trimmed legs that donned a fresh pair of boat shoes. His manly scent had already filled her condo.

She took a deep breath and closed her eyes. Upon opening them she noticed him walking toward her.

"I hope you like these." He presented a bouquet of red roses. "Your mom said you'd love them."

Tristyn gasped. "You got these from my mom's shop?"

"Yeah," he scratched his cheek. "She just about beat me up when I walked in, and your father threatened to make me leave by force."

"My daddy doesn't play but I'm sure you remembered that." Tristyn chuckled. "He didn't pull out his rifle, did he?"

Trey's eyes grew wide. "I forgot he had that but no, thank God he didn't."

"There's so many flower shops. Why did you go there?"

"I wanted to apologize to them for hurting you." He stared into her soul and asked, "Ready?"

Boy was she ever.

Trey dove into his chicken fried steak and potatoes while Tristyn scooped a mouthful of shrimp and grits into her mouth. After swallowing he said, "Tell me how you've been, what you've been up to, what I've missed."

"I wish I had a huge update, but life has been lowkey. I guess I shouldn't complain about something like that because other people have been going through it. I just found out that Georgia thinks Aaron has been cheating on her their entire marriage."

"Wow," Trey set his fork down and took a sip of his lemonade. "Men like him make the rest of us look bad."

Tristyn nodded through the guilt that kept pinging her gut. "But other than that, things are copacetic. I get up, go to work, hang out with my girls, and eat and sleep. A little boring but I'm blessed. No complaints."

"Good." Trey looked up from his plate and a smile lifted in the corner of his mouth.

"Oh! I did open a business at one point."

"Really?"

"Yeah," Tristyn shook her head. "I started making body butters. It was a few years back. I was good at it, and it took off, but it was too much. That's when I realized I don't really like working for myself. The pressure to grow, and make more products, and post on social media, and run customer service was a lot so I got out."

"Did you ever enjoy it?"

"I liked making the products but that was it. I still only make it for myself, my mom, Georgia, and Aiyanna. Maybe I'll make a male version for you."

Finished with his food, he leaned back and crossed his arms across his chest, a smooth grin resting on his face. "I'd love that."

"What about you? What's been going on in your life?"

He threw his arm across the back of the booth. "Not much. Same as you, working and sleeping. I make sure to visit Mama and Derrick up here once a month. Other than that, I work."

"What do you do?"

"I'm an architect."

Tristyn made her shoulders dance in the booth. "Aren't we fancy?" They sat, smiling at each other like newlyweds. Tristyn tried not to get lost in the moment, but it was too late. She had always been a sucker for him. He could be on his last dollar in dingy clothes and she would still follow him around like a love sick puppy. He was everything she looked for in a man. His height and muscles struck her visually while his sweet, loving, and caring nature called to her emotionally. The fact that he appeared to have come up on the financial side was definitely a plus.

"So, I was able to cancel my hotel reservation. Is the invitation to stay with you still open?" She decided right there that it was all or nothing. She had to see where this was going or else, she would regret not giving it a shot.

Trey scooted as close to the table as he could. "Yeah! Yeah, it's still open. I'd love for you to stay with me."

"Great." Although she still couldn't be sure if it was great news, she was officially shooting her shot to see if her future could be what she always dreamed it could be.

Just then, a slender waitress with full hips passed and the whole demeanor of the table changed. Trey's eyes were glued to the waitress's backside and Tristyn's were visually killing Trey. Typically, she wasn't the jealous type and truthfully, she had no right to be, but when it came to dealings with Trey, old habits died hard. Plus, she had just agreed to stay with him and for lack of better terms, re-get to know each other. That had to count for something. "I guess you liked what you saw."

Caught off guard Trey said, "She's pretty but nothing compared to you." He turned back around to look at the waitress once more. "I'll be right back."

Tristyn's eyes bulged as she processed him leaving their date to go and talk to another woman right in front of her. The waitress smiled hard as Trey leaned in closer. Tristyn crossed her arms over her chest and narrowed her eyes. If he considered this making up with her then it was clear this was not what she wanted. She pushed her plate away and grabbed her purse.

Trey watched the waitress walk away and turned to see Tristyn grabbing her things. He rushed over, "Where are you going?" No answer. "Tristyn?"

She glared at him and he began laughing. Rage engulfed her. "Sweetie, where are you going?"

"Home," she spat. "I will not be disrespected like this. Who do you think you are? What world do you live in where you think you can compliment me in one breath and then go and flirt with another woman right in my face?"

Trey shook his head and gently touched her arm. "Please sit down for a second."

"Get off me," she shook him off.

He sighed and sat down with an amused look on his face. "How are you getting home? I drove."

She bent over the table. "You think I don't know that? Have you ever heard of a taxi? An Uber? Lyft? I could take a fucking scooter if I wanted. I don't have to worry about not having a way to get home."

"Would you wait here for whatever you're going to use to get home? Please."

Tristyn looked around and saw people staring. She sat down, her voice lowered. She spoke clearly so he would understand every word. "I am going to wait outside. At this point you have no right to breathe the air I cough out my mouth especially when you can't even respect me when we're on a date."

"Who said this was a date?"

Anger flared as her voice rose again. "How dare you..."

Trey ignored her and started singing *Happy Birthday* with the approaching waitstaff. Seven individual slices of birthday cake, each with a single candle atop, were placed upon their table. Trey smiled and clapped along as everyone around their table joined in on the song. "Are you going to blow out your candles?"

"I hate you." She blew out all the candles as Trey doubled over in laughter and the waitstaff disbursed. "Is this what you were over there talking to her about?"

"Yes." He reached for her hand and held it. "You should know I'd never disrespect you like that."

Tristyn smiled slowly and nodded, the anger dissipating. "What's with all the cake anyway? You know it's not my birthday, right? Or did you forget when it was?"

He removed his hand and took out his credit card when the waitress dropped off the check. "I remember your birthday. It's August seventh, next month. These," he motioned to the cake slices on the table, "are for all the birthdays I missed."

7

PEACHES

7 YEARS AGO

Back at school, Trey sat in the cafeteria swirling his soup around in his bowl, eventually dropping the spoon. David wanted to see him and Derrick. The sooner that happened, the better. Their sister, Chelsea, also wanted to see them. Which was crazy because before today, they'd thought their father to be dead and they certainly hadn't known they had a baby sister. Now everything was moving at a pace that even Trey couldn't keep up with. He needed time to adjust to this new life.

Once they met and experienced an awkward as hell family reunion, everything would change. What would life be like with a father that came back into your life over ten years too late and had the nerve to bring a new family with him?

After Mama broke the news they'd sat for a minute, all in their personal state of shock. Mama focused on finishing her dinner. Derrick was stuck in a state of awe. Trey couldn't stop staring out the window, halfway expecting David to walk up the driveway, home from a long trip.

Derrick wanted to see David and Chelsea immediately but Trey wasn't so sure. There were just too many unanswered questions and they weren't only about their dad, he was curious about Chelsea as well.

Did Chelsea resemble them? Would they know upon seeing her that they shared the same bloodline? Were they complete opposites? That's probably what it would be seeing as though she was a woman. Or a girl...he'd just stick to baby sister.

Baby sister. That still sounded funky. Truth was he'd always wanted a baby sister to look after but did she want to be looked after? So much time had passed. What if she didn't want to be around them after they met? Nonsense, she was the one that reached out first. Of course, she wanted to know them and create a relationship. He was tripping. Right?

And his mama. What the fuck. She seriously led them to believe their father was dead when he was alive. Real alive. Should he be mad at her? Well, how could he be mad at the woman that had cared for him and Derrick by herself?

On the other hand, that was the same reason he was pissed at their father. He'd left Mama with two boys to care for. He was weak for that. Basically, he just walked out the door and said fuck them kids. And Trey was *them kids*. Their mama was scary, but she wasn't that damn scary. There wasn't a way in hell that their father was so scared of their mama that he disappeared and refused to come back around despite Mama's efforts to reconcile and at the least, apologize. And why in the world had Chelsea reached out instead of him?

He needed to clear his thoughts before his next class but when he looked up, he saw Tristyn walk into the cafeteria. Alone. Normally, she was always with a friend. A buddy. Some loser trying to make a move. But not this time. Momentarily pulled from his thoughts, the other thing his mama said rang in his ears.

Time passes fast.

This was it. She'd be a fool not to talk to him. At least he hoped so.

"Hey. Tristyn, right?" Trey fell into step behind her in the hot foods line. He'd already gotten his food but who was counting? He had to be hitting a growth spurt. Or, he had to be a man finally shooting his shot.

Surprisingly, her face lit up when she saw him. "Hey, cute guy from English. How's it going?"

One thing he'd always hated about his fair skin was how easily people could tell when he was overheated, embarrassed, or blushing. In this case, the flush quickly crept into his cheeks.

"You think I'm cute?"

"I mean, you're not ugly." She smiled and if he didn't know any better, he would've sworn that his heart stopped. Man, maybe it skipped a beat. It did something like flutter because his chest felt funny and it made him want to be closer to her.

"I mean, I guess that's a compliment."

Tristyn grabbed her food, Trey grabbed a burrito, and she walked to an empty table with Trey following close behind. "And I'm guessing you're gonna keep me company while I eat today."

This was his lucky day. Had she invited him to eat lunch with her? "If that's all right with you."

"We'll see." She took a bite of her burger. "Can you hold a conversation?"

"Depends on what we're talking about but I'll do my best."

She stared at him while she chewed her food. Her raised eyebrows suggested she was waiting on him to start.

He was fumbling. He racked his mind for the many things they could talk about and yet the only thing that came out his mouth was, "It's chilly out today."

"Wow." Her mouth actually fell open. "Yes, it is chilly out today. It was also chilly yesterday and it'll probably be the same tomorrow. We're right in the middle of fall and should expect more of the same weather pattern."

Trey envisioned kicking a goal in a soccer game and the goalie blocking it and then throwing it back in his face. This was the same, if not worse. Truthfully, he had a right to be fumbling. He was dealing with a lot and that was keeping him off his A game. Without the outside factors he still might have fumbled when trying to talk to the woman he'd had a crush on since the first time he saw her in class with two pencils holding her hair into a ponytail. When she'd removed the pencils and her hair fell down her back and around her face, he'd practically drooled all over his desk.

An awkward laugh forced its way out. "My bad, I just, you put me on the spot."

Tristyn shrugged and swallowed a mouthful. "I just figured that if you came over here to talk to me then you had something to say."

"That would make the most sense." Trey rested his arms on the table and smirked. "I see you're gonna keep me on my toes."

Tristyn's eyebrows rose and her head tilted to the side, just like Mama's did, except he knew Tristyn was judging him. "You're assuming we'll have conversations outside of this one, which actually, isn't a conversation."

"That depends on what you consider a conversation," Trey countered. "We're talking, aren't we?"

"Barely."

"It counts." They stared, each silently challenging the other until a small smile broke out on Tristyn's face. Trey returned it and for a tiny moment, he forgot about the fire at home.

8

CAN I

Trey switched from the loveseat to his sofa and stretched his legs out on the matching ottoman, crossing one ankle over the other. Pulling out his phone, he checked for notifications but there were none. He rose and looked for the remote to change channels but found it right where he'd been sitting. "Relax."

His mind was frazzled and his nerves were jumbled. It had been years since he and Tristyn occupied an intimate space for an extended amount of time. It wasn't just that this was the moment for reviving their relationship, but it could also be the straw that broke the camel's back if anything went wrong. He rehearsed topics to avoid, like their breakup, all while doing his best to prepare for anything and everything he prayed could happen during their time together. The possibilities had his heart racing and the memories of their heated moment in his old bedroom kept causing movement in his pants.

"It's just Tristyn. It's just Tristyn. Sexy ass Tristyn who's staying at my house. And she could be moving here." He dragged his hands down his face as the doorbell rang.

For her arrival he ordered sub sandwiches and according to the app, the delivery driver would be there any minute. He opened the door and his heart proved to be back to its old tricks. Tristyn stood there looking absolutely stunning.

"Hey!"

"Hey." He was in trouble. She'd changed out of her clothes from earlier and was now wearing clothes that clung to her curves. And her toes were out. In all his years, the only time he had a thing for feet was when they were together, and he wanted to drag her upstairs just to suck on them and listen to her little moans.

"I thought you were the food. You were supposed to call when you got off the highway."

"Decided not to. Can I come in?"

"Yes, sorry."

She stepped inside, lugging her weekend bags on her shoulder. A monstrous TV caught her attention first. To the left was a kitchen that looked as if it were actually used, and to the right, a black leather sofa, loveseat, and matching chair. In the middle sat a matching ottoman. The beige walls and dark laminate flooring made the room cozier.

"Your house is really nice. I'm impressed."

"Glad you like it."

"I didn't take you as a suburban cul-de-sac kinda guy but somehow you managed to merge the bachelor lifestyle with the suburbs." She spun around and caught him looking at her rear.

A guilty smile showed on his face.

"Best behavior, Trey."

"Yeah, I know. Let me show you to your room so you can get settled." He led her to the second level. Lining the stairway, a multitude of framed sketches in various sizes with Trey's signature took center stage.

"I forgot you were a sketch artist! I absolutely love these. They're beautiful."

A big smile grew across his face. "Thank you. I can draw one for your place. A housewarming gift for when you move here." Trey opened the door to the bedroom sitting right off the stairs and placed her bags near the bed. "You'll be sleeping in here."

His long stride carried him within arm's length, but he stayed back, avoiding palming her face because all he wanted to do was lay her down on the bed and make love to her all night. Small talk would be his saving grace. "How was your drive? Hit any traffic?"

"It was fine. Barely hit any traffic. For the most part the drive is nothing but farmland unless you're close to a city, but I'm sure you know that. Thanks for letting me stay here."

"Absolutely. I'm counting my lucky stars that you took me up on my offer. Someone up there likes me." When his eyes drifted from the ceiling and back to Tristyn, he knew he was in trouble. Already, he was back to staring at her lips, her cups, and those toes. Her hair, pulled into a ponytail at the nape of her neck, presented a youthful look but he knew there would be nothing kiddish to her if he pushed her down on the bed and rammed into...

"I'm glad I'm here. It'll be nice getting to know this new and improved Trey." Tristyn smiled, ever so innocently, unaware of the thoughts spiraling out of control in his head.

New and improved his ass. All he could currently process was fucking the shit out of her. He cleared his throat. "I'm glad you're here too." Reluctantly, Trey moved away and ran his fingers through his hair. Instead of brushing it down after his shower, he'd left it wild. With it being so short it turned into a short wavy afro. "Tell me something, can you still read my thoughts?"

Tristyn looked down at her feet and smiled. "Yes, but I don't have to read your thoughts to know what you're thinking. It's written all over you."

"Are you having the same thoughts?"

She smoothed her hair back to her ponytail. "I'll never tell."

He leaned against the wall and examined her, trying his best to read through her façade. "I don't know how I'm gonna keep my hands off you, especially knowing you're sleeping right down the hall from me."

Tristyn bit her lip, "You'll figure it out."

The corner of Trey's mouth curved into a smirk. "I ordered food and it should be here any minute."

"Perfect. I haven't eaten anything since our lunch earlier."

The doorbell rang. A chance for them to reset. "I'll get that. Go ahead and get settled." He practically ran from the room, skipping down the stairs. He had a long two nights ahead of him. There was no way he was going to make it when just looking at Tristyn gave him an erection that could cut through metal.

Trey placed his full sub on his plate with fries and sensed Tristyn in the kitchen with him.

"That smells delicious." Tristyn breezed into the kitchen.

"Your food is right there." Trey pointed to the sub already plated. "And I got you onion rings. I hope that's cool."

Tristyn hands paused briefly after unwrapping the sub. Trey internally cheered. It would be a slow burn to win her over, but he was up for the challenge. By remembering intricate details about her that included her favorite foods and flowers, it was in the bag. When they dated, they once stopped at a food truck and she tasted a Philly Cheesesteak for the first time. Weeks after, they continued frequenting that same food truck. Tomorrow, she would receive a floral delivery just like he sent while in college. He'd made it a point to send her flowers every other week because the smell reminded her of the time spent working in her mother's flower shop.

"Thanks for the food, Trey." She caught his eye.

He took a slow sip of his beer, allowing the liquid to fully absorb into his stream and then placed it back on the counter. "You're welcome. What would you like to drink?" He named a few non-alcoholic beverages and wines. "I also make a really good mudslide."

Tristyn leaned back. "I love mudslides but I'll pass for now and go with the wine."

He grabbed a vintage bottle and began pouring.

"Not too much," Tristyn stopped him. "I'm a lightweight."

"Is that right?" Trey raised his eyebrows. "Maybe I should fill it to the top then."

Tristyn playfully hit his arm with the back of her hand. "This is fine, thank you." She shook her head as she took her plate and glass back into the living room.

*   *   *   *   *   *   *

They sat on the floor with their backs against the couch, entirely too close to each other. Each time Tristyn looked over, she saw every handsome feature on his face. His eyebrows, thicker than average, provided a simplistic rugged touch to the rest of his normally clean-cut face. His lips, still exactly how she liked them. The bottom lip, slightly plumper than the top, perfect for sucking into her mouth when they kissed. The eyes, grey with brown speckles. His skin, still the lightest brown that allowed people to mistake him for their whiter counterparts. He had since gotten a tan, proving he still preferred being outside as long as the weather held up.

"This was so good. Thanks for the food. I'm gonna have to run ten miles just to work off all these calories," Tristyn chuckled, noticing the stubble beginning to appear on his face. It was such a turn on.

"I'm gonna get a little more wine. Do you want anything? And where's your bathroom? You only showed me to my room. You're a horrible host with a one-track mind." The corner of her mouth lifted into a grin.

"Well, I did feed you." He pointed to the door down the hallway that led to his office and Tristyn walked off without another word. Needing to stretch his legs, he moved from the floor to the sofa.

Tristyn emerged from the kitchen with another glass of wine. During her short reprieve she decided to give into her feelings and move their night along. She didn't know whether it was the wine, or the easy-going familiarity of being around Trey, but all she wanted was to be closer. She followed his lead and sat next to him on the sofa, angling her body toward him. "Can I be honest?"

Trey licked his lips. "I'd prefer that but I'm nervous about what you're gonna say."

A soft smile crossed her face. "Right before we ran into each other I had a dream about you."

His left eyebrow raised, a trait she had always adored. "What kind of dream?"

"A naughty one." She zeroed in on his lips. When would he kiss her again? She urged him to be on his best behavior and here she was hoping he would break her rules.

He nodded his head slowly, seeming to ruminate over his next move. "Did you enjoy it?"

"Loved it." Her body was so close that she could feel the heat from his body. During the short time she'd been there she'd spent the entire time checking him out when she thought he wasn't looking. Now they were smack dab in the middle of Netflix and Chill and had partaken in libations that loosened her up just enough to feel all the feels. And she was feeling all the feels.

"You know, we never finished our dance at the reunion."

He looked at her out the corner of his eye. "We didn't, did we?"

"Nope."

"How about we finish that then?" Trey switched off his TV and connected his phone to the speaker hidden behind his loveseat.

Tristyn took his outstretched hand and stepped into his arms. She felt as if she were the love interest in one of those old love songs. If Trey's arms were the wrong ones to be inside of, she sure as hell didn't want to be in the right ones. His embrace was everything. She felt protected in his strong arms. Safe with her head snuggly fitted underneath his chin. Secure with his heart beating wildly in her ear.

His hands, that had remained in the safe zone for the last two songs, started roaming more urgently along her back, gripping the material of her shirt. She had to kick this into high gear so he knew it was completely consensual on her end. Her next move, purposeful.

"Zaddy," she purred. The only times she'd called him that in the past was when she was about to do things she hoped no other woman had done to him since.

Trey stopped in his tracks. "Tristyn," his voice held a warning she wasn't about to follow.

"It's been a long time," she damn near whispered.

"Yeah." Both were suspended in time. Each awaiting the other's next move.

"That ends tonight." She was more than sure. Her body craved to be reunited with his. With the intake of his breaths increasing two-fold, she knew his craved the same. Only an act of God, warning her that the path leading to Trey was the wrong one, would stop her tonight.

She inched even closer and placed her hand on his chest.

Trey's eyes narrowed, crinkling in the corners. Brief seconds ticked by. Tristyn knew he was debating his next move. "I think you've had too much to drink."

"Trey, I'm very levelheaded," she slurred the last words.

"Or at least somewhat levelheaded," Trey joked.

"I have a clear head and believe me, I want you."

9

RIDE GOOD

CURRENT DAY

If there was anything to stop the wicked visions dancing around his brain, he would shoo them away. Tristyn was going to be the death of him tonight whether they slept together or not. Her gestures, words, and those damn body movements were driving him in-fuck-ing-sane. It was all a slippery slope and he hoped she felt just the same.

Tristyn's eyes narrowed to a slit and she pulled her bottom lip into her mouth. "Do you remember how I used to dance for you?"

"Whoa!" His voice cracked when her hand reached inside his pants to pull his phone from his pocket. She switched the song.

"I have something for you."

Trey's heartrate increased. He knew. He hoped, it was what he thought it was.

"Want a show?"

It was exactly what he thought it was. One of Tristyn's hobbies in college to stay in shape was pole dancing and when she felt frisky, she would show off what she learned. No man in his right mind would decline a personal show from her.

Eyebrows on ease and a tilt at the corner of her mouth sent her hips swaying. She dropped it low and slowly eased back up, pushing against his groin. Trey second guessed his good guy act. How necessary was it really to keep it up anyway? She said she wanted him, and he definitely wanted the same.

"It's only a dance. Can't handle it?" Seduction slipped off her every word.

Trey had yet to make a move. Had yet to touch her. All he could do was watch and try not to drool. He elected to be completely honest. "No."

It was bad enough that she had shown up at his door wearing tight shorts that if she bent over, he was sure he would see the bottoms of her squeezable ass. Then, her cut off shirt reminded him of all the nights he'd started at her belly button and kissed his way up and down her body. And the heels. Goddamn. She was trying to kill him. Now she was giving him a strip show.

"That's too bad, Trey." She continued her seductive dance, turning around and dropping her hands to the floor. Her ass bounced, jiggling wildly against his pelvis. His breath caught when she lowered to her haunches and her shirt flew off and covered the lamp. Those breasts. Those goddamn breasts. And her unzipped shorts. Fuuck.

He could no longer imagine being honorable around her but he had to. Didn't he? The notes of the next song floated through the air and his heartrate increased even more. Trey wondered if the old song *Slow Motion* by Trey Songz indicated what he was about to get himself into. Nah. Slow motion was for men ready to romance their women, not one that had been deprived of his woman for seven long ass years. Once he dove inside of her, he'd be lucky to last seven seconds.

He pulled her ponytail, as he'd been longing to do. Tristyn's head jerked backwards, her body curving back up to press against his. She turned her head around to look at him. "You must've forgotten the rules. Touching is not allowed at my show."

Trey's voice, lower and more gravelly, informed her, "Show's over." His hands enjoyed every inch of her skin as it travelled up to her chest, cupping a breast in each hand. He squeezed.

She moaned out loud, bringing Trey to attention. "Trey, no one has ever touched me like you do."

Tristyn spun around, Trey tilted his head down and brought her mouth to his. Passion overtook his body. "I'm about to do to you what I've been fantasizing about for the past couple of days and baby, you might never walk again."

Her lips grazed his and her hands caressed the back of his neck. She managed to breathe out, "Promises, promises."

Right as he was scooping her into his arms his doorbell rang.

Tristyn's hand on his chest stopped him in his tracks. She checked her watch. "Who is at your door this late?"

Trey shrugged his shoulders and glanced at the door. "I don't know, baby."

"Is it a booty call?" Accusation spit from her mouth.

"I'm not expecting anyone." Trey attempted to kiss her again, but she turned her head.

"Go tell whoever it is to go away." She walked away from him and hooked her bra back together.

"If I don't answer they'll probably go away." Trey hoped, but had a gut feeling that nothing good awaited the opening of his door.

Stopping in her tracks, Tristyn's head jerked toward Trey. "All of your lights are on. No one would drive over here this late, ring the doorbell, only to leave after hearing the music. Open the door."

He knew she knew. Her female intuition had to be persuading her to find out who was ringing the doorbell. Didn't she know that curiosity killed the cat? As much as he wanted to hold his ground, he wouldn't win this battle. He moped over to the door. Knowing, hoping, it wasn't who he thought it was on the other side. His hand grazed the handle and he bit his lip. Could he get around this? No, he couldn't. He snatched open the door and cursed under his breath. Yep, this wasn't going to be good.

Eve. The one and only woman he regretted sleeping with in his entire life. The one who appeared to have more than a few screws loose. The one who falsely claimed ownership over his body and refused to take a restraining order for an answer. If he believed in violence, he would've hired a hitman.

In the beginning, their relationship had gone smoothly enough, but one day, things had changed and he was sure it had something to do with the alcohol he started smelling on her breath. She started calling him constantly. The final straw in their relationship was when she yelled at the receptionist at his job for not pulling Trey from an important meeting when she called. When he broke things off, she disappeared, until a month ago when she started calling again. He didn't know what she wanted but he was sure it was nothing important.

"Go home, Eve." Trey attempted to shut the door in her face, but she barged past him into the living room. "Eve, get out my house!"

Her eyes immediately narrowed in on Tristyn. "You sure didn't waste any time getting over me. I knew you would have a bitch over here tonight. That's why I came over. I had to see for myself. Did I mean anything to you?"

"No, Eve, you didn't."

Tristyn laughed under her breath. "I know this chic did not just call me a bitch."

Trey glanced at Tristyn. Eve was ruining his only chance. "You gotta go, and don't call her a bitch."

Tears rapidly appeared in Eve's eyes, as if she had been holding onto them, waiting for the perfect moment to drop them. "How could you say I meant nothing to you when you were everything to me? And to leave me for her?" She gestured toward Tristyn.

"You were gone way before her, Eve."

"All right now," Tristyn talked over her crossed arms. "You got one more time to bring me into something I have nothing to do with."

"How dare you talk to me!" Eve screamed past Trey.

"Eve!" Trey tried to pull her attention back to him. "You're drunk, as always. Go home. Get out. Just go." Eve, a woman of average height, average weight, average looks, average strength, proved difficult to push out his home.

Eve broke out of Trey's grasp and marched toward Tristyn. "You are the worst type of woman. You think you can just waltz in here and take something that doesn't belong to you."

Tristyn, possessing a level of calm he'd never seen, advised Eve to get her finger out of her face. Before Trey could get over there, Tristyn smacked Eve's hand down and pushed her back.

Eve responded by pulling Tristyn's hair. Trey watched in bewilderment before stepping in. He never would have guessed that the name calling would escalate into an all-out brawl. When he jumped in between the two he was scratched on the face by one and slapped in the nose by another. What seemed to take several minutes was over within seconds.

"That's enough!" He pulled Tristyn off Eve and flung her to the couch.

Tristyn froze and Eve pulled herself off the floor. "Eve, get out before I call the cops. And you know as well as I do that you don't wanna be caught over here. And don't ever come back!"

Eve stopped with her hand on the doorknob. "Trey, you were everything to me. I don't know what I did to make you act this way, but I don't deserve this." With mascara running down her cheeks and a drop of blood on her swollen lip, Eve ran out of Trey's house in tears.

Trey palmed his fist in his other hand, unsure how to proceed. Tristyn's smoothed ponytail now had strands of hair pulled into loops at the top and her face remained twisted out of anger. All he wanted was to comfort her and make sure she was okay. "Princess, are you..."

Not a word was spoken as she put her hand in the air to stop him in his tracks.

Trey tried another angle. "I ain't know you could fight like that."

"Shut up, Trey," Tristyn's eyes shot daggers through his soul.

Ruined. What he had believed would be a magical reunion had quickly gone downhill with one ring of the doorbell. "If I had any idea she was coming...I had no idea, Tristyn."

She breezed past him without a word. "I can't stay here. I just-I gotta go. This is, this is..." she searched for the right word.

"Ridiculous?" Trey offered.

"Yes! Don't do that!" She snapped.

"Do what, Princess?"

Her nostrils flared. "You know what I'm talking about and stop calling me Princess. You don't deserve to use that endearment with me. You lost that privilege a long ass time ago. Fucking asshole."

"Tristyn, I didn't do anything. I had no idea she was going to stop by and had I known, I damn sure wouldn't have answered the door. That bitch is crazy, you saw it."

She pointed her finger in the middle of his chest and lowered her voice. "Don't fuck with me, Trey."

He moved her hand away from his chest and to the side. "I know you're upset but stay. We gotta talk about this. You're drunk and I don't want you going anywhere like this."

"I am not drunk!" She screamed. Her eyes narrowed and she walked closer, causing him to take a few steps back. "Now I see what you're about." Her voice lowered. "How many women do you entertain in a month? Better yet, how many per week? Do they all just fall under your spell and end up heartbroken when you leave?"

Trey stared at her blankly. "Tristyn, listen," he reached out but she backed away. "With you back in my life the only woman that matters to me now is you."

Tristyn's eyes squinted even more. "I am not a conquest or a one-night stand. I am wife material and if you thought anything less of me then you were mistaken. Fuck you, Trey."

"Fuck me?"

"Fuck! You!"

"I know you're a little upset but..."

"A little upset? I'm pissed! I could fry an egg on my head I'm so heated right now. I got into a fight. I am a grown woman. What do I look like fighting someone? I could go to jail." She walked in circles continuing to rant and rave to no one in particular.

Trey plopped down on the couch and rested his head in his hands. A large sigh escaped as he pulled on his hair. He had to do something. He was not going to lose her again. He lifted from the couch. "Listen, I don't want you to leave next week, tomorrow, or even tonight. I meant what I said about wanting to get to know you again. You're right, you're not a conquest or one-night stand, you are much more and I know that. Princess, I need another chance with you. What just happened, please don't blame me for that. She means nothing. I swear that to you and whoever else I have to swear to for you to believe me."

A hint of a gleam showed in her eyes and Trey knew he had a chance to correct the evening. He continued, "Please don't let what happened tonight ruin anything that we could have going. I promise I will find some way to make it up to you. All I'm asking is for you to let me try. And then after that, if you decide I'm not worth your time then I'll leave you alone. But please, stay the night and let me make things right."

"I don't know, Trey. Think about it, how did we get here? Are things not moving fast to you? Every time I'm around you we almost end up in bed together and we literally ran back into each other two days ago. Two days ago." She held up two fingers.

"We can't help that there's chemistry between us, baby."

They participated in a standoff before Tristyn's shoulders sagged and she released a short breath, shaking her head.

The entrance. Trey took it. Tristyn was second guessing her choice to leave. The anger was slowly being replaced with tenderness. "Whatever you want, whatever you need, I will do it for you if you stay. I don't know what I would do if I lost the chance to get back in your life. And for me to lose it in this manner, due to someone that means nothing to me, I would die. And then I'd die again."

Her features softened.

"I have a restraining order against Eve."

"You do?"

"Not a real one but I told her I did. I thought it would make her fall back. But I'll get a legitimate one if you want me to. You call the shots in my life now."

"Trey, that's also ridiculous. We're not together and as of right now, I'm not sure you have another shot with me."

"If you're not sure then that means there's still a chance." Crinkle lines appeared in the corners of his eyes as he smiled.

Tristyn pushed past him. "You are on thin ice. I'm going to bed."

"So that means you'll stay?" He asked her retreating back.

"Goodnight, Trey."

"Night." Trey smiled as she walked up the steps. Despite everything, there was still a chance for him to win her over.

10

RIDE OUT

God had done it. An act of God had put her bad judgment on display. She'd stayed as Trey requested, slept off the wine, and with a clear head, it was time to make life decisions. Tristyn's life was going well until she ran into Trey. She had a loyal, sexy, boyfriend that cared for her, wanted to give her life meaning, and fly her around the world. Her job was stable, and she was damn good at what she did, but since running into Trey, she'd already managed to jeopardize her entire future.

She blew out a deep breath and flung off the covers to relieve herself, almost afraid to look in the mirror for fear of seeing a scratch or bruise that Eve left as a reminder of her time there. She was too old to be fighting off deranged exes and if that's what a life with Trey meant she had to look forward to, she didn't want any parts of it.

It was time to get back to life in Cleveland with her stable job, her friends, family, and Jacob. Finalizing a life away from Trey would be difficult but she would make do. Her life was good enough and she could spice it up, add some fun. Shit, she would try skydiving if that's what it took. And in time, Trey would become a distant memory again, she hoped.

She would go through with the interview for follow through purposes only, and then use that as leverage to get a raise at her current job. Then, she would return home with a new look on life.

Pulling on socks, she opened the bedroom door and padded down the steps to have the talk she desperately wanted to avoid.

"Trey," she called out with no response. A bright orange sticky note on the kitchen counter greeted her.

Didn't wanna wake you because you looked so peaceful. I made pancakes and left them in the fridge. Gonna try and leave work early but if I can't I'll be home no later than 5 and we can talk. Again, sorry for last night. I'll make it up to you. Promise. ~Trey

He made walking away even more difficult. Opening the door to the fridge her eyes delighted her. He still remembered and made her favorite, chocolate chip pancakes but was there...Reddi Whip, yes, after all this time he remembered her favorite breakfast. She stared at the plate debating her next move until hunger got the best of her. "Why is he like this? All thoughtful and shit. And sexy as hell. God, I hate him!"

She popped the pancakes into the microwave right when Trey's doorbell rang. Her heart skipped as memories of last night flooded her conscious. "Not again."

Needing to know if Eve had the nerve to venture back, Tristyn ran to the window and peeked through the curtains. A delivery van was parked in the driveway and a man stood with a bouquet of flowers. She bit her lip as she debated answering the door. She opened it just in time to stop the driver from putting the van into reverse.

He opened his door and yelled out. "I didn't think anyone was home."

Tristyn forged an excuse. "Sorry, I was in the bathroom."

"Oh, that's all right, ma'am. I have a delivery for Ms. Tristyn Miller."

She froze in her tracks.

Noticing her pause, the driver asked, "Does she not live here? I thought this was the right address." He validated the address on the house against the address in the system.

"No, she does. I mean she doesn't." Flustered, she said, "I'm her."

The man's face questioned her as his eyes narrowed.

"I'm sorry, I just woke up and haven't had my coffee yet. I'm no good until I get a little caffeine in my body."

Seeming to finally understand, he handed over the arrangement. "I know what you mean. I'm the same way. Well, these are for you. Enjoy and have a good day."

Tristyn carried the arrangement inside and set them on the kitchen counter. A beautiful display of two-dozen white calla lilies and white roses in a glass vase, treated her senses. Right in the middle was a card signed by Trey.

She smiled as she held the card next to her heart. Yep, she officially hated him. More than that, she hated she had to leave.

Her phone rang. Trey. "Hey Sleeping Beauty. Are you just now waking up?"

"I am."

"I see you got the flowers."

"I did." Tristyn quickly glanced around the house for cameras. "How did you know?"

"I got a delivery notification. Do you like them? They're obviously not from your mom's but hopefully they're comparable."

"They're very nice. Thank you."

"You're welcome." An audible sigh escaped his mouth. "I told you I was gonna make it up to you and this is just one way I'm doing that. I am so sorry..."

"Trey, stop apologizing. It really wasn't your fault." Where had that come from? She was caving, falling right back into his trap. It *was* his fault. It was *always* his fault.

Trey blew out a breath of air. "Well, it's just, I wanted everything to be perfect. I'm trying, Tristyn, to make up for every bad thing I've done to you, whether that was indirectly or directly, last night or forever a go."

She remained quiet. All of her being pulled her toward him but the one part, the part that mattered, warned her to run.

"Okay," Tristyn spoke again.

"Well, I should be there around five or so. I hoped to be able to take you out, but I can't get out of here early. We're right in the middle of this huge project. If you need to leave, there's a spare key in the drawer next to the silverware. Don't worry about setting the alarm."

"Okay, thanks." Silence hung in the air. She knew he wanted to say more but she cut it short. "I'll talk to you later."

Tristyn ended the call and held her phone against her chest, a single tear threatening to fall. She looked to the ceiling and rapidly blinked. She had to get out of there but first, breakfast. The microwave beeped a reminder that her food was done and for a moment, she let the chocolate chips take her away. Trey had always been an exceptional cook but only expressed his talent on special occasions. The pancakes melted in her mouth, and she moaned. "Damn these are good." She rolled her eyes and stuffed in another mouthful.

On her phone, the uncancelled hotel reservation called out to her. Before she could talk herself out of it, she clicked on the phone number to initiate the call.

"Good morning, my name is Tristyn Miller and I was supposed to check in last night but I got hung up and couldn't make it. Is my reservation still active?" Tristyn listened while the receptionist tapped buttons.

"Yes, it is. We allow no-shows twenty-four hours. After that, the reservations are automatically removed from the system. When can we expect you, ma'am?"

Tristyn checked her watch. "I'll be there in about thirty minutes."

11

ALL FALLS DOWN

7 YEARS AGO

He told himself he was going through with this for Derrick's sake but that wasn't entirely true. He wanted to know. Wanted to see. He needed to do this so he could make a final decision to either forgive their father for disappearing or hold a grudge forever. He was prepared to do both.

A young girl met them at the door of a small one-story house in a sketchy neighborhood. Locs reached the girl's shoulders, a nose ring dotted her nostril, and her skin held much more melanin than Trey and Derrick combined. Her oversized jeans hung low on her hips and her sweatshirt was big enough to fit Trey comfortably. She was different, presenting an earthly vibe that neither he nor Derrick showed any interest in. Trey could clearly see over her head, but she was taller than he expected. Other than having the same nose, she looked nothing like them. This was their baby sister, Chelsea. He fought the urge to hug her. Next to him, he saw Derrick quickly swipe his eyes. Allergies, apparently.

Her whole face and posture changed when she registered who stood on her front porch. "Oh my God! You're finally here! Dad," she called out behind her.

Her arms outstretched, she wrapped an arm around both of them, pulling them down to her height. "I can't believe it. You're actually here. Best day ever."

Trey wrapped one arm around her. Derrick did the same. Now, apparently, Trey also had allergies. They stayed like that, enveloped in a ball of emotions, until the click of a camera taking a picture behind them interrupted the moment. Trey opened his eyes to see an older man, the spitting image of Derrick. It was life altering.

Yellowing eyes on a man with only one leg, who also, apparently had allergies, stood there smiling at his phone. "I've waited a lifetime for this."

"Dad." Careful not to knock David off balance, Derrick fell into their father's arms and sobbed. The only other time Trey saw his baby brother cry was when his little league baseball team lost the series in the first four games. Neither of them showed emotions, much more preferring to keep them bottled. Their mama, similar to them, only dropped tears during the sad parts of animated children's films. She didn't cry at weddings, funerals, or even when their dog died. Trey had always figured she identified with the fake world more than the world they had to live in.

More cautious than Derrick, Trey inched into the home behind Chelsea, who had yet to stop chancing glances at them. Their home seemed to be stuck in time. The aged furniture, the lights with the yellowing shades, the carpet a lighter tan only underneath the furniture, the dust layered atop of the box TV sitting on the floor, all stood out against Chelsea. He wondered if it was as overwhelming for her as it was for them but soon decided it wasn't. Already, she had proven to be more daring than them, more willing to take chances, ready to reach out to strangers regardless of the risk of rejection.

She'd been dealt different cards though. Her mom had died and now her dad was sick. For the first time, he wondered, as a minor, what would happen to her once her dad, rather, their dad, died. Was there other family that would take her in?

"Let me get you some tissues." David walked off to the bathroom and brought back a roll of toilet paper. "I don't have the tissues from the box, but this will do just fine. I figure if it's soft enough to use on our asses then it's soft enough to use on our faces."

Laughter rang out around the room. Derrick and David seemed to be the spitting image in looks and personality.

"Daddy! Don't say things like that." Chelsea made her way to the sofa and took a seat. "They don't know you like I do."

Derrick beamed next to David. "That sounds like something I would say."

"That is definitely something you would say," Trey agreed. "Our mama is always getting after him for having something snappy to say."

"You're a smartass, too?" Chelsea nodded to Derrick.

"I wouldn't say that but..."

"You are," Trey interrupted. "Don't even lie. You can't go a day without being sarcastic to someone. And if you're not saying something it'll be written all over your face."

"Apparently, I get it honestly."

Chelsea laughed. "Daddy is always talking back to someone. It doesn't matter who it is. I bet if the president was here Daddy would find something smart to say to him, too."

David waved it off and sat back in his light brown recliner. "Oh, hush, child. I'm not that bad. But if people don't want me to say something smart then maybe they shouldn't say stupid shit. It's not my fault that these muthafuckas are dumb as all get out."

Derrick jumped up from his spot on the sofa. "Thank you! Somebody finally understands me. People are dumb. It's not my fault that I repeat back how stupid they sound."

Again, they all laughed until their bellies tightened. This felt right. This felt like...home? But it didn't feel like home more than it felt like home at Mama's. This was different, but still, home. Trey hadn't known what to expect and that had put undue stress on him to the point where he had forgotten to study for a test. Thankfully, it was in one of his easier classes and he'd received a B without having looked at the material. He wouldn't make that mistake again. With the pressure to help out Mama, the stakes to graduate at the top of his class were high.

"How is your mama doing?" David, along with the rest of the room, looked at Trey, waiting for him to answer. It was like he had read his mind. Was that the father son connection at work?

"She's doing fine." Trey glanced at his watch. "She just got off work and should be on her way home now. She started to call off and come with us, but we persuaded her not to."

"Now why would you do that? It would've been nice to see her after all this time and make amends."

Trey chuckled under his breath and shook his head, leaning forward on the sofa. "Nah, I don't think you wanna do that just yet."

"Yeah," Derrick chimed in. "Mama still mad at you and you don't wanna be on her bad side."

David rocked in his recliner and lifted the footrest. "Oh, Gloria, still the same after all this time. Her temper was something I always loved about her. Well, I loved it until she'd turn that on me and boy did she turn on me sometimes. For the littlest shit." He cackled. "I remember this one time, you boys couldn't have been more than two and six years old, well she asked me to take this casserole out the oven. I'll never forget. It was a Sunday, and the football game was on. Don't you know I forgot to take it out and it was burned to a crisp! Ooh wee she cussed me out so bad. But I made up for it that night if you know what I mean. She forgave me." His eyes glossed over, and he rubbed his chin. "Yeah, that was a good night. And I had to buy her some flowers and chocolate the next day like it was Valentine's. Good to see she's the same old Gloria though. I loved that woman to death."

Loved her to death. Trey struggled with that statement. If David loved Mama to death, why the hell didn't he come back? His mood immediately soured.

Derrick glanced at Trey and then spoke. "If she came it would've been all bad. You on Mama's hitlist."

"It can't be that bad," David rubbed a hand over his bald head.

"It is." The chipped tone on top of Trey's two words left an awkward sensation in the air. Since the tension was already sliced, he added, "You left her to take care of us with no child support, no forwarding address, no nothing."

Derrick's young eyes penetrated Trey's vision. He wasn't specifically Team Mama, but he sure as hell was Team Give a Nigga a Chance. "Trey, man, we can talk about that another time."

"Yeah, maybe another time," Chelsea suggested.

Trey grinded his teeth from side to side before his Adam's apple bobbed and he clapped his hands. "Y'all right. Another time. I'm sorry for ruining the moment."

David lowered the footrest and leaned forward, zoning in on Trey. "Trey's right. What I did was wrong, and I've regretted it since the day I ran. I shouldn't have done that. I thought about coming back every day."

"Why didn't you? We needed you and come to find out you said fuck us and created a whole new family like we weren't shit to you."

"Trey! Not cool." Derrick rarely raised his voice, this time notwithstanding, but with his voice beginning to quiver, it wouldn't be long before he challenged his big brother.

"All I can say now is that I should've come back for you. I had a million excuses back then as to why I never returned. Too much time had passed. You had aged out of needing a father. Gloria hated me. You didn't want me in your lives. I couldn't be the man that two boys needed. As I said, a million excuses, when truly I was just scared of the wrath I would receive when I came back.

"Being sick has a way of reminding you that it's never too late to do anything, even if it's to admit that you were the crappiest kind of human being to walk the earth. All the apologies won't make you feel any better. Coming back into your lives now, if you accept me, won't right my wrongs. I only had Chelsea reach out because I wanted to see the men that you had grown into, and to apologize, even if you don't forgive me. I'd hoped to get into this a little later but as I've learned, you can't control how life shows up.

"If I could get on my knees and beg for forgiveness, I'd do it, but those days are long gone." He looked into Derrick's eyes, studied him, and then gained a smile on his face. "Derrick, my baby boy who's not a baby anymore. You're my spitting image and instead of looking up to a father, I left you to look up to your brother, who shouldn't have had to stand in my spot as the man of the house. That robbed you of a genuine brotherly relationship with Trey, and I'm sorry.

"Trey, my oldest, I'm sorry I wasn't there to guide you into manhood. Instead, you had to step into it alone and figure out how to navigate relationships, personal and professional, on your own. You had to step into adulthood before you were ready because you took the spot that I should've been there to fulfill. You both deserved better and I'll be forever grateful to Gloria for doing such an incredible job raising you two."

Chelsea looked as if she wanted to shrink inside of the sofa and disappear. She'd curled her legs into her chest and sat, looking at the floor. If there was any group of people Trey wanted to protect, it was women, and he hated that he'd made his baby sister uncomfortable.

He looked at David. It was too early to offer forgiveness, but he'd done what was asked of him, to listen. Trey nodded, "I'm gonna get some air."

Derrick stood along with him. "I'll go with you."

Trey stopped him with his hand in the air. "I'd appreciate if you didn't. I'll be back."

The warm, crisp air soothed him momentarily, but he couldn't stop thinking about what David's return meant for his family. It could be the beginning of the end. He released a deep breath

The slap on the back of his back startled him. "You been out here kinda long big bro." Derrick stood next to him, looking at the street to see what had garnered Trey's interest long enough to keep him outside.

"This life crazy enough for you yet?" Trey returned.

"It's just getting started." Derrick, the deep thinker, thought hard and loved harder. He believed in love at first sight and soulmates. He knew that when he found the right one, he would propose immediately and they would live well into their nineties, bearing a basketball team's worth of children.

Trey, on the other hand, kept it straight. Life was not grey, but pure black and white. He maintained a life of saying and meaning what he thought. Mama constantly reminded him that things were consistently not what he imagined them to be, to which he responded, grass is either green or brown, alive or dead, there is no in between.

"Let's go back in," Trey suggested

"You cool?" Derrick studied him.

In time he knew he would be. "Yeah, I am."

Back inside, Chelsea stood, twisting the thin ring on her pinky finger. "Is everything okay? You're not leaving, are you?"

Trey knew right then, that he could never leave Chelsea like David had left them. "Nah."

Relief splayed all over her face, her eyes brightening the entire room. "Thank you."

A knock sounded at the door. "I'll get it." Chelsea squeezed past them and grabbed the food from the delivery person. "Food's here. I ordered chicken because I figured that was something we'd all eat."

"Why'd you think we like chicken? Because we're black?" Derrick asked.

Chelsea froze. "Oh, you guys don't like chicken?"

"He's messing with you," Trey pointed at Derrick with his thumb. "Of course, we like chicken. We're black."

"You scared me. I shouldn't have made any assumptions." Chelsea placed the food on the table next to the paper plates and cups. "Daddy doesn't cook anymore since he got sick and I'm still learning. I thought about letting you be my test dummies for this one recipe I found online but I didn't wanna scare you away too soon."

For the rest of their time, neither party broached subjects remarkably close to running away from the past, David's sickness, or apologies, until, "I'm really glad you boys joined us. I don't know if you can tell but at this point in my life my days are numbered. I, uh," David paused. "I don't have much time."

"Daddy," Chelsea blurted out. "Can I ask you something in the kitchen?"

David, who looked to be deep in thought, took a moment before pushing his chair away from the table. "Sure, sweetheart. No problem."

12

You

The day from hell, at best. Trey's firm was contracted to design a new mixed use shopping development and today, it had all went to shit. One of the interns was fired after discovering that instead of spending his time drafting over the last week, he had been gaming and building his online audience. To get back on schedule, two full time architects were pulled from their daily tasks. To make matters worse, the other intern, who also happened to be the development owner's daughter, snitched, and Trey was called into an in-person meeting that lasted an hour past five. Seeing Tristyn was the only thing that brightened his day, and he couldn't wait to walk inside his home.

But Tristyn's convertible wasn't in his driveway. He directed his phone assistant to send her a text to see what time she'd be back. If needed, he could order dinner or take her out if her day had been as long as his. He smiled. It already felt like they were in a relationship and he couldn't wait to experience more days of coming home to her face.

He kicked off his dress shoes and sent them flying to the corner before heading upstairs to change his clothes. The current environment at his job, relaxed to encourage optimal creativity, wasn't something he adhered to. Everything from sweatpants to jeans with safety pins were allowed but as the lead, who often was invited to meetings with millionaire business owners wearing the likes of Brunello Cucinelli and Balenciaga, neither of which he could confidently pronounce, he preferred to wear more upscale and casual professional attire.

He checked the rest of his notifications, preferring to keep the phone close while waiting for Tristyn's response. He paused in the middle of the upstairs hallway and walked backwards three steps. His arms dropped to his side. Tristyn's things were gone.

He pushed the door open more, it knocked against the stopper with a thump. Eyes scanned left to right and back to the middle, where he originally dropped her baggage next to the bed. Trey's teeth ground against each other and he lifted his phone to call Tristyn. It rang continuously before going straight to voicemail. As bad as he wanted to throw it against the wall, he needed it to be in working condition more.

He tried calling her once more with the same result. He flexed his fingers and practiced deep breaths. Thoughts ran crazy in his head. She'd left. She'd really left. "Fuck!"

He should've known by her tone when they spoke earlier that something wasn't right. Had she returned home? Was she coming back? Would she still visit Northrup tomorrow? Was she at...the hotel?

Trey bounced off the bed and ran downstairs. Tristyn mentioned cancelling her reservation at a Marriott hotel and there was only one in the area. His luxury pickup truck revved out of his neighborhood.

Maroon loafers carried him to the front desk, quietly making the statement to the few attendees in the lobby that he was a man on a mission. He had always stood out amongst his peers whether for his looks, his eyes in the bedroom, or his strict sense of fashion. He hoped everything would come in handy as he tried to sweettalk the woman associate at the front desk.

Right as he was walking up, she was tapped on her shoulder by a man who sent her on break. "Fuck my life." He smoothed his hands down his face and plastered on a white toothed smile. Maybe the man would be gay.

A brown-skinned beauty darted in front of Trey, chasing a loose toddler. Her breasts bounced inside her strapless top, enhancing her free nipples. "Excuse me," she caught up to the child and snatched him up.

His eyes followed the movement and so did the man's behind the desk. They were interested in the same sex. God was not smiling on him today. "Good evening, sir, are you checking in?"

He had to think fast. "I'm actually trying to see if my friend left her room already. We were supposed to meet in the lobby," he checked his watch, "about ten minutes ago. Can you call up to her room to see if she's left?"

"I'd love to, what's her room number?"

"She didn't give me that. I didn't even think to ask just because we were meeting in the lobby. I'll give you her name."

"That's not going to work, sir. I need her room number."

A muscle in Trey's jaw flexed. "Why do you need her room number if I'm providing her name?"

The associate, identified by Jay on his name tag, stared at Trey. His entire demeanor changed. "We're not going to have a problem, are we? Surely if you were really waiting for your friend, instead of stalking her, you could have called or texted her to see if she was running late. Something about this is off."

"Surely, "stalking" is a harsh word to use for someone wanting to check on his friend."

"Surely, you're right, Sir. My apologies."

They remained in a standoff, the associate's fingers still refusing to tap in Tristyn's name, Trey still refusing to walk away. He needed to find her. He needed to talk to her. He needed her to answer her phone. He needed all that to happen more than he needed to press the issue.

"Look, okay," he leaned over, resting his elbows on the counter. He ran his hands over his head and blew out a breath of air. He attempted to reason, man to man. "My girl, she used to be my girl back in the day, I ran into her and she came up to my house and shit went sideways. All I was trying to do was get back with her, make her feel comfortable, and then my ex showed up at my house and they ended up fighting. It wasn't my fault. You feel me?"

Jay nodded, a touch of sympathy in his eyes. "Yes, I do and that's quite tragic, but I still can't help you. Sorry. You're welcome to hang out in our lobby. We have water and tea. If you'd like some fresh coffee, I can brew a batch. It'll take about five minutes."

Trey's fingers gripped the associate's counter. He wanted to shake Jay, but it wasn't his fault. He straightened his fingers and then balled them back into a fist. "I understand. Thanks."

He walked away and sat in the lobby seating area. There was a good view of the front doors and elevators so maybe, just maybe, if Tristyn was staying there, he would see her if she left her room. It was a long shot considering it was already late and she had probably ordered food and taken it back to her room. Speaking of food, Trey looked around and finally smiled. A sign for a restaurant and bar pointed down a hallway. As much as he didn't want to leave his spot, he needed to see if she had ventured into the restaurant.

He scanned the restaurant. Tristyn wasn't there. It'd been a slim chance but now he was at least sure she wasn't there. He turned around to leave but when he heard a laugh, his stomach lurched. Tristyn. His chest lifted slowly as he took a deep breath. Her laugh had always done something to him, and he was a having a hard time figuring out how so much time had passed, yet, his heart still loved her like time had stalled.

His eyes scanned the interior once again. He still didn't see her but there was no other laugh in the world that would cause him to have the same reaction.

A waitress stood at a table in the corner, talking to a patron with a large smile on her face. Tristyn had to be in that booth just out of view. His purposeful strides carried him over and he greeted Tristyn with a grimace.

She'd seen a ghost and that was exactly the reaction she had left him with. As much relief that spilled through Trey's veins, a load of feelings pursed through his body, akin to an earthquake. He slid into the booth on the opposite side of the table.

The waitress looked between the two of them, the negative energy overflowing. The vibrant conversation from a second earlier, now gone. "Can I get you something?" she asked him.

Eyes trained on Tristyn, he talked to the waitress. "Manhattan. It seems as if I need something to relax me. I've been extremely tense since I got off work. Really, really rough day."

"Sure thing. I'll get those drinks and be right back to take your food order." She walked off, looking over her shoulder to assess the situation once more.

Trey bent his head to the left, eliciting a slight crack of his neck. The longer they sat without speaking, the more upset he became. He flexed his fingers again.

When he spoke, his voice cracked, emotions getting the best of him. "Tristyn."

She looked down at the table and rolled her lips into her mouth, a habit Trey remembered her doing only when uncomfortable.

"I called you about fifty times and sent you a bunch of texts. Why didn't you tell me you were leaving? We could've talked. I told you I would make it up to you. That I would do anything to make it up to you."

Her shoulders slumped and she looked everywhere but at him.

"After all our history, don't you think that your departure deserves more than telling me nothing? Leaving without a word?"

Tristyn snorted and crossed her arms over her chest. Her eyebrows lifted and her eyes thinned to near slits. "Are you sure you wanna ask me that?"

Trey balled up his hands and released them. Checkmate. "Is that what this is about? Are you getting your revenge?"

She uncrossed her arms. Voice lowered to keep from disturbing others, she hissed at him. "Revenge? *Clearly* that's what this is about. It couldn't possibly be that you're so into living the bachelor life that you have women coming over at all times of the night that want to hurt anyone that you're with. It couldn't possibly be that you're still leaving your mark on women and making them think they have something with you when they don't. It couldn't possibly be that I saw a piece of myself in Eve and I felt for her." Her hands covered her heart, tears pricking her eyes. "If I didn't go into a reclusive stage after you left, I could have easily been Eve."

The waitress set their drinks on the table. Her lighthearted conversation from earlier shifted into a quieter, purposeful tone. "Did either of you want to order food or are the drinks fine for now?"

Tristyn's hands supported her head, covering her face. Trey reached into his wallet and pulled out a fifty-dollar bill. He handed it over to the waitress. "We're taking our drinks to our room. I don't need any change. Thank you." The waitress dismissed herself.

"Let's talk in your room, Tristyn. Is that okay?"

She nodded without looking at him, grabbed her drink and purse, and walked out the restaurant. Trey followed.

"This is a nice room."

"Can we just get down to business?" The door closed behind them and Tristyn swung around to face Trey. "Why are you here? How did you even find me?"

Trey shrugged. "Kismet."

"Fate did not help you find me, Trey."

"It sure as hell didn't keep me away, Tristyn."

"Trey."

"Tristyn."

She growled and kicked off her shoes before walking to the dresser to grab her drink. Trey followed her lead. One glance at the glass in his hand and he decided to down the contents. At one time, she was his all. He'd known she would be his wife, that they would tackle the worst problems together. That they would argue about what colors to paint walls and how low he should mow the grass. Then it had changed after a conversation between Mama, Derrick, and him. It was a conversation he never regretted taking, but it was one that led him to make bad decisions that negatively affected Tristyn. He could've handled the fallout better but at the time he had been so lost in his grief that he could barely crawl out. Getting into her good graces, her arms, was all that mattered now.

He wasn't the man that left without a word and he wasn't the man that would ever do it again. "Princess."

Tristyn spun around so fast that her hair flew into the air, some getting caught in her mouth. "Don't call me that, Trey. There is no love or camaraderie between us."

"There was, and we can get that back. There was also friendship. And the passion we thought was gone was back like it never left."

"Ugh, don't remind me. That was a mistake that I'm glad was interrupted."

Her mind spoke the words clear enough but her body movements said otherwise. Trey had always been able to read her better than others. "That's a goddamn lie." Ever so slightly, Trey's chin tilted higher, challenging her.

"You're so arrogant," Tristyn leaned against the edge of the dresser. Trey's height intimidated most but not her. He had often joked that she was the only one he let boss him around.

"And I'm also aware. You may have changed your mind, but your body hasn't realized that yet." He involuntarily licked his lips while he remembered the wild times they would share after his basketball games. She loved his subtle take charge personality and he intended to remind her of that. He was tired of getting close enough to touch her but not close enough to truly feel her.

"The only reaction I'm having to you is an itchy, allergic reaction to your being." She stood upright and emphasized her point with every step toward him. "Being around you irritates my whole soul. Invisible scales pop onto my skin when I'm near you. You bring out the worst in me and I become someone I don't even know. Next thing I know, I'm yelling at you, or someone else. You are an infestation underneath my fucking nails." Her forehead reached his chin and her nostrils flared. "You don't know when to stop. I left because I didn't want to be found. But of course, you missed that part because you think everyone wants you."

"You left because you're scared. I get that but I don't have any intention of hurting you. Not this time. Not ever again. Princess, please..."

She looked off to the side and moistened her lips, an act that brightened the brown speckles in his eyes and darkened the grey. The intensity that followed was something that only appeared for her. He'd tried to change that. Tried to give to other women what he put down on Tristyn, but had failed. Being with her brought his body alive and he was anxious to hear her cries of pleasure. He had been deprived too long and at least, now, he knew there were zero chances of interruption. Fuck a conversation, he needed her now.

He took a step forward, much to her surprise. When his hands reached out to cup her face, she didn't stop him. Was it truly fate that led him to her, or had she purposely allowed him to trail her so they could finally start a new chapter?

Tristyn closed her eyes in anticipation of Trey's lips on hers. Trey held back until she reopened them. He couldn't help the smirk that appeared across his face. After everything, she still wanted him just as much as he needed her.

The atmosphere warmed immediately when their lips finally connected. It was gentle, slow. The memory of long make out sessions reclaimed space in his memory. Her lips were soft, the right alternative to his firmer ones. He let up for just a second and she took the bait, sucking on his bottom lip. She moaned and her arms wrapped around his neck, pulling him closer.

He hadn't planned for this to happen. Genuinely, he wanted to talk so he could work his way back into her heart, but as soon as his lips touched hers, he knew the continuation of last night was a must. This time they were both in their right mind and by the sounds of it, Tristyn was ready to take a trip down memory lane.

Trey's tongue forced its way into her mouth. Tristyn reciprocated more forcefully. That was one thing he'd loved about her, she had never been shy in expressing her need for him. She was the only woman in his life that he had *almost* had trouble keeping up with sexually. When Tristyn needed him, it was hard to stall her roaming hands until they could make their way someplace private.

Because of her sexual thirst, they enjoyed making love, fucking, and participating in oral satisfaction in more places than he could recollect. Of those places, the most memorable had been on his mother's bed. He regretted that but boy, had they done a number on those sheets. They had barely gotten the freshly laundered sheets back on the bed when Mama pulled into her garage.

Trey walked her backwards until her legs hit the bed. Their lips parted briefly as he laid Tristyn atop the plush comforter. Through the slits of her eyes, she welcomed his body on top of hers. The kisses were slow, controlled, the opposite of the blood that rushed to every limb of his body. He kept reminding himself that after all this time, Tristyn deserved the full experience. A reacquainting of their bodies.

His hand slid up her thigh taking in all her curves. When he hit the spot at the juncture of her pelvis and the top of her leg, her muscle twitched and her back arched, pushing her breasts against his chest.

Through shaky hands he smoothed the hair from her cheek. His eyes searched hers. "There's no stopping me once I start so if you don't want this..."

Barely above a whisper she said, "I want this." Her hands caressed the shadow growing on his chin and Trey held them in place. They were so soft just like her body that kept urging him to continue.

A warning lingered in the air. "I'm serious, Tristyn. I..."

"So am I. I said don't stop."

A growl emitted from deep in his chest. Trey placed a multitude of kisses from the bottom of her ear, continuing down her collarbone, stopping at her clothed breast. He sucked through her shirt, wetting the material so that her nipples poked through. He continued his journey, ending at the button on her jeans.

Lips slightly parted, eyes closed, Tristyn reached down and gripped the bottom of her shirt, lifting it over her head while Trey unbuckled her pants, pulling those and her lacy red panties from her body.

Trey's jaw flexed, she still kept her body groomed just the way he liked, and he wondered, if for a second, if she had gotten that done just for him before she drove up. He made his way back to her womanhood but paused. "You don't know how often I dreamt of this." A kiss to her left thigh. "Fantasized." A kiss to her right thigh. "About this." A kiss to the bottom of her stomach, down a little further, and one more kiss to one of his favorite places on her body. "I'm not moving until you're shaking in my hands."

He kissed his way down to her sweet, manicured toes, lifting her leg in the air. He put her big toe in his mouth, slurping before moving on to the smaller ones. Meanwhile, his other hand caressed her other foot. She'd always had the prettiest feet and surprisingly, he looked up to see her massaging her breasts, causing him to freeze. She was so sexy. He had to taste her.

Tristyn gasped as he dove in. He took his sweet time savoring her juices. If this never happened again, he would make sure that he remembered how every drop tasted. His tongue ran in circles, causing her body to jerk in pleasure. Her soft moans bounced off the walls illuminated by the streetlights, and he wondered how he had ever left. When her rate of breathing doubled, he increased his speed, causing her to tightly ball up the sheets at her side.

"Trey," she rocked her hips along his tongue, seemingly bringing more delight to him than her. "Don't stop." Her breathing quickened and spasms rocked her body while she screamed out his name repeatedly. Trey licked up the drops of bliss that had exited her body.

She lay limp on the bed. He ran his tongue along her clit once more for good measure. Her body jerked and he raised up on his knees watching her chest rise and fall to the beat of his own heart. He smirked, he still had it. He trailed kisses back up to her face.

Tristyn finally released the sheets in her grip and opened her eyes. Trey had pulled off his shirt but his pants were still on. She raised her naked body up and rested on her elbows. "You are taking entirely too long."

"You were always impatient."

Tristyn sat up, her breasts swaying as she scooted closer to him. "I'll just have to help you move faster."

Drawn to her full breasts, he could do nothing but welcome her into his arms. Nibbling on one ear she whispered, "You don't get to make me wait for this dick two nights in a row. Tonight, I get what I want, when I want it."

She slipped her hand inside his pants. Physics defied him as he became harder than he thought possible. When he responded with a low groan, she directed him to take off his pants before joining her back on the bed.

He inserted two fingers inside her. She cried out and grabbed his shoulders for support. "Is this what you want?" He sounded nothing like normal as his voice took on the sound of a caveman placing claim on his woman. She stroked him faster to the movements of his fingers inside of her.

"Yes!" She cried out.

With his resolve quickly fading, he gently pushed her down on the bed and positioned his naked body above hers. His throbbing erection urged him along. In one swift movement he eased his way inside. He studied her, eyes closed, arched back. Everything felt right. And for Trey, Tristyn certainly felt like home. He let out a deep groan and began rhythmically sliding in and out of his love. She met his every stroke and within minutes he knew he wouldn't last much longer.

He sucked in a breath. "Ooh shit. Wait, baby. Wait."

"What?" Tristyn scraped her nails along his back.

Trey tried his best to stall his rising climax. His large hands gripped her hips and held her still. "Don't move."

"But Trey, I don't want you to stop," Tristyn whined. His hands were of no use in trying to keep her steady.

"Well, you're going to have to..." Trey stopped talking, knowing he couldn't hold on any longer. He sucked in air and gripped her hips tighter. As if his life depended on it, he plunged in and out making Tristyn scream out his name as they reached their climax together. Trey groaned as he adjusted Tristyn's hips back onto the bed and looked down into her smiling face.

His breath stilled. Beneath him lay his all. His everything. His future. Hopefully, she felt the same but if not, he would make sure she did soon.

Feeling the need to apologize for his short performance he said, "Sorry."

"Don't be," she caressed his face and pulled him down for an intimate kiss. "We're not even close to being done tonight."

He couldn't help but laugh. He pulled out and walked to the bathroom, not bothering to cover up. "You always were greedy," he called over his shoulder.

She stretched her body and climbed under the comforter. "You call it greedy, and I'll call it unsatisfied."

Trey's neck jerked backwards, and he slow turned toward Tristyn. He had something for her unsatisfied ass when he was done cleaning off. Through the doorway, her frame created a perfect female silhouette under the covers. Sexy without trying.

He licked his lips and sank back into the bed, hands caressing her ass. "You don't look unsatisfied to me."

She moaned softly and adjusted her head to look at him. His finger trailed the crack of her ass down to her pussy, playing at the entrance. She curved her back upwards to provide more access. Her body, free of blemishes, purposefully placed tattoos, and piercings, called out to him.

Once before, they'd challenged each other to see how many times they could go in one night. They'd reached five before Tristyn tapped out right before Trey, who was determined to last the longest.

He leaned closer to whisper. "Are you tapping out on me already?" The challenge he'd hoped would spark a memory, lit a fire in her eyes.

"I'm waiting for you to get it up." She tilted her hips higher, urging him to keep playing.

"Baby, I thought that was your job."

Tristyn scooted closer and felt for his manhood, which grew at her touch. "Perfect," she commented, disappearing under the sheets.

Trey lifted the covers just in time to see her mouth close over the most erect part of his body. "Oh, hell yeah," he struggled speaking as he watched her lick from the bottom to the tip. He faded into bliss as he put the covers back down. Her tongue performed a juggling action with his boys and he knew that if she kept it up he would explode, and he didn't want that.

"Tristyn," he breathed deeply as she continued, the rate of her stroke increasing. "Baby...shit," Trey's head hit his pillow and his eyes closed again. Unable to say much else he used his strength to pry her off.

Tristyn interjected. "I want to repay you for that magical tongue of yours." She started making her way back down, but he stopped her.

"If anyone should be repaying anyone it should be me." With that, he left her on her knees and approached from behind, plunging deep into her with venomous force. He quickly established a rhythm. This time he made sure not to disappoint. They tried four different positions that ended with Tristyn on top rocking him to the most intense climax he'd ever experienced.

He didn't know how long they slept but when he opened his eyes, sunlight was already peeking through the curtains. There was just something about her that made him behave much differently than he did with other women. He wanted to protect her from every roving eye that crossed over her body. He needed to protect her from every possible thing that could hurt her now and in the future. His

90 ✳ Chichima Cherry

body craved her and longed to hear something as simple as her laughing from one of his corny jokes.

"What are you thinking about?" Tristyn's voice dragged him from his thoughts. Before answering, he reflected on his thoughts and then caressed her cheek. "Nothing you need to worry about, but I will tell you one thing, I am not letting you go this time."

"Trey..." Tristyn swallowed hard.

"Let me finish. There's a lot of things I'm not afraid to admit this time around. I swear I haven't stopped thinking about you since we ran into each other, and I don't even want to. Whatever I gotta do to keep you around, I'll do it."

13

U Deserve

She shouldn't be in this position. Trey shouldn't be here. But they were, and it was phenomenal. If someone would've told her that her freaky dream about her ex would spark a chain of events that led to them having incredible makeup sex, she would not have believed it.

The only question left to ask was, *what now?* Trey appeared to think they were getting back together and she would've been feeling it had she not just cheated on her boyfriend. She needed to break up with Jacob but how? She could go with the classic *it's not you, it's me,* but he deserved better and had deserved better for a long time.

"You still heading out to Northrup today, right? What time you gotta be there?"

Tristyn pulled the covers up to her chin and snuggled lower, wanting only to lay and bask in the afterglow for the rest of the day. "I told them I'd be there around nine."

His naked body came closer to hers and he lifted her face. "I'll drop you off. Then after work I'll pick you up and we can do something fun. Just enjoy each other."

"That sounds nice." Tristyn rolled away and reached for her cell phone to check the time. Slightly despondent, she replied, "I'm gonna shower and get ready."

Fifteen minutes later, she was ready to conquer Northrup but Trey was a hell of a distraction. He sat on the edge of the bed, hands cupped together with only his boxers on, looking like he was posing for the cover of GQ Magazine. Her body spontaneously lit up but she had to get dressed.

She attempted to make conversation even though Trey's eyes were reacting to her body. "I thought you'd be dressed by now and complaining that I was taking all day."

All night, she imprinted his body into her mind but seeing it in the daytime was another thing. With his eyes drifting downward, stopping at each batch of curves, it was obvious they shared the same thoughts, but she needed to stay on track.

"Damn, Tristyn."

"Trey." She snapped her fingers. "My face is up here."

An involuntary chuckle escaped his lips, but the sexual tension remained. "Yeah, I know, just, damn."

Tristyn laughed as she attempted to use the towel to cover up more. "Is that a compliment?"

"Hell yeah."

She shook her head. "You are something else."

He stood up, creating an intense presence.

"You haven't gotten enough?"

"I never could when it came to you."

She shook her head and held up her hand. "Nope. Not right now. I need to get to Northrup. And don't you need to get home and shower before you go to work? You do have a job, don't you?"

"I can do what I want. I'm practically the boss." He bit his lip and pressed his groin into her rear, pinning her against the counter. "I'll be quick."

"Unh uh, Trey." Tristyn grabbed her clothes and makeup bag, squeezing out of Trey's grasp. "I'll be ready soon. Put your clothes back on."

Trey's head dropped to his chest. "Stingy ass."

"Keep talking like that and I'll show you just how stingy I can be." She shimmied into a fluorescent yellow fitted dress that stopped right above her knee and pulled on her striped blazer to match. Accessorized with a few bracelets, rings, and a floral decorated necklace, her outfit was completed all before Trey's shirt was on. The final touch was to pin her hair into a bun at the crown of her head.

"I don't know how I'm supposed to control myself when you're out here looking like that. My dick is hard as fuck right now." He followed her back into the bathroom and stopped beside her. His hands ran up and down her hips. His voice automatically shifted back to a low groan. "I swear I'll be quick."

Tristyn wanted to but stopped. "And I know you won't. Plus, I'm not letting you wrinkle my dress." She turned back to the mirror and caught Trey's eyes.

"We look good together."

As much as she wanted to disagree, she couldn't. They were perfect together, at least in the mirror.

14

ESSENCE

7 YEARS AGO

Tristyn was sure she was being punished for procrastinating but surely, she couldn't have been the only one to leave one of her prerequisite classes until her senior year. The group project, accounting for eighty-five percent of her grade, required partners. Those partners were assigned by the professor. Her original group of three was now down to just she and Trey after the other member dropped the class after receiving an F on the first test.

She was now forced to hold several conversations throughout the rest of the semester with the same person who had already proved he could not even talk. On the other hand, she was extremely attracted to him and had been since he walked into class the first day with his hat turned backwards, a hoodie, and dark grey Adidas sweatpants. The simple outfit had done her libido in. She'd done her best to stay away from what she assumed was a player, but since he approached her in the cafeteria, all she'd done was imagine several scenarios where they satisfied their primal urges.

Her friend, Georgia, often teased her about being so in tune with her sexuality. In Georgia's words, specifically, she was as big of a hoe as the men but Tristyn didn't see if that way. Tristyn wanted love, marriage, kids, and everything that came with it, but until then, she was enjoying her freedom. The problem was, she refused to enjoy such privileges with Trey as long as they were partners on a project they were dependent on in order to graduate. Mixing pleasure, a lot of it if she gauged that on the imprint in his pants, with the necessity of getting an A on this project, could become complicated and convoluted, neither of which she was a fan. Yet, she fantasized about the stupid man almost every day. She hated having to discuss historical villains outwardly while drooling over him on the inside.

To get their project done ahead of schedule, Tristyn suggested they meet at the campus library twice a week. With just the two of them, they each needed to do more work than the other teams. Trey agreed to anything she said, which as far as she was concerned, was a godsend.

Now, they were mandated to spend time together. And unfortunately, Tristyn was falling under his spell. To make matters worse, she'd never been able to hide her emotions. What people saw was what people got. If she was tired, her shoulders drooped. When happy, her eyes turned a lighter brown. When upset, her voice quivered. And when she saw something she liked, her eyes squinted, her legs crossed so tightly she could strike a match between them, and she couldn't help biting the corner of her lip.

"We should just have sex."

Tristyn blinked rapidly and straightened her face. "What, what did you say?"

Trey leaned closer to the table.

"I said we need to just go ahead and have sex. You look like you wanna pounce on me right now and if you do, even in this library, I'm not stopping you."

Tristyn's cheeks blushed before her face stoned. There were only a few students there tonight and just the thought of sneaking off somewhere left her wondering if they should just get it over with. "Trey, I do not want to have sex with you. All I want is to get a good grade on this project so I can graduate. This class is the only thing standing between me and my capstone course next semester and I will pass this class."

"You're lucky then because with me, you can have the three g's." He counted out on his fingers. "The grade, the graduation, and the guy. Oh yeah, you can also have the Big O. If you don't know what that is it means…"

"I know what the "O" stands for, but I'll pass."

Trey smirked, "So you'll keep the grade, graduation, and the guy, huh?"

"Shut up," Tristyn chuckled. "Let's get back to work."

15

FLY

Bob Lamb waited for Tristyn at the receptionist's desk. When he recognized her, his face glowed. "Tristyn! So nice to see you!"

Northrup occupied the entire first floor of a three-story office building with a unique modern design.

Tristyn's heels clicked across the shiny floor. She held out her hand and put on her best corporate voice. "Bob, nice to finally meet you in person as well. Happy to be here."

"Believe me," he shook her hand, "we're happy you're here as well." Tristyn followed him into the executive suite, which sat on the opposite side of the building from the other employees. "I've been telling everyone how you were coming for a visit. Everyone, not just me, is excited."

"The pressure is on."

"As long as you live up to your resume there's no pressure at all." Bob held open the door for her to walk through.

"That's easy." The executive suite was quiet, with the décor transforming from bright and airy to expensive luxury. Dark carpet spanned wall to wall and the receptionist's desk in the room reeked of overpriced hardwood.

"As you can see, this is the executive side of our offices. When we first moved here everyone sat on this side. It's hard to believe, but only ten years ago we started with five employees, then grew to seven. Next thing I knew, we were at capacity over here, so we expanded. Now we're almost at capacity on both sides and debating whether to rent out another floor or buy our own building. It's been a ride."

He clasped his hands and knocked on the door of the human resources office, a space occupied by a woman named Victoria Lamb. Next was the vice president, Joe Lamb. It wasn't uncommon to see all of the upper management hold the same last name in smaller companies, and it wasn't a concern for her as long as the promise for her to climb the corporate ladder didn't pose a problem.

Bob led her down the hallway back toward the front of the building. "This would be your office. I hope it's up to your standards. We have a decorating budget that allows you to update your office space every five years and it's very generous. Since this would be your first year, you'd be able to get the office up to your liking."

Tristyn took in the environment, checking out her office. "I don't even think I'd need to update this."

"Well, the monies stay whether you use them or not. If you change your mind after a year here, you can decorate then. Would you like to meet the team? They're in a meeting in the conference room but we can barge in just to introduce you. Then we can go in my office and talk specifics. How's that?"

She nodded. "That'd be great."

In the conference room she met her team of ten who could've posed for a commercial on diversity. It felt as if every age, gender, sex, race, and classification was represented. She couldn't have asked for a better start. The team, small and mighty, managed payables, receivables, and the accounts. They were ready and willing to grow under her leadership, she just had to make sure she was prepared to take on the task.

"Have a seat." Bob handed her a bottle of water and sat behind his glass top desk. "What did you think of the team?"

"They seem like a great group. Hardworking."

"They sure are, which is really important. We've been working on this government contract and I expect it to be completed by next year. I couldn't have created a better team if I did it myself. Oh wait, I did create the team. I hired them!" Bob cackled so hard it was tough for Tristyn not to laugh along with him. By the end of their chat, Tristyn was in love with Northrup. The work would be the biggest challenge she ever took on, but she'd never shied away from something like that before.

16

Love of My Life (An Ode to Hip-Hop)

Trey arrived in the afternoon to pick up Tristyn from her meeting. His body had gone shaky at one point, his nerves reminding him how much he needed Tristyn to fall in love with Northrup. "How did it go?" he asked as she climbed into his truck.

"It was almost perfect. The team is driven and self-motivated. The last person who led the team implemented some great tools that helps them work faster and more efficiently. I'd have some big shoes to fill and honestly, I'm nervous about taking on that kind of responsibility. I've always only been responsible for myself. If I fail, it doesn't affect others. At Northrup I'd be responsible for the team and the work."

"Don't go second guessing your skills, baby. I haven't seen your work, but I know you're smart as hell and I know you'd kill it. You got brains and beauty. I'd give you two weeks, tops, before you were in there and putting in new ideas that were ten times better than the last person's."

Had he become the perfect man? Every item on her checklist, had she ever made one, was being checked off by Trey Dalton, of all people. A nudge toward her deciding to take the job pushed her further to the edge. "Thank you, Trey. That was really nice of you to say."

"I'm serious. You know I don't just say shit to say it. Ain't nothing changed there."

Tristyn released her bun and smoothed her hair over to one side of her shoulder. The weather was absolutely perfect and the warm breeze bouncing off her face through the open window convinced her that life could actually be what she dreamt it could be.

"Guess what," Trey pulled her from her thoughts.

"What's up?"

"You know I said we could do something fun before you left, so since you're leaving today I took the rest of the day off," he finished with a smile.

Tristyn raised her eyebrows. "You sure know how to make a lady feel special."

"That's the goal," Trey winked.

"What are we doing for the rest of the day? It's only a little after noon."

"First, I need to head back to the office to finish a couple of things but that shouldn't take too long. And," he grabbed her hand and squeezed, "you get to decide what we do. If you wanna see a movie then we'll see a movie. If you wanna Netflix and chill again I'm *really* good with that."

A smile broke out across her face. "Trey, you are ridiculous."

He released her hand to turn the corner. "So I've been told. But seriously, I'll even take you shopping if you wanna do that."

"Now I know you're desperate. Shopping! Really, Trey?" She laughed until her body quaked. From experience, Trey hated shopping more than he hated peanut butter and jelly, claiming that it wasn't the taste he hated, but the unnatural consistency.

"I don't know about that. If you still hate shopping as much as you used to then I'm going to have decline. Remember when you were trying to impress me back in college after you got your college refund check and you took me and Georgia shopping? You were so mad by the time we left."

"We were at the mall for five hours, Tristyn, and all you bought was damn lotion and a candle."

"Ooo someone is still mad about that," Tristyn teased. "And Georgia was so mad at you for being mad at me." She laughed harder.

"Yeah, whatever. So, what do you want to do?"

"I know I don't want to see a movie, and this even surprises me, but I don't wanna go shopping."

"What!" Trey put his hand over his heart and gasped in an overly exaggerated manner.

Playing along, Tristyn said, "I know. I'm just as shocked as you."

"Well, you have twenty minutes to think about it. After that, the decision is mine." Trey bit his bottom lip before focusing on the road ahead.

*   *   *   *   *   *   *

"I got it, Trey." Tristyn walked up the stairs to Trey's bedroom, where he had gone to change out of his work clothes. She was about to knock when she overheard him talking.

"I'll try and call you tomorrow...I miss you too...Yeah, work has been crazy busy...Maybe I can fly you out soon...I'll look into flights later...Love you, too. Bye."

Pain wrenched through Tristyn's gut. There *was* another woman. Why hadn't he said anything? She supposed the same reason he hadn't asked her about Jacob. Except, that he was treating her like he wanted to marry her all the while he was sweet talking another woman, probably leading her to believe the same thing. Maybe she shouldn't break up with Jacob.

Her time with Trey truly was a fling and now that she didn't want it to be, that seemed to be best. She raised her hand to knock just as he opened his door.

"Hey," she said more casually than necessary.

The color dropped from his face. "Hey. I'm all changed."

"I see."

"Was just finishing up a call."

"Right." It was awkward. That was clear. Each one wanting to ask questions about who the person on the phone was and how much Tristyn had heard. "I, umm, I figured out what I want to do." She shook off the mental fog and put on her poker face. Things had changed but she held all the cards. If she wanted to move forward then she would but until then, it was a fling and nothing more, but still..."Was the call important?"

"Nope. You said you figured out what you wanted to do?"

"Yeah, but that can wait. You look flustered. Everything okay?" Her hands lightly caressed his pecks. "Is it work or?" She trailed off.

"I don't want you to leave. That's all." He pulled her close for an intimate hug.

He lied right to her face. Tristyn fumed inside but couldn't let on that she had been eavesdropping. But was it really eavesdropping if it was accidental? It was more on the edge of overhearing.

"I'm going to miss you, too." She returned his hug and let it go. "On the bright side, guess what we're doing for the rest of the day."

Trey released her, curiosity written all over his face. "What's that?"

"There's go kart racing around here. I saw signs for it when I was driving in." Tristyn looked into Trey's blank face, waiting for him to say something.

"Go Kart racing?" He scratched his cheek.

"Yes!" Tristyn glowed from excitement despite Trey's lack of enthusiasm.

"You know, when I said you could pick something I thought for sure it would involve sex. Dinner and sex. A movie and sex. Talking and sex."

Tristyn crossed her arms over her chest. "Really, Trey?"

He emitted a sly smile and shrugged.

"It's nice out and I haven't done something like that in a long time. It'll be so much fun."

Trey caved. "Okay. Anything for my princess."

Tristyn squealed and clapped her hands. "I hope there's funnel cakes. Oh, and maybe some fries and Italian sausage, ohh, and some lemonade."

He led her downstairs. "I get it. We're only going for the food."

"One can only hope and pray that there's carnival food there. They'd be crazy to not at least have food trucks serving it. We also need to drive separately because if I ride there and back with you after expending all my energy I won't wanna drive back home."

"See, now that could work out. Go have fun, then come back here or your hotel, and end with sex. Go karts and sweaty sex."

"I'm going to pass," Tristyn said with a smile. "Don't you think you've had enough sex to last a month? At least."

"Never." Trey leaned against the wall.

She giggled. "Figures." Checking her phone, she looked at Trey who was not so subtly checking her out and licking his lips. "You are a mess. Stop!"

Caught, Trey burst into laughter and shrugged his shoulders. "What can I say? You're a beautiful woman with a beautiful heart. You're smart and your pus..."

"Don't even finish that sentence!" Tristyn held up her finger and warned him, causing Trey to laugh even harder.

"Do you even know what I was gonna say?"

"Yes. And I don't wanna hear it." Tristyn playfully hit his arm.

"Girl, you're going to hurt yourself. Don't you know I'm made of bricks? I was only going to say that you're pushing fifty, but you still look twenty."

"You're a damn liar!" She pushed him out the door.

Go Kart racing turned out to be the best idea she'd had in a while. They'd stuffed themselves with all the food she requested and driven various courses until she'd felt sick. Now, she found herself not wanting to leave.

"I know you were against the idea at first but what do you think now?" Tristyn asked as they walked to their cars.

"It was cool," Trey said modestly, as if the day was comparable to any other.

Tristyn screamed while pointing at him. "You had fun and you know it."

"It was all right." Trey refused to give in.

"Oh please, you laughed so loud when I ran off the course after taking a corner too fast. I thought you would crash too because you were laughing so hard."

They laughed and Trey's voice turned serious. "I did have fun. I haven't had that much fun in a long time and I'm glad I let you talk me into going."

"Good. I'm glad because I did too. Although I must admit I am beat," she added with a yawn.

"Getting old girl."

"Who you callin' old? If my mind serves me correctly, you're the one over thirty."

"Well see, that's the problem. Your mind doesn't serve you correctly but I'm close enough. Also, I'm not the one yawning."

"Touché, Trey," she eyed her feet as they reached their cars.

They endured an awkward silence until Trey pulled her into his arms and kissed her. "I'll probably be down to see you this weekend," he said at the spur of the moment.

"So soon?" Tristyn bit her lip, feeling the fire under her feet to figure out what to do with Jacob before Trey popped up.

"I know but I'm already missing you and you're standing in my arms." Trey charmed her and Tristyn couldn't resist.

"You're a smooth talker." In her arms was the reason that women had been practically tripping over each other just to get a look at him and she felt like the luckiest woman in the world. Broad shoulders, smooth complexion, deep voice, a smile to die for, and curly dark hair stood glued to her body.

"It's true though. Do you mind if I stay with you?" A hint of naughty splayed on the edge of his smile.

Her conscience warned, *Bad idea. Very, very bad idea.* Her lips said, "If you stay with me, we might not leave my condo the entire time you're there."

Trey kissed her lightly. "I have no objections to that."

They stared at each other, each trying to prolong the inevitable. Feeling a tear well up she turned her head. Having her composure back, she placed her hands on his shoulders.

"Oh, Princess, don't say it." He forced a fake cry and rubbed at his eyes.

"I have to, Trey. Gotta get on the road and get back home. I have to work in the morning."

"Speaking of, did you decide whether to take the position at Northrup yet?"

She shook her head, "Not yet."

"Well, if you do, you get the two m's. The man and the money. Win-win. But even if you don't take the job, I'd be willing to commute for you. Make some changes. We'd make it work. I promise."

"I'll keep that in mind."

"That's all I ask." Trey pulled her in for one last kiss.

Tristyn wanted to melt. Why had no one been able to kiss her like Trey? His mouth pried hers open and their tongues began their own wrestling match. With their bodies pressed together she felt her heart rate increase to match his and his hands soon wandered down past her waist.

She broke the kiss, not wanting to put on a show at a family park. "Trey," she warned, placing his hands back at his sides.

"I know, I know."

Tristyn searched for her keys. When comfortably seated she looked over at Trey who was standing with his arms propped on the ledge of her door. "What's wrong? You look like something is on your mind."

Just as Trey began to speak, he stopped.

"You okay?"

Trey sighed. "Yeah. Umm, drive safely and I'll see you soon." He gave her one last kiss and shut her door.

17

SHARE MY WORLD

"My little brother, Derrick, is coming for senior night."

Tristyn leaned into Trey on his black futon. It was the only stitch of furniture in the apartment other than a tall light in the corner and a portable tray that doubled as a dinner table and desk. Making more money at his internship, he'd finally been able to afford an apartment with a roommate. Tristyn still lived in the dorm, preferring to do as little moving as possible since she would have to uproot in six months anyway. She still couldn't believe graduation was so close.

"That's so exciting! I finally get to meet him!"

"He's excited to meet you, too."

"You told him about me?" Tristyn lifted her head from his chest to search his face for answers. Though Trey hadn't been secretive about his family, he also hadn't been forthcoming. All he'd told her was that he grew up with his mom and younger brother in Cleveland, where she was also raised. Other than that, everything else was a question. To hear he'd talked about her to his family brought unexpected joy.

They hadn't been dating long but they'd grown to be good friends and even better lovers, often finishing each other's sentences. They'd been inseparable since the night after turning in their paper, when Trey had shown up at her door with a box of condoms. Tristyn pulled him inside her room by his shirt and they released sixteen weeks worth of built-up tension. That was the longest semester of her life. Trey later admitted he hadn't been with any other girls during that time because he knew they wouldn't hold a candle to her. With only one more semester left, Tristyn was finally getting her wish for him to open up more.

"Yeah, I told my mama about you, too."

Tristyn sat all the way up. "Really? You told your mom and brother about me?"

"Why do you sound so surprised that I talk about you?"

"You don't talk about them much with me, so I figured it was the same on the other side. What do they think?"

"About what?" Leaned back, his arm outstretched to accommodate Tristyn's incessant need to snuggle, Trey paid more attention to the basketball game than her questions.

"About me. Do they like me?"

"Yeah, they think you're cool."

"Trey!" Tristyn hit his chest with a pillow.

"Princess, why you gotta resort to violence? They like you, okay?"

"Is your mom coming too? To drop off Derrick? Or is he driving?"

"I don't know." He jumped up when a player dunked over another player. "Oooooo!"

"Trey, baby," Tristyn tugged at the hem of his shirt. "I know you wanna watch this game, but I really need to know if your mom is coming. Can you find out?"

Trey sat back down and turned his attention to Tristyn. "Why do you need to know?"

"Because if she's coming I wanna make a good impression on her. I'll need to buy a new outfit, make sure I can get my hair done, make a nail appointment. I need to be ready. I'm really excited to meet your family."

"I'll ask, okay?"

"Thank you."

Trey kissed her temple before jumping up on another dunk.

18

You're Mines Still

CURRENT DAY
A knock on the door almost caused Tristyn to spill her cereal bowl onto her carpet. She'd told herself after the last mishap that she wouldn't eat in her living room, but she was a glutton for punishment. Still in her short satin nightgown, she slipped her feet into her favorite fluffy slippers and padded to the door.

The milk in her bowl swirled as she ducked down as if the man behind the peephole could see her. Not only did she look like it was early in the morning, but she had forgotten Trey mentioned coming into town, and had conveniently forgotten to break up with Jacob.

"Princess, it's me. You gonna open the door?"

Tristyn bit her lip and grimaced, despising the mess she had gotten herself into. All the air deflated from her body, and she unlatched the door.

Trey handed her a bouquet of tulips. "These are for you." He bent down and kissed her forehead.

"You're always bringing me flowers." She inhaled the floral scent, momentarily closing her eyes. "Thank you."

A small smirk lifted in the corner of his mouth. "You're welcome. May I come in?"

"Yeah," Tristyn replied quietly. "These look like they're from my mom's shop."

"They are."

"Did Daddy threaten you again?"

"He didn't speak at all, so I think that's progress."

"It is. I'll talk to him."

"No need. I deserve it and it'll change over time."

"Have a seat. I was just finishing breakfast." Her cereal in one hand and the flowers in another, she walked the few steps to her open kitchen, placing the bowl on the bar counter that separated the areas. She looked up to find him watching her. She cleared her throat. "I didn't think you were serious when you said you were coming this weekend."

"I was definitely serious. I missed you as soon as you left. Even though you weren't there long, my house felt empty." He walked over to where she was standing, officially invading her personal space. Suddenly, the thin satin material of her nightgown didn't feel like enough coverage.

"Is it a problem that I'm here?" He watched closely as she cut the ends of the flowers and put them into a vase.

"No, it's not a problem. I just wasn't expecting you."

He stalled her hand, studying her face. "What's wrong?"

She wanted to lie but she'd done enough of that. "Trey, I'm still in a relationship. I didn't break up with Jacob."

"Oh," he smirked and leaned back against the bar counter. An entirely different reaction than she'd expected.

"Oh? That's it?"

"I have to admit I thought he'd be gone by now, so I am curious as to why you didn't break up with him yet."

Tristyn focused on anything but Trey. It wasn't that she wasn't going to break up with Jacob. It was just that she hadn't yet. It was hard to hurt someone you cared for and for that, she was avoiding the difficult conversation she didn't want to have.

"You need to let go of that white dude."

"How do you know what he looks like?"

"I saw a picture of you and him on your IG."

She lightly gasped. "You follow me?"

"No."

Tristyn couldn't help the smile that followed. "You were IG stalking me?"

Trey scratched his temple and shrugged. "Maybe." Trey watched amusement spread across her face. "So, you're breaking up with him today? Now?"

Tristyn protectively crossed her arms over her chest. "Well, aren't we cocky? Why do you think I'm breaking up with him instead of calling off whatever this is between us?"

"A feeling."

"A feeling?"

"Don't act like you're not still in love with me."

Tristyn's mouth dropped open. "Wow. We spend a couple days together and suddenly you think I'm in love with you. If your head gets any bigger you won't be able to fit through my door when I kick you out."

"I can tell you right now, you will be mine again, Princess." He moved in closer to kiss her but instead of touching lips, he ran smack dab into her hand.

She badly wanted to be with Trey, but she also felt like, just maybe, she should keep Jacob in her back pocket in case Trey was in another relationship. She chewed on the inside of her cheek, trying desperately to ignore the rush of feelings that bombarded her each time she glanced in his direction.

"How are we going to be together if I have a man and you have a girlfriend?"

Trey reared back as if Tristyn had slapped him. "I told you I'm not with Eve."

"I'm not talking about Eve."

"Then who are you referring to? I don't have a girlfriend."

She started to speak but then stopped, wondering if she should admit to overhearing his conversation. Could she have misread his conversation? Could she be making excuses for him because she *did* love him? After all, he was here, instead of with someone else. "It's just, I thought you would have one. You're a single, black, good-looking man, with a good job and no kids. How could you not have a girl?"

Trey stepped closer. "I've had girlfriends, but none lasted because they weren't you."

"Trey." She placed her hand on his chest to stop him from coming closer, but she'd never been able to resist him in any capacity.

He rested his forehead on hers. "I wanna be with you. What do I need to do, Princess? Tell me what I gotta do to get you to break up with your boyfriend."

Trey's hands desperately roamed her sides, his breathing becoming ragged along with hers. His breath caressed her cheek. "I'm still in love with you. I never stopped loving you."

Tristyn's mind willed her to resist when he came down for a kiss but knew she'd lost the battle when she felt her mouth respond to his. Traitorous body. Once again. He took full advantage of the moment by sweeping her mouth with his tongue.

His voice deep with need, he breathed out. "You're mine, Tristyn." His hands covered her skin more urgently, pushing her against the counter. He released a tiny growl when he pulled up her nightgown, discovering she wasn't wearing any panties. He boldly licked his lip and pulled it into his mouth.

Tristyn knew, at that moment, she was a goner. His hands squeezed her ass cheeks, making her whimper. Effortlessly, she was lifted onto the bar counter. With one hand, he managed to drop his pants and put on a condom. His breath in her neck, he plunged into her.

She screamed out. One arm wrapped around his neck and her other supported her body while he pushed into her, pulling back out only to go deeper.

Droplets of sweat started to appear at his temples. "Tell me you love me."

She could barely breathe, let alone speak, with Trey charging into her.

Trey's fingers dug into her skin, holding her closer than possible. "Say it, Tristyn."

"Trey-I..." Her orgasm threatened to choke her as did the realization that yes, she did love him. She never stopped.

His hips moved faster, harder. "You're mine."

Tristyn's knees shook, her body threatening to collapse on the counter. "Trey, I'm coming. I'm coming. I-I love you, Trey."

Trey's hips pounded into hers as he lost control. "Ugh, Tristyn. Fuck." He roared as he released his seed. Out of breath, he held onto her like he never wanted to lose her again. He kissed the junction between her shoulder and her neck. "I love you, too. Now break up with him."

19

SIMPLE THINGS

Trey helped Tristyn off the counter, not wanting to let her go. "You love me, huh?"

Tristyn bit her bottom lip. "I was caught in the moment."

"Dick game strong," Trey joked.

"Relentless. You are relentless. What am I gonna do with you?"

"I have a list if you're seriously asking."

Tristyn burst into laughter. "I bet you do." A moment filled with nothing but smiles passed between them before Tristyn said, "I'm guessing you weren't planning on going back home this evening."

"You guessed right. Is there room in your bed for me?" Trey wiggled his eyebrows playfully. "I'm sure your greedy ass is already ready for round two."

Tristyn fell into his chest and then her ears perked up to a noise in the hallway right before she heard keys. Her heart nearly jumped out of her throat. "Shit, it's Jacob! Go hide."

"For what?" Trey asked in his normal tone.

"Keep your voice down." She deserved this. How convenient that her boyfriend popped up right when Trey had done the same. Her only saving grace was that she'd already broken the news to Trey.

A wide smile spread across his face. "I wanna meet him."

"Are you crazy? Get in the back. Hurry to my room." She pushed him but he didn't budge.

The door swung open and Jacob entered. He paused when he saw Trey. "Hey, baby." Closing the door behind him, he surveyed the space.

Tristyn left Trey's side. "Hey, Jacob. I didn't know you were coming over."

Jacob ignored Tristyn and stared at Trey, who was casually popping a mint into his mouth. "You agreed to help me find a present today for my parent's thirtieth anniversary."

"Oh, no! I can't believe I forgot. I'm so sorry."

Jacob slow nodded. He had yet to move from the side of the door or take his eyes off Trey. Tristyn was sure that with Trey looking at Jacob with his head slightly tilted up, arms crossed over his chest, he was silently challenging him.

"Who's your friend?" Jacob also crossed his arms.

Tristyn tried clearing her throat, but Trey stepped in. He walked over with a smile on his face. "I'm Trey. Tristyn didn't tell you about me?"

Trey's relaxed nature did nothing to diffuse the situation and Tristyn internally freaked out, fearful of what he was about to say.

"No, she didn't."

"I'm her cousin." Tristyn's stomach bottomed out. Trey held out his hand, the hand that had just pawed at her ass while they'd fucked on her counter. She prayed it didn't smell like sex in there.

A beat passed before Jacob's expression relaxed. He shook Trey's hand. "Nice to meet you. Baby you didn't tell me you had family in town."

Tristyn rested her chin on her fist. "I didn't know he was coming. He surprised me this morning."

Trey chuckled, "It was a nice surprise though, wasn't it?"

"It was." She hated him and his cocky response. His cocky clothes. His cocky way that he took control of her body.

Jacob eyed the flowers on the counter. "Those are beautiful flowers. Also from your cousin? Trey?"

"Yeah," Trey answered. "Got them at her mom's shop. Hadn't seen her in a long time. She was so happy to see me."

Tristyn scratched her ear. She swore that someone other than her had to hear her heart thumping wildly.

"Well, Tristyn, I still need you and your womanly eye to come with me. Trey can come, too."

"No, Trey probably wants to go see his mom or something while we go out."

"No, I don't," Trey corrected her. "I'll catch up with Mama later."

"Trey, I haven't seen Jacob in a while and I need some private time with him."

"Right." She could see him gritting his teeth, but he silently nodded. He walked to the barstool to sit, immediately pulling out his phone. She knew she would soon get a text.

"I'll go change."

"I'll come with you," Jacob followed behind Tristyn. She stutter stepped but then realized it would be better for Jacob to come with her than for him to sit with Trey. Tristyn nervously ran her fingers through her hair. Out the corner of her eye, Trey's fist bounced against the countertop.

She pulled her cell phone off the charger in her bedroom and tapped a text to Trey. *I'll break up with him today*

He responded immediately. *If he touch you while y'all back there he can kiss his pretty boy face goodbye*

Jacob closed her bedroom door. "Is everything okay?"

Tristyn walked past Jacob to her closet. "Why do you ask?"

"There seems to be tension between you and your cousin."

She shook her head and huffed. As of late, there was always tension between them. It just happened to be of the sexual nature. "You know how family can be."

"It's nice to meet someone in your family. I feel like you keep them a secret. Or you keep me a secret. Is it because I'm Italian?"

"What? No! I am not ashamed of you in the least." She pulled on her panties and stripped off her nightgown, pulling on a plain t-shirt. She rummaged through her closet until she found a pair of cutoff shorts. When she looked over, Jacob was leaning against the door to her walk-in closet with a smile on his face.

Tristyn tensed, hoping he didn't notice. She could not, under any circumstances, allow him to come too close. It was bad enough that she hadn't washed off any signs of her morning romp with Trey. She absolutely could not allow Jacob to touch, hug, or kiss her. "What are you considering for your parents' gift?"

"I haven't thought about it, that's the problem. I'm thinking we can head to a jewelry store first though. See if there's anything there."

"That's a good idea. And you could get it personalized, too."

"See, that's why I love you. I missed you." Jacob stepped into the closet with her. She had trouble swallowing. The knock on her bedroom door was her saving grace.

"Tristyn?" Trey knocked again. "How do I work your TV?"

"Let me go help him," Tristyn slid past Jacob to answer the door.

Jacob nodded, a look of defeat splayed across his features. "Sure."

Trey held up the remote. "I accidentally logged you out of Netflix. Can you log me back in?"

"Sure thing." She followed Trey back into the living room with Jacob following behind her. She knew that Trey had purposely logged her out to get them out of her bedroom. Trey lingered close enough for her to smell his cologne and want to fall back into his arms. Instead, Jacob pressed a tender kiss to her temple and as much as she wanted to shrink away, she couldn't. On her other side, she practically felt Trey seething. She entered the password as fast as she could.

"There you go." She turned to Jacob. "I'll get my purse and we can go."

20

EXPECTATIONS

7 YEARS AGO

David specifically asked Trey and Derrick to come over while Chelsea was at work. Since meeting, they'd spent more time together, developing an understanding to let bygones be bygones. Trey didn't know how long David had left but his health seemed to have worsened with every meeting. Since he refused to go on the transplant list, it was only a matter of time, but the doctors had given him three to six months to live.

Derrick pushed David's wheelchair from the kitchen to the living room. "Need anything else?"

"No, I'm fine."

"And you took your meds?" Trey asked. Chelsea had called last week, complaining that David had stopped taking his medications. She'd pleaded with him to say something. Trey called immediately and convinced David to start taking the medications again, if only to make his end of days less miserable for Chelsea. He agreed. Something told him that this time though, David was lying.

David huffed, "Yeah." He hobbled out the wheelchair and into his recliner, lifting up the footrest.

"How are you feeling today, Dad?" Trey asked. David got progressively grumpier as time passed, a drastic difference between his attitude when they first met. Trey felt bad because Chelsea was having trouble dealing with the impending death of her dad while trying to hope for a miracle, work part time, and attend high school.

"Like I'm dying. But I brought you boys over because we need to talk. Chelsea doesn't like to discuss these things so that's why she's not here. Before we get started though, how have you both been since we last saw each other?"

Trey and Derrick exchanged glances before Derrick spoke up. "I have all As and Bs. I made the baseball team, but I only joined to keep my body conditioned. Next year will be my last basketball season. I don't know if I'm good enough to get a scholarship but I'm gonna go for it. I'm also in the entrepreneur program and I was partnered with the owner of a landscaping company. I really like what they do but I've only been working with him for a month, so we'll see. There's still time to hate it."

David nodded and then looked at Trey, a cue for him to begin. "I don't have much to report. I'm finally in my last semester so I only have one class left. I was able to move to full time at my internship, so I got a small apartment with a roommate. That's working out so far."

David nodded again and then looked down at the floor so long that Trey started to wonder if he'd fallen asleep. "Trey, as the oldest, there's much responsibility that you carry. But you carry it well and I'm proud of you. As you know, Chelsea doesn't have any other family than you boys. With her being a minor, she's going to be put into foster care. And let's be real, very few people foster or adopt teenagers. I'm scared just thinking about what could happen to her.

"This is hard to ask because I wouldn't put this on you if I had any other option, but I need to know she'll be okay without me." He paused, tears in his eyes. "I started saving money when I first found out I was sick. The money, in the beginning, was for Chelsea, so she wouldn't have to worry about anything while in the system. But then I thought about reaching out to you two, and when I talked to Chelsea, she was excited to know she had brothers."

"We were excited when we found out we had a sister," Derrick said.

"I thought about asking Gloria but in the end, I couldn't do that. So, Trey, I'm asking you to take in your sister after I'm gone. I'll provide for she and you financially. You just need to make sure she gets signed up for school and graduates. After that, I'm confident she can care for herself."

"Whoa, whoa, whoa." Trey held up his hands in protest. "I can't take care of Chelsea. I haven't figured out how to take care of myself yet."

"I understand that, and I wouldn't have asked if I didn't think you could handle it."

"Dad, I can't handle that. She's sixteen. How am I supposed to handle her dating and driving, and what about shit like clothes?"

"I saved up twenty thousand for this. And when my life insurance comes, it'll be distributed to you three equally to do whatever you want to do with it."

Derrick sat quietly until, "I hate talking about this. Can we stop?"

David ended the conversation with, "Trey, I just need you to think about this. Chelsea has lost a lot in her young life and right now, she needs family. Please consider it."

Trey hung his head before nodding. He already knew what he was going to do. The question was how to tell Tristyn he was about to become the father of a teenager. He couldn't ask her to do the same. Their lives were supposed to just be starting, not ending.

21

LOUNGIN (WHO DO YA LUV)

CURRENT DAY

"You seem off. Are you sure you're all right?" Jacob studied Tristyn across the table. Since they'd left, he'd done nothing but repeat questions and wave his hand to get her attention. So no, she wasn't all right. She was in a sticky situation and to get out of it she had to hurt someone that she cared for deeply.

"Yeah, I'm sorry. I'm fine, I just have a lot on my mind."

"Family issues? Does it have to deal with Trey?"

Did it? She wanted to cackle at his question. Instead, she settled on, "Somewhat."

Weekend shoppers walked along the shopping center's sidewalks, carrying bags of newly purchased items, smiling under the sun with their companions, unbeknownst that Tristyn's stomach was about to toss everything she'd eaten over the lunch time shopping break. They had yet to make it to the jewelry store because Jacob had started spoiling her with gifts, buying her shoes and a designer wallet despite her protests. She was sure that he'd take them back once she broke up with him.

She shook all thoughts of Trey from her head and placed a smile on her face. "I'll be better for the rest of our time together. I'm sorry."

Jacob's brown eyes lit up. "I can help you through whatever you're going through, you just need to let me in."

"I know. Thank you for that."

Jacob leaned back in his chair and eyed her, crossing his arms in the process.

A lull came on so she pointed to the store sitting down the strip. "You ready to see what that jewelry store has?" Even though Jacob's parents expressed wanting to spend time with them for their thirtieth wedding anniversary, Jacob was set on also purchasing them matching gifts of some sort.

His parents enjoyed wearing matching everything. Over the years they accumulated matching earrings, rings, outfits, shoes, glasses, and even matching shoestrings. According to Jacob, the only thing they had that didn't match was their hair color, but his mother was already trying to change that. His father went along with it because, as he said, "He'd be a fool to turn down such a simple request from the love of his life."

"Yeah, let's go." He pulled a hundred-dollar bill from his wallet and waved over the waitress.

Her hand in his, he guided them toward the jewelry store. The normally comforting gesture made her uncomfortable but he either didn't notice, or he didn't care.

"Any thoughts on the type of jewelry?" Tristyn scanned the contents of the store.

"No idea." He led her to the watches. "I was thinking I could do a his and hers watch but I could also do a bracelet option." He leaned over the counter and scratched the back of his neck. His muscles flexed through the material of his shirt and Tristyn wondered what the hell was wrong with her. He was rich, spoiled her, treated her wonderfully, supported her, and was sexy as all hell. Why the hell wasn't she in love with him after all this time? Why had she cheated on him? Was this some inner child type of thing where she was intent on thwarting her plans for real happiness?

A sales associate with too much bass in his throat approached. "What can I help you find today?"

Jacob looked at Tristyn for answers before standing upright. "We're looking for a gift for my parent's anniversary. It's their thirtieth so it needs to be grand. Money isn't too much of a concern as long as it's worth it. And it needs to be a his and hers of whatever we find."

The associate's eyes lit up. "That's a beautiful idea to celebrate thirty years together. I'm just trying to make it to three months and I already can't stand my girlfriend." He chuckled. "You two look like you're fit to make that same thirtieth year anniversary goal in the future. You can just feel the love between you two."

Tristyn didn't dare look at Jacob. Every glance her way was filled with love and compassion, and she hated it because it reminded her of how much of an asshole she was.

"I'm going to see what's over there." Distance. She craved distance to breathe. To think. A place where there was no room for Jacob to flash his smile, making her feel torn. A space where Trey couldn't walk in and confuse her heart.

"I see you're looking at rings over here. Trying to give your man over there a hint?" Another associate tilted his head while waiting for her response. Jacob steadily made his way toward them.

"What?" Tristyn looked into the case below her. Sure enough, she'd stopped walking right next to the sparkling engagement rings. Jacob's eyes checked their interaction, a smile daring to grace his face.

"No, I'm not, I wasn't looking at these."

"Don't get shy now, honey. Which one do you like? It doesn't hurt to drop a few hints so your man can start planning early. Am I right?" He asked Jacob.

Jacob raised his eyebrows. "He's right. Which ones do you like baby?"

Tristyn felt her cheeks turning pink. Her skin scorched and her stomach began its terrible twirl. She didn't want to get married or look at engagement rings when she didn't even know if she wanted to stay with this incredible man.

Her body shut down and she rushed out the store, brushing past a stunned Jacob.

Jacob was right behind her. His hands gripped the tops of her shoulders, massaging away the unease. His eyes stared at her, but she refused to look his way. "Baby, what's wrong? You know you can talk to me, right?"

Tristyn blew out a small puff of air and fanned her face as she felt tears bubble in her eyes.

"Oh baby." He enveloped her in a tight hug. "I didn't mean to put pressure on you like that."

Tristyn grimaced and wiggled from his embrace. "I just need some time."

"Take all the time you need. I'm not in a rush to get married and didn't mean to make it seem like I was rushing you either. I just thought you were throwing hints my way and I was rolling with it."

"No," Tristyn wrapped her arms around her torso, ignoring the people walking past them. "I mean, I need some time. Like, time away. We need to take a break-from our relationship."

Taken aback, Jacob put space between them like she'd physically pushed him. "What do you mean we need a break? I've already been more than patient-taking everything slow for you. Doing everything on your timeline. Even regarding the sex!" He glanced around, remembering they were in public, and then stepped closer and lowered his voice. "I grew our relationship with you for over a year, per your request, so you could make sure it was real before we had sex. I did this because I loved you and respected your claim to be some born-again virgin."

"Jake, that's not fair." But even as she spoke the words, she knew he was right. She'd made him wait but then given it up to Trey almost instantly. She was the worst kind of girlfriend.

"Is it me?"

"No!"

He put his hands on his waist, dropping his head before turning back to her. "I don't know why I asked that. I know what I bring, and *this* is not me. So, tell me, what is it?" His eyes narrowed. "Or, who is it? Maybe I should be asking that instead."

Although she wanted to confide in him, tell him everything that had happened, she couldn't bear to break his heart anymore. "I just have a lot of thinking to do about us and my job."

"What about your job?"

"I had a job interview in Columbus. I'd make much more money and..."

"*That's* why you went up there?" Jacob tried to hold back his anger by biting his lip but that only lasted a mere few seconds. "I'm guessing you're taking the job and that's why you've been acting different."

"I haven't decided yet."

"These are things that we could've talked about. I travel all around the world. Travelling from Cleveland to Columbus is not an issue for me. But let me guess, it's an issue for you. Do you still wanna be with me?"

She paused long enough for that to become her answer. Jacob rolled his lips into his mouth. "Wow, Tristyn."

Emotion clogged her throat. "I just, I just need time. That's all I'm asking for."

His head bobbed as he nodded. "I'm gonna go pay and then I'll take you home. You can have all the space and time you need."

22

Loveeeeeee Song

"Was Trey able to get off work?" Georgia sat cross-legged in the floating egg chair in Tristyn's single occupancy dorm room.

"I don't know." Tristyn focused on her latest splurge, thigh-high leather boots. They perfectly accompanied the shorts she was wearing tonight that left out a small slice of butt. With her relationship on the fritz, she hated to admit that she purposely chose the shorts just to see if she still had it.

In the chair, Georgia donned a checkered miniskirt, black booties, and fishnet stockings.

"I called him earlier and he didn't answer."

Georgia stopped the chair from swinging by lowering one leg. "He didn't answer the phone the last time you called either."

"Don't start, Georgia." As much as she hated to admit it, Georgia was right. Lately, Trey answered her phone calls much less often and returned them fewer times than that. In his words, everything was cool, but he wasn't the same man she'd grown to hold feelings for. As close as they had become, they were growing apart at an even faster rate.

"I'm just trying to figure out what his deal is. That nigga never used to let you out his sight and now he can't answer his phone. This is our senior year and we're so close to graduation that we barely have to show up to our classes. And he's not working that much either. So..."

Tristyn closed her eyes tight and spun around. Squeezing Georgia's face with her palms she said, "I just want to have a good time tonight at this step show. That's it. Can we do that?"

Georgia rolled her eyes. "In order to do that, does that mean we can't talk about the possibility of Trey cheating on you?"

Nostrils flared, Tristyn's words squeezed through her teeth. "That's exactly what it means. So stop."

"Fine." Georgia removed Tristyn's hands from her face. "Let's go bitch."

The sororities were showing out on the stage and for the first time, Tristyn wished she had pledged instead of letting a horror story stop her from doing what she knew she really wanted. Now, Tristyn regretted not going with her heart instead of her brain. What did it look like to stick with your heart? To blend it with the head? One was emotional. The other, logical. Could a person seamlessly blend emotions and logic?

Right now, logic told her that she was being stupid. Trey was up to something and he had to be cheating. There was no other reason for him to suddenly become distant. At least there wasn't any reason that he had communicated to her.

Her heart, on the other hand, told her that whatever Trey was involved with had nothing to do with her. Perhaps, he was unsure what would happen after college. Possibly even, something could be going on with his brother.

After that, her brain would gently remind her that if Trey was going through something, he could talk to her about it. Since he wasn't talking, the only possible deduction left was that he was cheating.

"Do you think Trey is pledging?" Tristyn leaned closer to Georgia to be heard. The Deltas were finished and the audience was hollering loudly as the Alphas made their way onto the stage.

"That ship has sailed, Tristyn." Georgia hollered when her crush, Aaron, made eyes with her. "Everyone already crossed so if he was planning on pledging it wouldn't be until next year. By then we'll have graduated. I mean, he could be planning on it but highly unlikely."

Tristyn nodded and sighed before looking at her phone.

Sorry I missed your call. Be there in 5

She hated that her heart leapt at the chance to see him, and she knew that tonight, logic would bow to emotion once again.

Tristyn's smiling face looked back up to Georgia's frown. "I hope you at least make him grovel before you give up the pussy tonight."

With one raised eyebrow, Tristyn replied, "No worries. He'll be doing a lot of groveling to make up for how distant he's been."

Georgia nodded to the figure behind Tristyn. "It starts now because your man is making his way over here. I swear it always looks like he's walking in slow motion. That's so weird."

Trey's embrace around her entire body comforted Tristyn in a way that she shouldn't have enjoyed. But it was Trey and damn if she wasn't the biggest fool for him. And his cologne. She hated him as much as she loved him. She closed her eyes and melted into all that was comfortable, normal, and sane.

"It feels so good to be next to you," Trey mumbled into her neck.

Georgia rolled her eyes and then refocused on her crush. "I'm gonna talk to him tonight."

Tristyn held onto Trey's arms still wrapped around her shoulders. "I heard he got a girl."

Georgia swung around to face Tristyn. "I am not concerned. If their relationship is solid, then his girl won't have anything to worry about."

She knew Georgia too well and was thankful that Trey didn't. Georgia's last statement, although for her, was also directed right at Trey. She would talk to her later. Georgia's intentions were always good, but this was Tristyn's life to live and she didn't appreciate her throwing jabs at Trey or their relationship.

At the afterparty, Georgia pointed to Aaron, who was chatting in the corner of the house party. "There he is. How do I look?"

"You look perfect, of course." Tristyn nursed a drink in a red cup. Beneath her, Trey caressed her thighs and ass. He'd finished his second drink and the longer they sat, the higher his hands went. Knowing Trey, he would soon try and lead her into an empty bedroom or bathroom at the party.

"But be careful, I thought I saw his girlfriend here."

"Once again, not worried." She lifted the hem of her skirt a notch.

"I'm not fighting anyone, Georgia," Tristyn warned. "I promise I'll act like I didn't even know anything was happening."

"Chill, Tristyn. I'm not like that anymore."

"Whatever. Just don't go over there provoking people."

Trey adjusted her rear against his pelvis, allowing her to feel his hard on. "You ready to go yet?"

"Not yet," Tristyn removed his hand from the inside of her thigh.

He rubbed his hands up and down her back, calming her nerves and igniting an inner fire. Trey always knew exactly how to get her ready. "Let's go upstairs."

Trey's lips on the back of her neck were the last straw. "Okay."

He lifted Tristyn onto the bathroom vanity and stripped off her shirt, immediately plowing his head in between her breasts. With the way he was attracted to her there was no way there could be another woman, she reasoned...but still.

"Wait, Trey, wait a minute. Can we talk?"

Trey continued kissing her chest. "You wanna talk right now?"

"I do." Tristyn lifted his head so they were eye to eye. An abundance of sadness that Tristyn hadn't seen before was present. "Baby, what's going on with you? We used to be together all the time and now when I call you don't answer. When you show up you act like you never even disappeared, as if it's all right for you to go MIA for days. If I did that you know you'd ask me what was up, too. You can talk to me."

Trey squeezed her hands. "I know, Princess. I'm just not ready to talk about it. That's all. I promise, I'm fine."

"Is it school? Family?"

"Tristyn, drop it, please."

She nodded. "I will if you make me a promise."

"What's that?" Trey hugged her lightly around the waist.

"Whatever you're going through, if it gets to be too much, promise me that if you don't feel like you can talk to me, that you'll talk to someone else."

Tristyn watched his Adam's Apple bob a couple of times before he nodded.

"Thank you."

Trey licked his lips and smiled. "It's been a long time since you came over. How about we go back to my place instead. I need to lay you on something soft."

"I'd like that a lot." Tristyn pulled her shirt back on and as they were coming down the steps, commotion greeted them. Tristyn knew exactly who was spurring it on. She smacked her lips and crossed her arms, cementing herself on the steps.

Georgia stood, in the middle of the party, arguing with Aaron's girlfriend. Aaron stood in the background, smirking, before one of his line brothers motioned for him to stop the commotion before it went too far. Aaron stepped in between them and asked for his girlfriend to leave. Just like that, Georgia had won, as she always did.

23

Happily Ever After

Georgia paused from covering Tristyn's dishes with bubble wrap, a lonely tear rolled down her face. She sniffed and quickly wiped it away.

"Georgia, you promised not to cry," Tristyn's voice broke. "We'll still see each other all the time. I'm only two hours away."

Earbuds in her ear, Aiyanna snapped her fingers and danced her way into the kitchen. She removed one and said, "I knooow y'all are not in here getting sappy! This is not a time to cry. This is a whole damn celebration! It is a time to turn all the way up. Our girl is moving and she's not *just* moving. She got a new job with a twenty-five thousand dollar pay increase." She held up her hand for one of them to high-five her.

Tristyn took the bait and their hands clapped in the air. "That sounds insane to me. Twenty-five thousand dollars. Some people don't even make that in a year and I'm getting it in addition to what I already make."

"Honey, listen!" Aiyanna preached. "This is a joyous time for all of us because you know that when you're unpacked, the first thing we're doing is coming up for a pizza, pajama, and wine slumber party."

Tristyn's eyebrows raised into the air. "That sounds so good. I can't wait."

"And might I add," Aiyanna continued, "that your condo sold in one week for fifty thousand over asking. This, my dears, is the best financial blessing Tristyn could have received. And that means everything is on you when we get there."

Georgia wiped her tears and gave a silent amen. Aiyanna continued, "Lastly, you're getting your happily ever after. You got your job and the man you have pined over for what seems like forever. It won't be long before we're bridesmaids and Godmothers. How do you feel?"

Tristyn looked to the two friends that had helped her through the past few weeks. There were many nights when she called them instead of calling to check on Jacob, just to see how he was doing. They'd assured her that she'd made the right decision to see what her future held with Trey.

Her days had been filled with tying loose ends at work, training her replacement, which thankfully, turned out to be Aiyanna, working with her real estate agent, and now, packing. The stressful transition was finally ending and she was ready to jump into a fresh routine.

"Honestly, I'm nervous, but excited. I'm going to miss you two, but I can't wait for our first slumber party. We're going to get so drunk." They laughed and hugged it out as a knock came on the door. "Let me get that. Probably the movers."

Four men stood in the hallway, one with papers and a clipboard. "Tristyn Miller?"

"Yes. A Plus Moving Service?"

"Yes." The one with the papers smiled, showing a gold tooth on each side of his mouth. "Are you finished packing?" He stepped inside and surveyed the space filled with various sized boxes.

"Almost." Tristyn left the door open for the other men to walk in. "We're finishing up the dishes but everything else is packed." She released a small sigh, looking at her friends. This truly was a new beginning. One that she didn't know she needed. Before she became the one to start crying, she turned away.

"Do I need to do anything?"

"No ma'am." He waved the other men forward and they went to work, wrapping furniture with plastic wrap, lifting it up and out of her condo. She'd never seen anything be cleared so efficiently. "I'll have you sign after we're done and that'll be it."

"We'll get out of your way then." Tristyn motioned for Aiyanna and Georgia to follow her onto her balcony, where she had stashed three seats and a bottle of champagne for when it was time to say goodbye.

Georgia stood with her glass in hand. Tristyn and Aiyanna followed suit. "I'm not gonna cry this time but you know I had to be the first one to start this toast. Tristyn, girl, sis, we been at this friendship game for too long so it's hard to see you going off on a new beginning without me, but I wish you the best of luck in Columbus."

Aiyanna followed. "In the short time we've known each other I've watched you kill the game in so many ways. Whether that be at work or in fashion, you walk through life with grace, style, and a little bit of sass and I love it. Girl they are not gonna know what hit 'em when you get up there and you better serve it up."

Tristyn's free hand flew into the air and she cheered. "You know I will!" They all laughed and clinked glasses.

24

LOVE ON TOP

The reconciliation between Trey and Tristyn had been exactly what he prayed for. It was a beautiful blend of the past, the present, and their future. They'd established an almost perfect routine of alternating homes on the weekend when she wasn't working, and he wondered if he should take it to another level and ask her to move in with him.

Her position at Northrup was taking up most of her time but her team was in the final stretch toward the end of their fiscal year. This weekend was the first one she'd had off since she started but the next few months were looking up and she promised him they'd spend so much time together that he'd be begging her to leave him alone. This evening, he planned something special but for it to work, he needed to get her out of his house for a few hours.

"Would you get dressed already?"

"Trey," she pouted. "I'm tired. Where are we going anyway?"

"An avian museum."

She lifted from his sofa to a sitting position. "A bird zoo? That's where our date is?"

"I was told that birds are very relaxing and that's what you need."

"A nap is also very relaxing and would be so perfect right now."

Trey released a smile and gently lifted her from the sofa. "Come on, you can nap later. It's a short trip just to get us out the house and away. When we come back, I have something special for you."

"You do?" He nodded and Tristyn turned to him, gripping the sides of his hooded sweatshirt. "What is it?"

"A surprise," he licked his lips and gave her a peck on the lips. "Go change. Wear something comfortable."

Apparently, the avian museum was the right move. Tristyn squealed as soon as Trey handed over his phone for the front desk associate to scan their tickets. "Aww, look at the penguins! They're so adorable."

Trey's nose immediately turned up. He was happy she was enjoying it, but he was turned all the way off. Those birds were wretched and all he wanted to do was throw them in a bubble bath.

"And they're getting ready to feed them." Tristyn squealed again. "Look how they're waddling with their little feet. Eek! And there's babies! They're so fluffy I just wanna hold them."

He followed her to the penguin exhibition where a woman sat in their exhibit, feeding them small fish. Another team member was on their side of the glass explaining what was happening, while allowing the children to ask questions. Tristyn held her hand up to ask one as well. At least she was enjoying herself and that was all that mattered.

After the penguins, they walked through the Wetlands Habitat where Trey swore it smelled even worse. He started to turn back around but Tristyn started giggling. When she'd gone to take a selfie, a flamingo had walked up and photobombed her.

"This is so great!" She walked in front of other birds like the herons and pelicans to see if they would photobomb her as well, but none took the bait.

Trey checked his phone for the time. Having spent over an hour there, they only needed to spend a short time more while the set up for Tristyn's surprise was completed. He wrapped his arm around her shoulders and kissed her gently. "I love you."

"I love you, too." He never tired of hearing her speak those three words. "Thank you for bringing me here. I didn't think I'd love seeing these birds but they're so stinking cute."

"Stinking is right but if you like it, I love it. Ready to go through this last exhibit?" Trey looked over the map. "The Rainforest Habitat. Says there's over thirty different species of free flying birds in there. And a sloth."

They walked in, a beautiful fifteen-foot waterfall greeted them from across the exhibit. Sounds of the many birds living in the extravagant number of tall trees, plants, and grass delighted them. They walked along the paved path that allowed them to explore.

It was all majestic until Trey stopped in his tracks. A peacock was steadily walking toward them on the path.

"Aww, I wonder if it'll put its feathers up?"

Of course, Tristyn loved it. She walked past the bird. Trey, on the other hand, couldn't pass. Every time he moved to the side, the bird walked to the same side. "What's wrong with that bird? I don't want no trouble." He tried again but the bird stared him down. He took a step back, ready to bolt, if necessary, causing her to giggle.

"Trey, it's not gonna bother you. If it was vicious, they wouldn't allow it to be in here."

"Then why won't it let me pass? Don't forget, it's still a wild animal."

Tristyn called to Trey from the other side of the bird. "It's not wild anymore, it's domesticated. Babe, just ignore it. It's not going to mess with you. Maybe it smells fear."

Trey tried taking Tristyn's advice but as soon as he started walking toward her, the peacock turned and trotted toward him, causing him to jump back. "What's wrong with this damn bird?"

Tristyn tried holding in her laugh. "He likes you. That's so cute."

"Tell him I don't swing that way." Trey edged back to the front door. "You know what, I'll wait for you outside. This bird is tripping."

Shrugging, Tristyn turned around. "Suit yourself. I'll be out when I'm done touring." She hadn't walked five steps before she screamed. She held her arms out to the side and looked as if she would cry any minute. All she kept repeating was, "That did not just happen. Please tell me that did not just happen. Trey," she cried out.

A team member briskly walked over with a frown to see what was happening.

Trey called from his place near the door, still not wanting to provoke the peacock. "What's wrong?"

"A bird pooped on me. It's on my ear. And my clothes. And it might be in my hair." She waved her hands to the side, much like the peacock, who decided to wave his feathers at the same time.

The laugh started small, but the more he watched Tristyn flail around, the harder he laughed. "Are you sure?"

"Yes! It's not funny."

The team member, now at her side, said, "Oh man! You got nailed," which made Trey laugh even harder.

"What do I do?" Tristyn cried.

"You can wash it off in the restroom." Knowing that the birds were safe, the team member's voice was much calmer. "If it makes you feel better, bird poop is ninety percent water."

Trey lost it. Tears squeezed from his eyes and he doubled over, having to support his weight with his hands on his thighs. "That means it's only ten percent shit on you, Princess."

Tristyn's eyes shot daggers at Trey as she ran past him. Before she disappeared into the restroom she yelled, "Keep laughing and I'll sick the peacock on you."

"Feeling better?" Almost back to Trey's, Tristyn was still pouting. He'd helped her wash it off, making sure none got in her hair or inside her ear. Then he'd stripped out of his sweatshirt so she would have something to wear home. No longer loving the museum, they left shortly after.

One glance at her and he started laughing again. "They say it's good luck when birds poop on you."

"Isn't that when they poop on your car?"

"Must be even better luck when it lands on you then."

"Whatever." Tristyn shook her head and went back to reading an online article. "I still can't believe that happened. I can't wait to take a shower. I feel so dirty."

Trey turned on his street. "You'll feel much better soon. Remember I said I had a surprise for you? Well, it's ready now."

Her spirits lifted and she looked at Trey's house down the street. "I almost forgot! Damn bird distracted me. What is it? Is it in your house?"

To avoid making her mad again, he avoided the chuckle that threatened to spill out. When would this not be funny? He put his truck in park and opened her door, helping her down. Inside his house, two massage tables were set up in his living room. Screens had been placed on the windows to darken the room and set the mood. A platter of meats and fruits sat in the middle and lavender was being diffused throughout.

Trey picked up a vase of sunflowers from his table and handed them over. He was grateful that his cleaning lady agreed to come over on her off day to unlock his house for the masseuse and accept the floral delivery. "You've been working really hard, and I wanted you to feel relaxed. I'm sorry the bird zoo messed that up but that was just my way of getting you out the house so I could get this set up." He gestured to the massage therapists. "Massages are first. After that is a manicure and pedicure. And I'll order whatever you want for dinner so that on Monday you feel rejuvenated enough to hit the ground running. I'm very proud of what you've been doing at Northrup. Tomorrow you can sleep all..."

Tristyn didn't let him finish speaking. She pulled him down and kissed him thoroughly. "Thank you. This means a lot."

"You're welcome. Now tell me how much you love me."

"You're so perfect that I could never *not* love you."

"Good. I love you, too. Forever."

25

Black Eagle

7 YEARS AGO
As members of the immediate family, Trey sat in the front pew of the small Baptist church with Derrick, Chelsea, and Mama. As much as he tried to avoid staring at the already closed casket, he couldn't. Their father lay in there, motionless. No breathing. No sickness. No nothing.

Members of the community came out, some he had crossed paths with, which he had trouble reconciling. Many approached the three to express condolences, pat one of them on the back, or recall a story. All he could do was nod; they knew David better than he did. The world had come to know a man that was loved, deeply, by every person he met. He was a man that never forgot a name, even if he only met you twice within a ten-year span. It was clear that the person that left them as kids was not the same person that had passed on.

An elderly woman with a cane sat in the pew behind them and tapped Trey and Derrick on the shoulders. Her frail body could barely hold onto her cane, but Trey could tell her soul was still only twenty-five years old. "You must be David's boys."

"Yes, ma'am," Trey nodded.

"I knew it. You two sure do resemble him. Uhm hmm." Chelsea and Mama also turned around. "You do too, sweetheart," she motioned to Chelsea but then refocused on Trey and Derrick. "I know your daddy ain't do right by you boys, but that don't mean he didn't love you just the same."

"Excuse me," Chelsea's small voice interrupted the woman. "How did you know Daddy?"

"We worked together at the plant. I'd still be working there if I hadn't been injured. Uhm hmm." She motioned to her bum hip. "Since my daughter lived out of state, your daddy would check on me at home. Long after I left rehab and your dad medically retired, he still came to visit. Brought me a meal every week. Always talked about you three. Had a picture in his wallet of you boys, and you too," she nodded to Chelsea. "He was a good man despite his past and I pray he realized that before he died. I think he worked real hard to be good because he regretted leaving. I'm so happy you all met before he went on Home."

Now came the regrets of not asking Mama to tell them more about David. Trey should've asked those hard questions so he could know him like the world did. Now he couldn't do any of that and he felt sick. The finality of death taunted him, displaying the various decisions he could have made in order to have a relationship with his father that started long before David got sick. With his stiff body there, now all he wanted to do was give the man a long hug. Cry into his shoulder. Tell him he was forgiven. Tell him he was loved.

But it was all too late. Too damn late.

Trey bent over, resting his elbows on his thighs. His heart thumped irregularly through the benediction. An incoming headache caused Trey to squeeze the bridge of his nose a little too tight. He involuntarily said, "Ouch."

Derrick rubbed his back. When Trey sat up, he asked, "You cool?"

No, he wasn't. None of them were. But he nodded and locked his hands together. Even at David's funeral, all he could think about now was Tristyn. He had been awful to her, and she had done nothing wrong.

When Chelsea called to inform he and Derrick to come over because it wouldn't be long, Trey had stopped talking to Tristyn and he had no idea as to why. Over a week later, she finally stopped calling and he was relieved. He didn't deserve her.

To make matters worse, he never even told Tristyn about David or worse now, that he died. Nor did he tell her about Chelsea and how he was thinking of moving both of them out of the state. It wasn't that he was embarrassed about his situation. And it certainly wasn't that he thought she would judge him; she wasn't that kind of person. It was just that...she didn't deserve to be caught up in his mess and because of that, it was better for them to part ways.

The minister's voice snapped him back to reality. "Pallbearers, please come to the front."

Trey and Derrick stood with four other men. Chelsea stared at her feet, as she had done for most of the service. The walk out of the church was what started it. Trey tried to hold it in. The sob of all sobs. First, it felt like his stomach shook from the inside. The shakes travelled from his heels to his fingers. His breathing was affected, and it felt as if his oxygen was cut off. He gasped for air. His legs, as strong as they were, transformed into putty.

A voice in the distance yelled for *somebody to help that boy* before somebody actually did.

26

FOREVER

Trey used his copy to let himself into Tristyn's apartment. She was half dressed in her bra and panty set, jewelry, and heels. Her dress lay flat on top of her bed and she stood in the bathroom mirror, pulling a flat iron through her tresses. "Are you planning on being late to your own party?"

She huffed. "I'm hurrying and I won't be late especially if you let me drive."

"Hell no. You're not driving, especially if we're running late."

"That's exactly the reason I need to drive." She cracked a smile before stealing a glance at Trey in the mirror. "Thank you for coming with me."

"You're welcome." He put the lid down on the toilet and sat down to keep her company. "You're lucky I know how important this party is or else I'd have you up against the wall right now. I feel like you're doing this to me on purpose to assess my resolve."

"What do you mean?" She focused on curling the ends of her hair.

"This," he motioned to her body. "Look at what you're wearing. Whenever you walk around like this, you're just waiting for me to pin you down on the bed."

"Listen, I don't want to put on my dress until I'm ready to go. I don't want it to get messed up. I didn't purposely put this on to tease you."

"And why do you already have on your heels?"

"I don't know." Tristyn spun around in the mirror to view the back of her hair. She'd placed curls through her normally straight hair to look a little more elegant and professional. Her hair tickled the small of her back and she noticed Trey swallowing. If it was any other time, she would give in, but not tonight. "Done. What do you think?"

"I love it." Trey stood up and kissed her on her forehead. "I know how you get and there's nothing to be nervous about. When you get up there and you look up and see all those people, I want you to think this in your head. Repeat after me," his hands cupped her shoulders. "I'm a boss bitch."

"Trey, really?"

"Say that shit, Tristyn. I'm a boss bitch doing boss bitch things."

"I'm a boss bitch doing boss bitch things."

"Say it like you mean it. And put your hands on your hips like Wonder Woman or some other female superhero."

Tristyn did as he suggested and straightened her back. With authority she said, "I'm a boss bitch doing boss bitch things."

Trey smiled. "One more time for good measure."

Tristyn nodded and added more hutzpah. "I'm a boss bitch doing boss bitch things."

"That's my princess," he slapped her on her butt. "Now go put your dress on so we can get out of here. This is the one thing you can't be late for."

"I'm a boss bitch doing boss bitch things!" Tristyn's arms flew above her head. She trotted over to her dress and slipped inside. Needing to make a statement she had chosen a skintight turtleneck red dress that hit right above her knees. The color block sleeves, a darker shade of red, worked in averting the attention from her curves and up to her face. In her three-inch black heels, she felt like the boss bitch that Trey had just referred to her as.

Before walking into the event hall, Trey hyped her up once more. She half felt like when they walked through the doors, everyone would stop and applaud her. Instead, they continued with what they were doing.

Trey's hand glided across her butt and he winked. "The rest of the evening is about you. If you want me to stick by your side, I'll do that. If you want me to find a seat while you talk to everyone, I'm good with that, too. I'll be on watch for your cues though and when you get on stage to make your speech, I'll be cheering you on. You worked harder than anyone in that company and you deserve this award. Now, remember what you said earlier and go kill it. I love you."

Tears in her eyes, Tristyn bit the inside of her lip. "I love you, too. Thank you for being here with me and supporting me through this."

"Always and forever, Princess." Trey kissed her on the cheek and walked away to check their coats.

Tristyn didn't have to wait long before Bob spotted and waved her over. She looked over to check on Trey and as promised, he nodded, a silent urging to do her thing.

Standing in a cluster with Bob were a few members of her team and others she assumed were government officials she'd only communicated with through email.

"Tristyn! Here is our star employee."

"Hello, all."

Bob made his introductions. Among the group was Mary, Winnifred, Matt, and Zach. She'd worked with all of them during her time at Northrup. Zach, in particular, challenged her leadership most of the project, while Winnifred had been the most reluctant to share knowledge, for fear of being replaced. Matt was generally unresponsive, often popping in the email threads to ask questions that were already answered. If it hadn't been for Mary, she wouldn't have made the progress necessary to complete the audit by her personal deadline, one year earlier than Bob predicted.

"Mary, it is so very nice to meet you. I feel like you're my best friend." They hugged.

"Doll, it was refreshing to work with you." Mary, an older woman with large, round, blue framed glasses and a floral dress, waved her off.

"It is nice to meet everyone else as well," Tristyn added.

They all shook hands and Bob walked her around to introduce her to others in attendance. Occasionally, Trey walked over to make sure she was still doing well, but other than that, he stayed in the background with a proud smile on his face. Right before the awards ceremony, Tristyn made her way to the bar to get her first glass of wine.

"I never imagined I'd see you here."

If Tristyn lacked composure, she would have snapped the wine glass in two. She turned around to see Jacob. The dashing smile on his face, the complete opposite of surprise on hers.

"Jacob, oh my god. What are you doing here?" In the past she would've immediately reached out to hug an old friend but in this case, she wasn't sure it would be welcomed.

However, when he opened his arms, she stepped into his hug. He breathed a sigh of relief, holding onto her like an old lover would. "Well, I'm a private government contractor."

"I never knew that."

"It's through one of the companies I own. One of my employees is being recognized so I came. Do you work for the government now or are you also a contractor?"

"I'm also a contractor. I work for Northrup. Our responsibilities were on the auditing side and it's what I've worked on since moving here. I'm also receiving an award tonight."

"No shit! Congratulations, but I'm not surprised. You were always focused. It looks like moving here was good for you."

"It was," Tristyn smiled modestly and took a sip of her wine. Jacob was dashing in his suit, but she expected nothing else. The gold cufflinks with a matching men's brooch holding a diamond in the center made him standout among the guests. The shoes with the gold studs lining the toes were simply to continue the display of wealth.

"I'm happy for you." He looked down at the floor before asking, "Are you happy?"

The question, Tristyn knew, was loaded. *Are you seeing anyone? Do you regret our breakup? Is there still hope for us?*

His eyebrows raised when she didn't answer. "Should I take that to mean that you won't be happy until we're back together?" His laugh at the end did nothing to assuage her feelings that he was fishing, evaluating how to slide back in.

Before she could respond she caught sight of Trey heading their way, eyebrows furrowed. She had to get rid of Jacob. While she didn't expect Trey to cause a scene, she erred on the side of caution. The last time Trey had seen Jacob he'd worn his jealous streak proudly. She had no idea how he'd display it now with them officially in a relationship.

"Well, I *am* happy. I love my job. It's a lot of work but I enjoy it. I also, umm, met someone."

"Ouch. I can't say that I'm not surprised. Hurt, but not surprised. I'd be a fool to think you wouldn't move on. You deserve to be happy even if it's not with me." He took a heavy breath and then looked her in the eyes. "Tristyn, I would've given you everything you ever dreamed of. You know that, right?"

Tristyn looked in the distance and then back to him. "I do."

"It wasn't enough though, huh?"

"It wasn't."

Trey slid next to Tristyn, his hand gently placing claim to her hip. He nodded to Jacob and Jacob watched the movement, assessing the situation.

"Everything good over here?" Trey asked.

Tristyn recognized it as it was, a pure show of asserting his masculinity and she was not pleased, especially since he first introduced himself as her cousin.

Jacob stood a little taller and then a smirk, as he understood who Trey was, appeared in the corner of his mouth. He was a calculated man. Never outdone. His wealth accrued through a careful mixture of planning and slight mistakes that paid off. The words he spoke, the moves he made, were always deliberate.

"Ah, your *cousin* is here with you. Pleasure to see you again, cousin Trey. Everything is well," Jacob finally responded. He lifted Tristyn's hand and kissed the inside of her wrist, his lips lingering long enough to prove a point. "It was nice catching up with you. Congratulations on your award."

"Thank you, Jacob."

"Tell your boyfriend, whoever he is, that he's a lucky man and to watch out. With as beautiful as you are, I'm sure your exes would do anything to get back into your life." Jacob took one last look at Trey before walking off with his drink.

Tristyn didn't know who to be more upset with. She turned to Trey. "Is your ego okay now that you proved I'm with you?"

"My ego is just fine," Trey gritted.

"Good." Tristyn swung around and walked away. Inside her clutch, her phone chirped. Jacob. *Call me when you're done playing around with your "cousin"*

27

WHILE WE'RE YOUNG

CURRENT DAY

Trey hung his head and turned around to wave over the bartender. His intention had not been to upset Tristyn but seeing her chatting with Jacob had unexpectedly caused his temper to flare. Jacob's smug smile and warning afterwards had upset him even more. "Manhattan, please."

"Attention guests." The man Tristyn had introduced as her boss, was on stage announcing that the awards ceremony was starting. Trey made his way to his table, his unbuttoned suit jacket flowing behind him. Tristyn was already seated and didn't bother acknowledging him when he sat beside her.

He leaned over and whispered, "I'm sorry." When she didn't respond he added, "I was an ass."

Tristyn cracked a smile, so he sat back in his seat and rubbed her thigh.

The emcee of the night welcomed everyone. "Thank you all for coming to the Government Ball. It's like Thanksgiving because tonight we are giving thanks to all our wonderful contractors and employees that assisted us in our achieving our goals. Our taxpayers trust us to put our best foot forward and without each of you, we wouldn't be able to do so. Tonight is about what you all have done on our behalf."

Trey didn't hear anything else the emcee said. His hand on Tristyn's thigh was there to form a truce but the more he rubbed it, the more he heated up. Without even looking over, she stopped him from sliding further up her thigh. He slid his hand off her leg and crossed his arms in an effort to control his urges.

Bob was welcomed back to the stage to introduce his company. He quoted statistics, timelines, and achievements. Tristyn turned to Trey and leaned over. "I think I'm the first one in the company to be called up."

Trey squeezed her hand to encourage her.

"The person I'm calling to the stage now is our newest employee but with her work ethic and the way she learned the processes, you'd think she had been at our company the longest. I'm not embarrassed to say that we stole her from another company back in Cleveland." The audience chuckled lightly. "But she's not leaving us, right, Tristyn?"

Tristyn mouthed *No* from her seat.

"Good!" Bob's swiping of fake sweat from his brow made the crowd roar. The introduction he continued with filled Trey with a sense of pride. Over the last few months, he'd watched as Tristyn stressed, filled in for employees that called in sick, and provided guidance to her team. She worked hard and her efforts were finally being recognized.

"Tristyn, come on up here." Her hips swayed to each side as she walked up the three steps to join Bob on stage. Trey loosened his tie, slightly warmer than before.

Bob took her hand in his and spoke into the small microphone. "I present this Small Teams Excellence Award to Tristyn Miller for her work on the Fiscal Year End Audit. Through hard work and dedication, she and her team of just ten employees gathered and analyzed documents to establish extensive, strategic goals to resolve variances in just a few short months. We are positive that this will lead to the government receiving an unqualified opinion on the audit." He turned to Tristyn, "Would you like to say a few words?"

She nodded and stepped forward. "I spent a lot of time planning my life but recently it's been left to fate. This job is just one of the things that fate brought into my life and it's one of the best decisions I made, so don't worry Bob, I'm not going anywhere.

"I'd first, like to share this award with my team. Without them, I wouldn't be receiving this. We kept our eye on the goal and I'm so very proud of us. I joined them earlier this year and they welcomed me and allowed an outsider to provide direction. I honestly can't say that I would've done the same if a stranger came into my life and started telling me what to do."

She allowed a small break for comedic pause, as Trey suggested when she practiced her speech.

"Together, we met our goal a year earlier than expected. For those of you unfamiliar with numbers and aged balances and auditing, I want to break down a few things. We successfully reduced a suspense account's balance from over a billion dollars to only three hundred seventy-five million. We worked with other agencies to put internal controls in place to keep that balance stable. We familiarized and taught classes to other agencies on identifying trends, standardized guidance and distributed it, and more. This required all of us to put in mandatory overtime in the evenings and on weekends, sometimes missing important events. Everyone on the team is phenomenal and I look forward to enjoying many more years with Northrup."

Trey's chest expanded. Tristyn nailed her speech and didn't miss a word. He was the first one out of his seat clapping, the rest of the room following suit.

Back in her seat, Trey kissed her cheek. With the continuation of the awards ceremony in swing, Trey leaned over, his lips hovering dangerously close to her ear. "You did an amazing job. I'm sorry for upsetting you earlier."

"You're forgiven," Tristyn placed her hand on top of his that rested on her thigh.

"I'm also proud of you."

"Thank you."

"I wanna show you just how sorry and how proud I am." Tristyn adjusted in her seat and Trey knew she understood. He licked his lips and motioned for her to follow him out the room. Before rising he added, "Trust me, it's worth your while."

Trey breezed past Jacob's questioning eyes and waited for Tristyn in the hallway. While keeping busy earlier, he had come upon an empty supply room when searching for the restroom. He hadn't expected to make anything of it, but life with Tristyn always held an element of surprise. Just when he thought she was standing him up, she appeared looking like the goddess that she was.

"Just like old times." She took his outstretched hand and he led her to the supply room.

He backed her against the door, hands gently caressing her hips. "I'm proud of you."

She looked up at him. "You said that already."

"And I'll say it for the rest of our lives." There was no question on whether Tristyn was *the one*. The only question was whether she knew he was the one for her. By her lack of response, he'd either thrown her off or she didn't believe it, both of which he could remedy.

With her gaze low and zeroed in on his lips, he fused hers to his. She moaned into his mouth, her fingers flowing through his hair. One thing he loved was Tristyn's unabashed need to massage and gently pull his short hair when falling into the abyss of passion. He'd have to fix it afterwards. Or maybe, he'd leave it wild just for Jacob to see.

Tristyn's moans became more urgent. He badly wanted to take his time, in this moment of making up and proving his love, but he knew he couldn't keep her, and by the look on her face, she wouldn't mind. Determination to please her as fast as he could, make her forget about Jacob, took over.

His hands roughly pulled her red dress over her hips and up to her waist. Lust filled eyes looked down as he lowered to his knees and lifted her thick thigh over his shoulder. His finger moved her panties to the side before he dove in. Gasps of pleasure rushed out of her mouth. Trey briefly lifted his head to remind her to be quiet. She nodded, her head falling to the door behind her.

His tongue knew its way around her body and its favorite thing to do was to drive her crazy. The way her breaths increased and she lost all control drove him mad. He wondered how he'd be able to stop there when done instead of lifting her against the door and driving into her to provide the ultimate experience.

Tristyn loved when he started slow but tonight, he was changing it up. He flattened his tongue and ran it up and down between her lips, rough and fast.

"Oh my God." Tristyn's back arched away from the door.

Oh, how he wished he could see her breasts bouncing right now. Over and over, he flicked, sucked, and sipped his fill of all of her. When she was close, he inserted two fingers, massaging her g-spot.

She put her fist in her mouth and her eyes rolled back into her head. Trey watched her face change and that made him go to work. He pushed his head further into her pussy and she rolled her hips into his face.

"Yes, fuck my face, baby." He groaned and massaged his dick through his pants. She swirled around his tongue while his fingers plunged deep into her and pulled back out. His free hand gripped her ass and squeezed. Tristyn's breaths became ragged and she froze and then shook violently. Her legs gave out and Trey caught her.

"Damn, Tristyn." Trey stood and Tristyn leaned her head against his chest. He still supported her weight but gradually, she started to stand.

"Trey," Tristyn's breathy tone did nothing to ease the pain in his crotch. "That was incredible."

He licked the remainder of her juices from his lips and pulled a pack of mints from his pocket. "I know. You're so loud sometimes. I hope no one heard you."

"Was I?" Her eyes widened just as her mouth did.

Trey shrugged. "Kind of but we're so far away from the action and everyone should still be in the ceremony. I doubt anyone was walking around here."

"I hope so." She supported her full weight and smoothed her dress. "I hope you're ready to finish this back at your place when we get outta here."

"I stay ready." He held open the door. His hand on her lower back guided her back to the reception hall. "You're right, Tristyn. This was just like old times."

28

WITHOUT YOU

CURRENT DAY

Tristyn's stomach growled. Trey was supposed to have picked her up over two hours ago so they could drive back to Cleveland to visit his Mama, who complained that he'd been gone too long. What really upset her was that they were supposed to enjoy a late lunch before hitting the road. Now, it was nearing dinner time and she was starving. She had purposely avoided lunch, fully expecting to devour an appetizer, entrée, some wine, and to share a dessert with him.

Tristyn twisted the top portion of her hair into a messy bun, leaving the rest hanging down, and huffed. Upon hearing the doorknob turn at the front door she spun around and stomped out her bathroom. Trey tossed his keys on the entryway table and faced a sour faced Tristyn. "Princess, I apologize for being late." He held his hands in the air for her to grab but she ignored them.

"Two hours! I've been waiting two hours. I'm starving, Trey."

"I know, and I'm sorry. Did you eat a snack?"

"No!" She debated throwing a shoe at him. "You told me you'd be thirty minutes late, forty-five minutes at the most. I called you after an hour and you didn't pick up or give a courtesy text or anything. That's rude."

"Princess..."

"Don't call me that when I'm mad. Do I look like a Princess to you when I'm mad?"

Trey sighed and dropped his head. "Tristyn, I am deeply sorry for making you wait."

Tristyn crossed her arms over her chest and rested her weight on one leg. "And what else?"

"What else, what?"

"What else are you sorry for?" It wasn't enough to be sorry. For them to work through any issues that arose, it was important that they understand each other enough to know why they made each other mad.

Trey's eyes darted to the ceiling as he thought. Then he snapped his fingers. "I'm also sorry for not calling you back?"

One eyebrow rose on her face.

"And for making you feel scared because you couldn't get in contact with me?" More of a question than an answer, Trey could only hope that Tristyn's anger was dissolving.

Her arms dropped. "Finally, we're getting somewhere. Trey, I was worried sick. I thought something happened to you. All you had to do was send a quick text to let me know what was up."

"And then you wouldn't be mad?"

"Oh, I'd still be mad." Tristyn turned on her heels and called over her shoulder. "I'm starving, Trey."

"I know baby," he called after her. Mumbling, he plopped onto her sofa. "Two hours late and she's still not ready."

"Because I didn't know if we were still going!" Her yell from the other room startled him. She had sonic hearing when she was hangry.

His forearms flexed while loading her suitcase into the backseat of his truck. "We're only going to be gone for the weekend. That's two outfits, max. Why do you need a suitcase and a carry-on?"

"Plus shoes, accessories, and makeup, Trey. What if something happens and we need to stay longer? Or what if I dirty an outfit?"

"What are you, a toddler?"

She handed over her carry-on. "You are on my nerves already."

Trey licked his lips and performed a mental reset. "How about we grab something to eat before we hit the road. You wanna eat at a restaurant or is a drive thru fine? I need to get some food in your belly ASAP before you bite off a chunk of me."

Tristyn's eyes narrowed. "You're so damn funny."

"Hilarious," Trey mocked before swooping in to nuzzle her neck.

Unsuccessful at holding in her laughter, Tristyn playfully pushed him away. "I don't care what we eat just get me to the closest place open. Now."

He followed her around the truck and kissed her pouting lips. "Your wish is my command." Making sure her feet were inside, he shut her door.

Cheeseburger in hand and milkshake mixed with peanut butter chips in the other, Tristyn danced in the passenger seat. It was a far cry from the dinner she thought she'd be eating but it was hitting her tastebuds perfectly.

Trey watched from his seat and shook his head. As soon as he finished his double bacon cheeseburger they would get on the road. "Here I thought you were evil. Turns out you were just hungry."

With the food in her stomach and her hunger pains at bay, nothing could make her mad. She bounced her shoulders along with the music. "Now you know to not let me get that way again."

"No worries there. I learned my lesson. That won't happen again." He leaned over the console and waited for her lips to touch his.

"Trey!" Tristyn scrunched up her face. "My mouth is filled with food."

He bit his bottom lip. "I don't care." When she didn't budge, he sat up straight and started the truck. "Fine. Be ready to give it up later."

"I got you." Tristyn winked and went back to dancing. "This is soooo good! You'd never think this was from Dairy Queen!"

Trey rolled his eyes and a chuckle escaped as he merged onto the highway. "Yes, you would."

*   *   *   *   *   *   *

"Is that my baby?" Mama peeked around the corner from her kitchen. With her sleeves rolled up, flour covered her hands up to her elbows. "I knew that was you. It's about time you got here. I've been waiting all day for you to finally..." her voice trailed when she saw Tristyn behind him.

Her eyes darted between them, and she stopped walking. "Glad to see you could get off work, Tristyn! Let me wash my hands so I can give you a hug. It's so good to see you. And have a seat, honey, while I talk to my son in the kitchen."

Before she walked away, she nodded repeatedly with a thin smile on her face. Looking to Tristyn she said, "It's about time my son got his act together, huh?"

"I'm standing right here, Mama."

Trey helped get Tristyn settled, setting up the TV. "Be right there, Mama."

Tristyn sat on the tan loveseat in front of the bay window that was flanked with plants of varying sizes. Across from the loveseat was Mama's oversized brown faux leather recliner. No one was allowed to sit there even when she wasn't home. She claimed the chair was fitted for her height and weight and when someone else sat there, it screwed up the proportions, which took three days of sitting to get it back to normal.

"Want any water?" Trey asked.

"I'm fine. Go talk to your mama."

Trey dragged his feet into the kitchen, where Mama was waiting.

"I don't have any problem speaking my mind, Trey." Mama dropped chicken into the flour and shook the bag.

"What's wrong?" Mentally he prepared for a lecture he knew he was too old to receive. Only when Trey had done something wrong, did Mama pull him to the side and remind him that he might be an adult, but she was his mother and would continue to be even after her death.

"I love Tristyn," she started.

"Unh unh, I'm not going down that road. I love you but you're not about to tell me you don't think she's right for me. I will not entertain that."

She paused with the bag in her hand, her neck swiveling to the side. "Boy, shut up. You are not about to tell me what to do in my own house. You will listen to me without interrupting."

Trey thought of saying something more but bit his lip, his teeth grinding in the process.

"Now, I love Tristyn and am so glad she's back in your life..."

"But?"

"What I tell you?" Trey held his tongue. She continued, "You better be sure that you're ready to walk down a real road with her. No more playing games. No more using people, or letting them use you for that matter. You are too old to not know what you want."

Trey's chin rolled to his chest. "I know, Mama. I am serious this time."

Mama smacked her lips and crossed her arms. "So that means you've talked to her. That you've righted your wrongs? That you explained that you changed and would never do that again?"

"I'm working on it."

She pursed her lips into a thin line. "Working on it ain't good enough. Not this time. Past hurts have a way of lingering into the future when they're not addressed. I'll never forget her calling my house trying to find you after you didn't even bother to say goodbye. She thought you died. I felt terrible for her and all I could say was, "You deserve better. Move on, honey."

"You owed her more, Trey. Tristyn is just as sweet as can be, she's strong, and she loves folk for who they really are. She wouldn't have looked at you any different when you told her about David and Chelsea. And she would've battled that with you. You didn't give her a chance to prove how good her soul is. She's not like other women. You're also not like other men. In that way, you two belong together, but you need to make sure her pain isn't gonna pop up when you least expect it. Address it now."

Trey fought back tears. "When I tell her she gonna leave me. She'll think I chose Chelsea over her, and I did. She won't forgive me for that. I don't wanna chance that so soon."

The lines on his Mama's face softened. "Trey, you were young, and it was so very brave of you. Not many other men would've taken on that task, but you did, and that should be applauded."

"Thanks," Trey cracked a smile.

"You were always different from other boys your age. That showed in how you took on responsibility after David left. I tried keeping most of it from you, but you were perceptive. You've always been that way. When you decided to care for Chelsea I wasn't the least bit surprised. You have a large heart, don't be ashamed of that. Frame it that way and you'll be fine.

"As a man, I'm sure you'd do things differently now. That's what matters. And now, you're going through another level of growth where you need to be an even bigger man and admit your faults."

Trey's gaze drifted to the floor and he nodded his head repeatedly. "I know."

"Good." Mama tested the oil to see if it was hot. Seeing that Trey hadn't moved, she joked, "I blame your grey eyes for your stupidity.

The women let you do whatever you want. You used that to your advantage. You and your smartass brother."

"At least now, I only open my eyes for Tristyn."

"Keep it that way. And one more thing, are you still using condoms?"

"Do I really need to answer that? I'm practically thirty."

"I had a dream about fish, so someone is pregnant. I'm just trying to narrow down who it is."

Trey shook his head, laughing. "Yes, no worries there."

Gloria pointed a wooden spoon at him. "Good, now get out my kitchen. Food will be ready in a bit."

"Man, Mama, I hate when you say that. What's a bit? Is that fifteen minutes or two hours?"

"It'll be ready when it's ready." Mama smiled behind his back. "Your brother will be here soon."

29

10 Seconds

Tristyn cuddled deep into the crook of Trey's arm on Gloria's sofa. On her other side, Derrick nursed a beer, sipping and laughing at a rerun episode of *The Office*. Mama snored lightly in her recliner, her house shoe feet twitching every now and then. Shortly after four, Tristyn was on her way to sleep as well. She wasn't sure if it was the food that had elevated her comfort level to the point where all she wanted to do was sleep, but she couldn't get there fast enough.

"Don't go to sleep," Trey whispered into her hair. "We're still going to Georgia's, right?"

"Yeah, we have to since we're in town. It's been too long since I saw her. I bet the babies are getting so big. They grow so fast when they're little."

"They do but we can also see them tomorrow if you're not up to it today, you seem tired. You could also do lunch with Georgia and Aiyanna tomorrow, just you three."

Derrick moved to the edge of his seat to look around Tristyn at Trey. "You're going to Georgia's?"

Trey smirked, "You're so thirsty. Leave that woman alone. She don't want you."

Derrick smacked his lips. "Time will tell."

Tristyn's hand caressed Trey's chest before pushing off to stand up and stretch. "She's married, Derrick."

"I haven't forgotten." Derrick downed the rest of his beer. "Y'all heading out? I'm gonna go, too. I got some admin stuff to finish for work."

"Your ass needs to get an assistant. You make more than enough to hire one," Trey said.

"I will when I find a good one." Derrick walked off to the bathroom.

"Take a plate to go," Mama mentioned behind them. "Don't leave me here with all this food."

Tristyn hadn't realized Mama had awoken but that was normally how it was with her. She dozed off quietly and then woke up just the same as if she'd been included in the conversation the entire time.

Trey towered over Tristyn. "I'll go make them."

Left behind with Mama, Tristyn attempted small talk. They hadn't yet bonded like a mother would with her son's girlfriend. Mostly, they had a growing relationship during their previous time together but since they'd gotten back together, they hadn't talked much yet.

"Dinner was delicious. Thank you for cooking. It was nice to see you after all this time."

Mama released the footrest and it lowered into the recliner. "You're welcome. I'm happy you're back with my son. You're good for him, you always were."

Tristyn sat back down, waiting for Derrick to come back, suddenly having to use the bathroom. "Thank you. I'm happy we're back together, too. I've had other boyfriends but to be honest, none made me feel the same way."

"You're in love with him?" Mama crossed her arms over her chest and tilted her head to the side.

Absolutely, but why was Mama asking? Was that why Mama had taken Trey into the kitchen when they arrived? And the way she was looking at her, was there a right way to answer the question? If she said she wasn't, Mama might ask why not. If she said yes, was the next question going to insinuate they get married soon? She did not want to be in the hot seat.

"Umm, well..."

Derrick returned. "Mama, I'm heading out too, but I'll be back to check on you in a couple days."

Mama stayed focused on Tristyn even though Tristyn tried escaping to the bathroom. "Come back tomorrow, Derrick, I need you to fix a few things."

"Okay." He bent down and kissed her forehead. "See you then."

"Tristyn," Mama caught Tristyn before she turned the corner.

"Yes?"

"What's your answer?"

Tristyn turned. "I'm not sure."

Mama nodded and excused her just as Trey walked in with two paper plates covered in foil. They all said their goodbyes with Trey promising to return the following month with Tristyn.

Before Trey pulled onto the empty street, he stole a glance at Tristyn. "Can I be honest?"

"Of course."

"I never liked Aaron in college. It was just something about him that was off. I'll play nice tonight for you and Georgia, but that's it."

"That's all I'm doing, too. I never liked him either, but for some reason, Georgia fell in love with him as soon as she saw him. I especially don't like him now since I know he's been playing her their whole marriage. Georgia is too good for him."

"If she ever decides to leave him, Derrick is more than willing to replace that bum."

Tristyn chuckled. "I know. Georgia knows too because I told her he has a crush on her."

"It's more than a crush," Trey corrected. "That boy is in love with her."

Tristyn laughed deeply. "It's a crush, he doesn't even know her."

"I promise you, Derrick is in love with her and has been since the first day they met. I guess it's similar to how you said Georgia knew she wanted to be with Aaron when she saw him."

"I honestly think she would give Derrick a chance if she weren't with Aaron. Before, Derrick was too scrawny and was a baby. Now, I feel like, if she saw him again, she would be interested. But I don't know, he's still pretty young. I couldn't see him leaving his young and fun life to be with a divorced mother of twins. Then he'd have to be all responsible and deal with a baby daddy. I just know Aaron would make Derrick and Georgia's life a living hell just because he's an ass."

"Derrick would deal with it though. He'd change his whole life for that woman. Bet." A vibration in his pants pocket stopped their conversation. "Speaking of the devil now." Trey answered his phone. "What you want? You miss me already?"

Tristyn chuckled as they pulled into Georgia's driveway. The autumn sun had already started setting and casted a beautiful glow on her home. The up lights on their quaint three-bedroom home highlighted the shrubs and flowers Georgia tended to when the weather allowed.

Tristyn exited the car to walk up the driveway to Georgia's house. Trey followed a few steps behind, still on the phone. Tristyn started to knock but stopped short when she heard the yelling. They were at it again.

"Is that them?" Trey motioned to the house.

She could only nod her head. This environment was awful for their babies and Georgia soon needed to decide what to do. It was just as toxic for their babies to be in that environment as it was for Georgia.

The door burst open. Georgia stood with tears running down her face, trying to push the double stroller out the door. When she saw Tristyn, she simply said, "I can't do this anymore."

Tristyn rushed forward into action. "I'll get the stroller. You have anything else you need to get?"

"Our bags. Umm, my bags and the baby's bags."

"I'll help," Trey stepped around Tristyn and assisted. Inside, Aaron sat on the couch, a shot glass sitting on the table next to him. To his side, another woman. He couldn't help but to shake his head.

Tristyn focused on buckling the babies into their car seats while Georgia threw a bag in her trunk. Trey exited Georgia's house with more bags, stopping next to Tristyn.

"What's going on in there?" She harshly whispered.

Trey squeezed the bridge of his nose. "There's another woman in there on the couch and I'm assuming Georgia didn't invite her."

"Are you kidding me?"

"I wish I were."

"The fucking audacity," Tristyn started to stomp past, but Trey grabbed her forearm.

"Baby, don't. Things need to cool off in there and I don't want you making it worse."

Tristyn flexed her fingers repeatedly, trying to calm down. "I won't say anything to him. I'm just gonna see if Georgia needs help bringing anything else out."

A smile that Trey didn't expect, appeared on his face. "Princess, you know you don't believe that." Trey's eyes darted to the ground before he smiled again. "Derrick said he don't believe that either."

"Both of you can shut it. I forgot you were still on the phone."

Trey said, "I would've too but this nigga won't shut up. He so concerned about Georgia he 'bout to have a heart attack." He turned his attention back to his phone. "Derrick I'm gonna call you back once we get Georgia settled...No, I don't know where she's going yet." He looked to Tristyn. "I guess we gotta figure that out. I'll get her a hotel for the week while things settle." Tristyn thanked him with her eyes. "You sure you wanna do that? Hold on, I'll put you on speaker."

"Can you hear me?" Derrick's voice flowed through the night air.

"Yeah, repeat what you just said."

"She can stay with me."

"Did you forget she has twin babies that are now walking?" Tristyn reminded him.

Derrick chuckled. "I did not, I am very clear on that. And that's why she can't stay in a hotel. It's not enough space and they probably won't even have a tub or kitchen for her to take care of them the right way. I just closed on my house a few months ago."

"Congrats," Tristyn said absentmindedly.

"Thanks. I have five bedrooms that include two master bedrooms. One is a first-floor master that she can take over."

"Derrick, why did you buy a house with five bedrooms when it's just you?"

"I liked it."

Tristyn waited for him to say more but he didn't. "Okay, thank you very much for the offer. I'll pitch it to her."

"Just tell her she's coming here. She doesn't need to make any more decisions tonight. Take that off her shoulders. I'll be up waiting when you all get here."

"All right, bro. I'll text when we on the way." Trey ended the call.

"Derrick is a lifesaver."

Georgia walked back outside and stopped in the middle of the pathway leading to her driveway. Tears threatened to spillover, but she held them at bay. She had wasted too much time trying to resurrect a failed marriage and she was tired and mad.

They were kids when they met but she had fallen in love with how he took charge of everything, allowing her to just be, for the first time in her life. Back then, neither owned a dime after student loans kicked in but Georgia had creativity, and Aaron had business acumen. Together, they grew a t-shirt designing business. It wasn't until after the birth of their twins that their business had slowly started failing. The toll of taking care of newborns stunted her creativity and even though Aaron didn't specifically say it, she knew he blamed her.

She cracked her knuckles, realizing she forgot her keys. She knocked on her door. "Let me in, Aaron, I forgot my keys." She knocked harder but still, Aaron didn't open it.

If it wasn't for needing to transport the twins in Georgia's car, Tristyn would've suggested they leave the car, at least for the night. It was obvious that Aaron had no intention of letting Georgia back in.

"Aaron!" She continued banging and kicking the door. "Just open the door so I can get my keys and then we'll be out of your life. Aaron!" When he still didn't open the door, she kicked the door with all her strength, but it didn't budge. "Fine, I got something for you and your hoe," she screamed through the door.

Tristyn's ears perked up. Georgia breezed past her with a blank stare on her face and her eyebrows low. She opened her glove compartment and pulled out a nine-millimeter gun. Aaron would either be scared into submission tonight or she would be leaving her home as a wanted woman.

Tristyn's eyes bulged and she ran after Georgia. "Georgia, put that back. You really don't wanna do this."

Georgia heard none of Tristyn's pleas. The door rattled as she banged and kicked on it like the feds. "You got five seconds before I blow this shit down."

Three seconds later, she cocked the gun and aimed at the frame, shattering the lock. With significantly less effort, she pushed it in, despite Tristyn's begging.

Trey glanced around the neighborhood to see if any lights had gone on inside the houses. He prayed no one called the police. Not wanting to leave the babies in the car alone, Trey called after Tristyn to not get involved. Tristyn shut him out and continued to beg Georgia to just grab her keys so they could leave.

Aaron's panicked eyes greeted Georgia.

"Get the fuck up," Georgia commanded much too calmly. Aaron remained in a trance. "You know what, never mind, keep your ass in that seat. Baby, look at this mess. Our door is ruined. All I wanted was my keys out my own house. I have a right to my keys *and* my house but somehow along the line you really thought that I didn't. That's crazy, right?"

His mistress, visibly distressed, scooted away from him to a chair across the room.

"I feel like we need to talk about that. About this. All of this."
Georgia motioned around the room with her gun, causing everyone
to duck. Perched on a window ledge, she smiled, happy to finally
have his attention. Her voice, lower, without an ounce of emotion.
"One would think that after six years of being married to an adul-
terer, that I wouldn't be surprised, but I am. I *am*, Aaron. I am very
surprised. And hurt. You really kicked me and our babies out of our
home." She turned to the mistress. "How can you be with someone
that would do that to his own children? That's not insane to you? He
literally has no fucking morals. Not one!"

The mistress averted her eyes, refusing to look at Georgia or
Aaron.

Finally able to find his voice, Aaron spoke up. "Georgia, sweetie."

Georgia crossed her legs and smiled. "Yes, Aaron."

"I, I don't know what to say."

"Saying you're sorry is a good start," Georgia shrugged.

"It doesn't seem like enough." Aaron kept his eyes on the gun.

"That's because it isn't, Aaron Brown," she spat. "It fucking isn't!
I should ruin your life like you ruined mine. You will never understand how much pain you caused me. What about our babies? Do
you care anything about them? About me?"

Tristyn watched in horror from the door. Georgia had always
been crazy, but in a good way. It was something they joked about
immensely. While Tristyn hadn't figured Georgia was capable of
pulling a gun on someone, she had always felt like it could be a possibility. Now, here they were. While she didn't feel as if this situation
warranted this sort of reaction, she didn't blame Georgia. To lock
your wife and children out of the home they built was inexcusable
and, in her honest opinion, punishable, but certainly not by death.

"Georgia," Tristyn called out.

"What!" Georgia looked at her, but then the features on her face
softened. It was like she saw Tristyn and realized the gravity of her
actions for the first time, snapping out of it.

Tristyn spoke softly. "Your babies are waiting for you in the car."
Georgia slowly nodded. "You just came in to get your keys. Right? I
think Aaron would love to get them for you. Wouldn't you, Aaron?"

"Yes." Aaron's head bobbed up and down. "Let me get them for
you." Aaron's footsteps were quieter than the room, his eyes never
leaving the shaking gun in Georgia's hand. Instead of taking the
keys to Georgia, he placed them in Tristyn's palm.

Keys in hand, Tristyn called Georgia to her. "All right, how about we get going so we can get your babies in a bed for the night." Georgia nodded and walked over to her. "I'll hold that for you, too."

Georgia handed over the gun. Before she walked out the door she stopped and stared at the night sky. Without turning around, she took a deep breath, tears streaming down her face. "Aaron, in case you haven't figured this out, I want a divorce."

30

Gotta Move On

Trey and Tristyn carried the bags while Georgia placed the infant carriers on the floor. Georgia was in a daze. Her eyes glistened but tears no longer fell. Her back was slumped, but somehow her shoulders were still straight. Her tone, flat through every syllable. As she walked into Derrick's house across the freshly installed wood floors, her feet dragged.

"Where should I put our stuff?"

Derrick, squatting next to the babies, cooed at them, holding a pinky out for each of them to grab. "You wanna see your new room?"

He stood back up. "I figured it'd be best if you had everything you needed on the same floor with the twins, so I got the first-floor bedroom ready for you. That way you can get to the kitchen when you need. And the laundry room is right outside the garage," he motioned behind them. "The suite also has an attached bathroom so you're good there. I think that's everything you might need but..."

"It's more than enough. I appreciate you even allowing us to crash here." Georgia bit her lip, trying to hold back the onslaught of tears.

"It's my pleasure."

"We won't be here long. I just need to figure a few things out and we'll be out your hair."

Derrick, wearing pajama pants that sat low enough on his hips for his boxer briefs to show, walked closer. "Please, stay as long as you need. Believe me, you are welcome and if you need anything here that you don't see, let me know and I'll get it. You've had to worry about a lot lately so if I can take that off you, I will."

Georgia wrapped her arms around her torso. "Thank you."

"I'll show you where your room is." Georgia nodded and went to pick up the twins' carriers.

"Leave them here, Georgia," Tristyn shooed her away. "We can handle watching them."

When Georgia cleared the room, Tristyn crossed her arms. "What a night." Tristyn tried processing the night's events but was having the most trouble trying to do so. "I just can't believe Aaron did this to her."

Trey lightly rubbed the area between Tristyn's shoulder blades. "As much as I wanna agree with you, I *can* believe he did. We were just talking about how much of a bum he was on our way over there."

"I never thought he would take it to this level though. This is a new low."

"That? I agree with. However, fate seems to be working out in Derrick's favor just like it did for me."

31

Alone

7 YEARS AGO

"I got the job." Trey stood in Mama's backyard, hands stuffed in the pockets of his shorts.

Mama tended to her garden, pruning flowers before she moved to the vegetables. "You're telling me because you want me to be happy for you, but I can't do that. You are running away from your problems and that's not something that makes me happy. As a man, well, as an adult, which you are, you don't run away from things. You have to face life."

"Mama..."

"Still talking." Trey didn't say more. "You haven't faced the main person you owe an explanation to, and you know I'm not talking about me."

Trey ground his teeth. He'd already made up his mind that whatever Mama said, he was getting the hell out of the city. There were too many reminders of things gone wrong and the things he had completely ruined. He hated what he put Tristyn through, but it was too late to make amends and what was the point anyway since he was leaving tomorrow.

Mama huffed before pulling off her gloves and turning to face him. She remained seated on the ground. "You have always been my most responsible child. You never gave me any trouble. No fuss. No nuthin'. As a parent, you know that at some point, your good child will do something that you don't agree with. I expected something but I had no clue that David's return would send you into a tailspin."

"Mama, I'm not in a tailspin."

"You're certainly in something. Maybe it's not a tailspin." She shrugged. "Maybe it's...maybe it's grief. How are you dealing with your father's death?"

"I'm fine."

"Sure you are. That's why you passed out at his funeral because you're fine. If you don't wanna talk about it or you're not yet ready, that's to be expected, but you'll have to at some point, even if it's just to come to terms with whether you're happy or sad about the relationship ending before you decided whether you hated or loved the man that gave you life. Or if it's to decide whether you're upset with me because you feel as if I kept you away from him."

Trey stretched his head from side to side and rolled his shoulders, anything to take the attention away from the matter at hand. "I appreciate what you said and I'll keep that in mind."

"That's all I ask." When Trey said nothing more, she asked, "When do you leave?"

"Tomorrow." He cleared his throat. "I leave tomorrow, Mama. It's in Tennessee and I know that seems far away but it's only about a nine-hour drive. It's a really good job and I'll be able to send you some money every month."

"I'd rather have you here than to receive your money."

Trey kneeled next to her. "I gotta do this. I need to. I can't stay here."

"I understand but promise me two things."

"Anything."

"Get help. See a professional about the grief you're holding onto. You owe it to yourself. And also say goodbye to Tristyn. You owe it to her."

Trey's chin dropped to his chest. Both things, he wasn't sure he could do. They were the first promises to his mama that he intended to break. "I will."

"The graduation ceremony is on Sunday. Guess we won't be needing those tickets after all."

"Yeah, about that," Trey took a seat on the ground next to Mama. "I already talked to the office and they're going to mail my diploma. I finished all my requirements so the ceremony is just for show. You didn't really wanna sit in the sun and listen to the commencement speaker talk about stuff that won't mean anything next week, did you?"

"I wanted it all. I've waited your whole life to watch you walk across the stage to get your college degree. You're the first to do it in our family and yes, I wanted to celebrate you in that way. But if you're sure this is what you want, then that's what it is."

"It is." Trey waited for Mama to say something else. "There's one more thing."

"I know, that's why I was waiting for you to continue."

"You already know?"

"I don't know *what* it is, I just know there *is* a what. So come on. Out with it."

He wanted to tell it all. To tell how he came to his decision. Why he decided to move forward. What exactly he would do point forward. He hated to admit that he'd kept his secret because his mama's reaction to his declaration made him more than nervous. She wouldn't hate him, but a stern reprimand was on the horizon.

"I'm renting a two-bedroom apartment in Tennessee."

Mama nodded but stayed quiet.

"It's for Chelsea. I'm taking Chelsea with me."

Still, Mama said nothing.

"She doesn't have anyone. As you know, Dad didn't have any siblings, so she doesn't have any aunts or uncles or cousins. Derrick and I are the only family she has and I can't let her go into the system. Anything could happen to her. And I can't let her try and take care of herself on the streets." Trey rubbed his balmy hands together. "There was no way I could've asked you to take care of your dead lover's daughter. You can't afford..."

"Stay out of my pockets," Mama scolded.

"I just couldn't ask you to do something like that."

"You don't know the first thing about taking care of someone other than yourself."

"I know."

"But you'll do fine."

Trey's head snapped toward Mama's. Of all the things he expected her to say, that wasn't it. And support wasn't what he thought he would receive. It almost brought him to tears. "It means a lot to hear you say that. I'm nervous though. I don't know where to start."

"No parent ever does."

"It's not like I'm trying to replace Dad, I'm still going to be her brother, not her father."

"But you will be her guardian, which means you may need to make tough decisions. You'll need to guide her every day, but I know you can do it."

"You think I made the right decision to take this on? I'm still young."

"Don't talk yourself out of something you've already set your heart on. You thought it through?"

"Yes, I thought about it a lot and it's what I need. What I think Chelsea needs. We both need a fresh start."

"I can understand that but make sure you're not running away. Sometimes what we need isn't what is best for us or our loved ones. Your father, rest his soul, is a prime example of that." Mama tapped his knee. "All right, now help up your mama so I can cook you a proper going away meal. And call Chelsea to tell her to come too. It's about time I welcomed her into our family."

32

DO RE MI

The plan was to get on the road early in the morning so they could get home in time to prepare for the upcoming work week, but since Derrick was busy getting Georgia settled, Trey had gone to Mama's house to make repairs instead. As soon as he finished, he was heading back to Derrick's to pick up Tristyn.

That was three hours ago, and Trey should've been back by now. By her calculations, helping his mama would only take one hour, including driving time. She sent a quick text, *Everything ok? What time you coming back?*

Tristyn placed her phone on the dresser and removed the baby bibs, onesies, and socks from the trash bag filled with baby clothes. Georgia, who was nursing both babies in the rocking chair that Derrick bought that morning, sat with her head back and her eyes closed.

"I'll put the bibs in the top left drawer and the onesies and socks in the one on the right. That okay?"

Georgia nodded, swallowing before saying, "I don't know how I got so lucky to have friends like you and Trey and now, Derrick. No one has ever done something like this for me. Derrick really came through. If it was the other way around, I can't say that I would've done the same for some random chic and her kids."

Tristyn used a tissue to dab Georgia's face.

"I am extremely grateful."

"And you are extremely loved. This is how love feels. We got you, girl." Tristyn leaned over to kiss her cheek. "I gotta use the bathroom. Be right back."

"You just went."

"No, I didn't."

"Yes, you did. You went when I changed the twins and that was less than an hour ago." Tristyn stopped in thought, prompting Georgia to ask, "Are you pregnant?"

Tristyn's mouth dropped open. She went to speak but couldn't formulate the words. "No, I, umm, we never..."

Georgia gasped. "You're pregnant!"

"No! I mean, I don't think so." Tristyn crossed her arms over her chest, smoothing her hair from her face. "We don't always use condoms but I'm on birth control. I couldn't be."

"Nothing is one hundred percent."

"Don't say that."

"When was your last period? Any other symptoms?"

Tristyn rushed to grab her cell, desperately needing to check the app that tracked her cycle. "Oh, thank God." She sank to the bed next to the rocking chair. "I'm not late. My period starts tomorrow. Damn, those sixty seconds were nerve-wracking. I am *not* ready to be somebody's mommy."

Georgia nodded. "It is a lot of work, that's for sure."

"And you do it so well. I'm going to the bathroom and then I'm gonna get us some food. I'm starving."

Georgia watched out the corner of her eyes but then shrugged her shoulders.

"Hey Derrick." A fresh pep in her step, Tristyn walked into the large open kitchen. White cabinets and light colored wood floors glistened from the sun shining through the equally large window overlooking the expansive backyard. With the leaves scattered across the ground, the view was picturesque.

Derrick pulled a large pack of ground beef from the refrigerator along with eggs, onions, and cubes of Colby Jack cheese. "Hey Tristyn. I'm 'bout to make burgers. Want one?"

"Absolutely! I'm starving. I was just about to see about ordering something, but fresh burgers are always a good idea." Tristyn sat at one of the barstools lining the counter. "Have you heard from Trey? I thought he would've been back by now."

"Nah." Derrick, dressed in a black, unzipped athletic hoodie and matching joggers, moved fluidly in the kitchen. He pulled his sleeves up and dumped the ingredients and seasonings in a bowl. "Knowing Mama, she probably found some other things for him to do. Did you text him?"

"Yeah, I did a few minutes ago but he didn't respond yet. I hate when he does that. He did that right before we left to come here. Just went ghost for hours. I thought something happened to him." To be honest, she'd thought even worse and had flashbacks of when he left her without notice in college. And now, she couldn't help feeling the same.

Derrick peeked at her. "He's not leaving you, Tristyn. Trust me, he ain't going nowhere."

A clog of emotion she hadn't expected, caused her eyes to gloss over. "Can I ask you something?"

"You can ask me anything."

"Why did Trey leave me in college? Was it something I did? Was it all too fast?"

"You can ask me anything but that." Derrick avoided her by moving to the other side of the countertop to create the patties and place them on the baking sheet.

"Figures." Tristyn pulled her cell from her pocket to check for a response from Trey. Still nothing.

"You gotta ask him. It's not my place to tell you."

"Was it someone else?"

Derrick washed his hands and turned back around to face Tristyn. "Again, you need to talk to Trey. Only he can answer your question."

Tristyn shook her head and then shot Trey another text. "I would if he answered his damn phone."

A slight smirk emerged on Derrick's face and for a moment, Tristyn wondered why Georgia couldn't see Derrick as more than Trey's little brother. "I'll take you to Mama's after we eat. If you're there, Mama won't keep him any longer and y'all can get home. That make you feel better?"

Relief coursed through Tristyn's body. "Thank you. Now let me help you because I'm starving and you're taking forever." She bumped him out of the way with her hip, causing him to laugh, and she washed her hands in the sink.

Georgia's exhausted feet dragged across the kitchen floor behind them. "That smells yummy."

Derrick's eyes lifted from the skillet, pausing when he saw her. He cleared his throat. "You can have the first one."

"That's messed up," Tristyn pursed her lips. "I'm the one helping but she's getting the first one. All she was in there doing was feeding, burping, and putting her babies to sleep. Clearly, my job assisting you is harder than hers."

"Clearly," Georgia joked. "And also, fuck you."

"What are we eating with these burgers?" Georgia looked around. "You have potatoes? I have a taste for french fries."

"Pantry," Derrick responded. "But before you start cutting up potatoes, I'd like to show you around the rest of the house before the twins wake up from their nap. Tristyn, can you watch these burgers while I finish showing Georgia where everything else is?"

"Sure." Tristyn manned the skillet, watching their interaction, knowing it was a matter of time before Derrick worked his magic on Georgia.

<u>33</u>

I HATE YOU

CURRENT DAY

"I'm starting to wonder if you're embarrassed by me."

It was funny how fate worked to expose lies. Or rather, to expose truths. Twenty-four hours ago, Tristyn had praised the gods for allowing her to have Trey, and not someone like Aaron. Now, she could only laugh as she watched him argue in the driveway of his mama's house with an uncommonly gorgeous woman who was naturally shaped like an African goddess, and obviously, younger than she.

Their exchange was one of passion. The kind that only love could bring out. It was the identical expression of love and frustration that shone in his eyes when he looked at her during their arguments.

Derrick stopped short when he saw why Tristyn had stopped walking.

"Who is that?" She whispered, a knot perfectly formed in her gut.

"Tristyn," Derrick rubbed the back of his neck, unable to explain without exposing Trey.

Their argument continued. Trey's hands rubbed down the sides of his face. "You know it's not like that."

"Then what is it? Why doesn't Tristyn know about me?"

"Look, you know I love you, but I love her too, and I can't tell her right now. I will, but not right now. I just need a little more time. And I need for you and Mama to get off my back."

"Tell her before you go back home." The woman's voice softened. "You're not mad at me for giving you an ultimatum, are you?"

Trey's head tilted toward the sky, and he bent his neck in every angle. "I could never be or stay mad at you. And please, I ain't never had an ultimatum from you or Mama that I couldn't dodge." He kissed her forehead before pulling her into a hug.

Tristyn's breath became ragged, her stomach threatening to expel the burgers and fries from lunch. As much as she wanted to run, to leave him standing there and never see him again, her feet were too heavy to move.

She felt Derrick's voice before she felt the nudge forward. "Come on, let's talk to Trey."

"No," she shook her head violently. She wanted nothing to do with Trey. Ever. Again.

Derrick's head fell to the side. "Tristyn."

"No!" She yelled, causing Trey to look up with wide eyes. The smile on his face now gone.

"Tristyn." Trey's eyes rolled from Derrick to Tristyn. "What are you doing here?"

"What am *I* doing here? I'm sorry if I'm intruding on your affair."

"No, baby, it's not like that. I swear."

Derrick went to walk past but Trey roughly grabbed his arm. "Derrick, back me up."

"I'll talk to her after you lay in your bed."

Trey badly wanted to swing on him. He turned to Chelsea, the woman he'd been talking to. With her arms crossed over her chest, he knew she would be no help.

Tristyn turned her wrath on everyone. "So, Derrick, you knew Trey was cheating on me and you said nothing? And apparently, your whore and your mama knew about me too, so that means I'm the only fool here." Her voice rose with every sentence, not caring who heard her screaming. "My gut told me to leave you alone but no, I just had to put myself back into the same situation that hurt me the first time. I completely ignored all the signs. The time I was at your house I heard you talking to her, or maybe it was one of your other girlfriends..."

"Tristyn, I promise, there are no other girlfriends. There's only you."

"...but regardless, I should've left then, but I stayed. I should've left when you didn't show me enough respect to let me know you were running behind schedule. And now, here we are. Fool me once, shame on you. Fool me twice, shame on muthafuckin' me!"

Mama emerged from her house. "What in God's name is going on out here?"

"Reckoning day." Derrick, now standing next to Mama, explained.

"That's my sister!" Trey's outburst shocked them all.

"Do I look stupid to you? You don't have a sister!" Tristyn yelled back, tears now falling rapidly down her face.

Chelsea, standing in the doorway of the house, shook her head, disgust written on her face. "Should I say something?" She asked Mama.

"Only if you wanna get involved." Mama dismissed herself. "I'm going back inside to finish my nap. Only wake me up if hands are thrown."

Derrick stood next to Chelsea, resting his arm on one of her shoulders. "I kind of feel bad for him."

"I mean, he had it coming but I feel bad too. Let me go save his rotten ass."

"Cool," Derrick shrugged. "I'ma go see if there's anything Mama had left over for Trey to finish before she falls back asleep."

Chelsea nodded and then took a deep breath.

"Don't come near me," Tristyn warned Chelsea.

Chelsea kept walking. "He's telling the truth, he's my brother."

Tristyn blinked rapidly, trying to process the information. How could he have a sister he never told her about? His Mama only had the two, Derrick and Trey, and as far as she knew, she hadn't adopted anyone. Since Trey's father was dead and Mama never remarried, she assumed they were all in cahoots. "Don't bother covering for him. You're all fucking liars. I'm out of here."

Trey ran after Tristyn, now walking down the driveway. He grabbed her arm, which she snatched away. He grabbed again and stopped her. "I wouldn't lie to you. That's Chelsea, she's my sister. Please don't leave, Tristyn. I can explain everything."

"Like how your mother has a new twenty-year-old daughter?"

Chelsea hollered down the driveway. "I'm not twenty."

"Nobody gives a fuck how old you are."

Chelsea paused then walked away. "Yeahhh, better for me to go back inside until she calms down."

"Tell me Trey, who's the father?"

"My biological father. His name is David."

"Oh, right, the father that you never knew because he died."

"Well yes, but he's not dead. I mean, he wasn't dead then, but he is now."

"So you lied to me then?"

"No, I mean yes, not on purpose." Trey wanted to pull his hair out in frustration. "I can explain everything, and my family will back me up. I should've told you everything before now and for that, I am so sorry."

Tristyn spit at his shoes. "Fuck you and your lying ass family. I'm out of here." She snatched her bags out of Derrick's car. "Matter of fact, take me home. Now!"

Trey stood, staring, before he acquiesced. "I'll get my things."

*   *   *   *   *   *   *

Inside, Trey retrieved his keys. In the living room, Mama snoozed in her chair. In the kitchen, Derrick and Chelsea talked quietly. No one except him was in misery and no one seemed to care how he was feeling.

"Why you ain't tell nobody you were coming into town?" Derrick asked Chelsea.

"You know how I like to pop up. I heard about your new family."

"How?"

"Don't ask questions you don't want the answer to." Chelsea and Derrick stared at each other for a moment before she joked, "But seriously, how's it going with the new family?"

Derrick sighed. "Man, it's a beautiful thing."

"Well, don't forget they're not yours. You might have to give them back."

"We'll see about that. I need you to do something with me. I'd ask Trey but, you know."

"He'll be fine," Chelsea glanced over her shoulder. "What you need me to do?"

"Go over and see Aaron with me right quick."

Chelsea's tight belly shook as she released a laugh. "The fuck is wrong with you!" She quickly glanced at Mama to make sure she was still sleeping before lowering her voice. "Are you trying to get us killed? You can't show up at the house of a man whose wife and children are shacking up with you. What is your purpose, here?"

Derrick hung his head. "I don't know."

"Relax, you don't even know if Georgia wants to go back to that loser. Take it from me, don't go overstepping boundaries. If it's meant to be then she's right where she should be."

"You're right."

"I know."

"How can y'all act..."

Simultaneously, Derrick and Chelsea raised their pointer fingers to their lips to quiet Trey. Behind them, Mama lightly snored in her chair. Trey lowered his voice and subsequently, willed his adrenaline to wind down. "You two are acting like everything is cool when you know it's not."

Derrick leaned his hips against the counter. "Relax, bro."

"Don't tell me to fucking relax," Trey hissed, inches away from Derrick's face.

"Come on, Trey," Chelsea guided Trey away from Derrick. "Don't get mad at us when you know this is your fault. All you had to do was tell Tristyn the truth and you could've told her a long time ago, but you don't listen. You're always so damn secretive."

Trey bit the inside of his bottom lip, practically drawing blood.

Derrick slapped him on his shoulder. "Once she calms down and you explain it all she'll be fine. I don't doubt for a minute that you two aren't made for each other. All you have to do is not dig yourself any deeper holes."

"Exactly," Chelsea grabbed a glass from the cupboard and the jug of Mott's Apple Juice from the refrigerator. "Meaning, keep your mouth shut and wait for her to talk to you. Don't mess it up any more than you already have."

"Give me my shit." Trey stole the gallon of apple juice and walked out the door. Calling out behind him he said, "Tell Mama I said bye. Love y'all."

34

INCOMPLETE

7 YEARS AGO
"I'm sure he won't miss graduation."

Tristyn, on the other hand, wasn't so sure. Lately, she was unsure of everything. She was unsure if she and Trey were still together. She was unsure whether she had done something to upset him to the point where he no longer returned her texts, calls, or social media messages. Speaking of social media, he hadn't posted or shared anything in weeks. His mother said he was alive, but needed time, all of them did. Tristyn had no idea what that meant and prayed everything was okay.

What hurt the most was knowing that whatever troubled him, he hadn't felt safe enough to share it with her. He'd cut her off completely without so much as a word.

"How about we avoid talking about him?" Georgia's eyes pleaded for Tristyn to feel better. To fake it until she made it, at least for today. "Maybe he'll be there, maybe he won't. Either way it goes, you'll still be mad at him so let's at least be happy until we either do or do not see him."

Georgia placed her graduation cap on her head and then placed Tristyn's on her head. "Today is the day we graduate. Today is the day our lives change. You got a job. I got a job. Our futures are paved with gold, girl. GOLD! And I am engaged." She held her hand in front of her to admire her ring. The diamond was smaller than she wanted but Aaron promised he would get her a bigger one as soon as he found a real job.

"You're right," Tristyn found the energy to fake a smile. "Let's go graduate. We earned this and I'd be a fool to let Trey ruin this day. I only get one college graduation."

"Unless you go for your masters or doctorate or some shit like that."

"That ain't happening. One and done for me." They laughed as they walked out of Georgia's dorm room, arm in arm.

Trey hadn't shown. He'd missed his own graduation and now, Tristyn was really worried. She had to see him to make sure he was okay and thus, begged Georgia to drive her to his apartment.

"What are you going to say when you see him?" Georgia asked.

"Who knows."

"Maybe you could start with asking why the hell he's avoiding you." Georgia suggested from the driver's seat of her run-down Chevy.

The longing in Tristyn's eyes was evident. She did her best to enjoy the day. To enjoy the festivities. But she couldn't stop worrying about Trey. Although they hadn't known each other long, disappearing was uncharacteristic of him. Something had to be wrong. Whatever it was, she just wanted to hold him and tell him everything would be fine. That she could help him through anything. At the end of the day, all she wanted was to be with him. To love and grow old with him.

"I'll figure it out when I get up there." When she noticed Georgia's hand on the handle, she stopped her. "I need to do this by myself. I won't be long."

Hanging out in the hallway outside of Trey's apartment was his roommate, Mitchell. "Tristyn, what's up? Haven't seen you in a while."

She'd never liked him, but she put up with him because he was rarely home. "Just stopping by to see Trey really quick."

Mitchell told the caller on the line to hold on and then studied her so long it made her uncomfortable. "Trey's not here."

"Do you know when he'll be back?"

"I don't think he's coming back. He moved all of his stuff out."

Tristyn's mind took her to a million places, none were soothing. "When?"

"I don't know."

"Did he say where he was going?"

"Nah. Just left. He paid next month's rent so I ain't really care. He ain't tell you he was leaving? I thought you was his boo."

Tristyn slowly turned around, not hearing anything else Mitchell said. By the time she was back inside Georgia's car she could barely talk. "He's gone, Georgia. He left. And he didn't even say bye."

Georgia held her as she cried, soaking her shirt, and she knew, Tristyn would not get over this.

35

CALLING MY PHONE

CURRENT DAY

"What are you gonna do?" Aiyanna sat on Tristyn's sofa with her legs curled underneath her.

Georgia, stretched out on her chaise, laid under a soft blanket with fuzzy socks. For the hundredth time, she glanced at the playpen set up in Tristyn's living room. Normally, the twins' nap lasted three hours but because she was doing something without them, she swore they would wake up any minute.

Tristyn pulled tissues from the box centered between the three. She had taken up a spot on the sofa opposite of Aiyanna. The two had driven down earlier in the day after Tristyn had broken the news that she thought she was pregnant. Four positive tests later, she was confident that she was carrying Trey's baby and that her bladder might bust from all the water she had consumed.

"I don't know," Tristyn blew her nose. "This is completely unexpected. We used condoms and I was on birth control. To be honest I wasn't totally keeping up on my pill and was thinking of getting on a different kind, but I thought I'd be okay because we used condoms. I don't understand how two forms of birth control can fail. How is that fair?"

"No birth control is a hundred percent effective," Aiyanna mused.

"That's the same thing I told her last week," Georgia stretched, feeling relaxed.

"No need to state the obvious," Tristyn dabbed her eyes with another tissue.

Georgia said, "I knew you were pregnant. You were peeing all the time and you were hungrier than usual. Did you have any other symptoms?"

"No!" Tristyn shook her head. "I did eat more than normal but right before my period I always eat more so there was no reason to be suspicious. I never would've thought I was starving all the time because I was growing a baby. Then, when my period didn't come, I think I was in denial. A week later is when I started to worry. My period is never that late."

Tristyn cried on Aiyanna's shoulder. "Am I a bad person for not wanting this baby?"

Georgia kneeled in front of the sofa and rubbed Tristyn's arm. "No, Tristyn, you're not. You took all the necessary precautions and it happened anyway. You can't fault yourself for not wanting it."

"I don't even know how far along I am," Tristyn held her belly. "What if I'm past the date to have an abortion? What am I gonna do then?"

"You just missed your first period," Georgia smoothed Tristyn's hair. "You're probably only like, five weeks along."

"Me and Trey aren't even talking. How am I supposed to have a baby with someone I'm not talking to? This situation is so messed up." There was much to think about. What would she tell Trey? Would he want her to keep the baby even if she didn't want to? With her tears having slowed, she sat back up and Georgia took her place back on the chaise.

"Is he still calling?" Georgia asked.

"All the time. He won't stop. I'm surprised he hasn't popped up here yet. He just keeps asking for me to hear him out."

"Why won't you?" Aiyanna shrugged her shoulders. "You've given him chances before and it's clear you still love him, so why not listen? It's not like you have to be with him just because you listen to his story. Whatever he says, believe what you want, but I feel like you won't be able to officially move on until you get your closure."

Tristyn sat, waiting for Georgia to contradict Aiyanna. She had warned Tristyn not to get involved, knowing it would end with Tristyn getting hurt. Instead, Georgia sat, nodding her head.

"You agree?" Tristyn scooted to the edge of the sofa and rested her forearms on her thighs.

"I do," Georgia gave a sympathetic smile. "You're pregnant and regardless of what you decide to do, you owe it to yourself and your unborn baby to at least hear him out. See what he has to say. And you don't have to tell him you're carrying Trey Junior."

Tristyn cracked a smile.

"Or Trey Juniorita," Aiyanna added, causing Georgia and Tristyn to laugh aloud.

Georgia continued, "When Derrick was home the other night, he had Trey on speakerphone. He's a mess."

"Really?"

"Oh yeah. They're gonna stage an intervention."

"Is it that bad?"

Georgia snorted. "Definitely. I've never seen a more miserable man. Derrick was on Facetime with the rest of Those Gotdamn Daltons..."

"Wait," Aiyanna put down her drink. "*Those Gotdamn Daltons*?"

Georgia waved it off. "Yeah, apparently that's what they call themselves...Chelsea, Derrick, Onyx, Phoenix, Trey, and Xavier. But anyway, they're all planning on popping up at Trey's crib to get him back into shape. They were gonna do it this weekend but they wanted to go when Trey least expected it, so I think it's going down next weekend. And Chelsea had to book a flight, so there's that. I really do think she's family, Tristyn."

They sat in the quiet longer than necessary, neither of them knowing how to respond. Tristyn changed the topic. "So, Georgia, have you heard from Aaron?"

Georgia released a deep sigh. "I've heard plenty but none of it has been to my liking. Every time he calls saying some bullshit I hang up on his ass."

"What's he saying," Aiyanna's eyebrows squeezed closer together on her forehead.

"He saying he's not giving me a divorce," her head tilted to the side and she rolled her eyes.

Tristyn's eyes widened. "You gotta be kidding."

Georgia shook her head. "I wish I was. He said he'll never give me a divorce and if I file, he'll petition for full custody. For some odd reason he thinks we can work things out through counseling."

Tristyn gasped. After everything Aaron put Georgia through, she couldn't believe his audacity was still so high that he thought she could forgive him. "You can't be serious!"

Georgia looked them in their eyes. "Does it look like I'm playing? I'm so fed up. I should've killed him when I had the chance."

"There has to be something you can do," Tristyn sat back on the couch. "Have you talked to a lawyer to see what your options are?"

"Derrick called one of his friends who is a divorce attorney and she's supposed to give me a call next week."

"Oh," Aiyanna raised her eyebrows.

Grateful for the focus on Georgia, Tristyn smiled and pulled her legs up, resting her chin on her knees. "Yes, *oh* is right. How's that working out for you? And Derrick?"

Georgia could not keep the smile from spreading across her cheeks. "It's good. *Really* good. Almost great. He's so good with the twins, and with me. He's patient. And he takes care of everything. There's no comparison between him and any other man I've dated. We've completely invaded his space and he has no complaints. He goes to work and then comes home and plays with the twins, gives me time to get showered and recoup, I make dinner, and when I don't feel like it, he orders something. I still don't have any money or income and he doesn't even care. All he says is that he makes more than enough and is happy to spend it on something meaningful."

"Are we sure there aren't any other brothers lingering around, other than Trey?" Aiyanna bit the corner of her lip.

"Girl, shut up," Tristyn laughed, and Georgia waved away her statement.

"Shit, I'm serious. I need a man. I'm so tired of being single and lonely. I can only hang out with my friends so many times before I'm over it."

"So, you're over us?" Tristyn threw a pillow at her head.

"You know what I mean. I love y'all but neither of you can please me the way I need to be pleased. The dating apps are horrible and so are the men on them. You wouldn't believe the crap in these profiles. And I need sex. I miss sex," Aiyanna sunk into the couch and whined.

"You'll find your guy, Aiyanna," Georgia promised. "He's on the way."

"Tell him to hurry before my pussy dries up for good," Aiyanna hissed through the pillow covering her face.

When Tristyn finally gained her composure from laughing she asked, "There's not even one prospect?"

Aiyanna sat back up. "I saw this guy at a wedding I went to. He was a groomsman. When I tell you he was sexy I'm telling you he was sexy. I'm getting hot just thinking about him." She fanned her face. "He was so big, like, muscular. Even though he had on a suit I swear he might have played football in college or something. The suit looked like it was gonna rip and all I wanted to do was squeeze his arms, and his legs, and then jump on him."

"Be careful, that's how you end up like us, pregnant," Tristyn pointed at her.

"I wanna be pregnant and married. I'm built for that kinda relationship. It don't matter anyway because he was there with a girl. But if he wasn't, he probably would've been perfect for me."

"Your husband is coming, and I hope you meet him tomorrow," Tristyn warmly squeezed Aiyanna's ankle. "Matter of fact, I hope that guy breaks up with his girl and you two meet again."

"If not, I know for sure that Derrick's cousins are single," Georgia glanced at the twins again. "Maybe we can stage a meet up or something. But stay away from Phoenix, I doubt he'll ever settle down."

"That's the personal trainer, right?"

"Yep."

"Well, whoever you meet, we pray he moves you in and takes care of you for the rest of your life, just like Georgia's future husband, Derrick, is doing now," Tristyn giggled.

Georgia cut her eyes at Tristyn. "He's not my future husband. He is very sweet but he's too young for me."

"It's only three years, Georgia," Tristyn shook her head. "Give the man a break. He's certainly more mature than any man you ever met. He's damn near perfect."

"I don't wanna jump back into another relationship though."

"Then don't. No one said to marry him next year. Just keep him in mind."

Georgia's thoughts swirled in her head. "You're right. And also, call Trey."

36

PILL FOR THIS

CURRENT DAY

"Where are you?" Chelsea peered outside to the airport pickup window zone.

Derrick responded through the phone. "We're pulling up now. We're in a red Escalade."

"Who's driving the Escalade?"

"It's X's."

Chelsea stepped closer to the glass, not yet wanting to step into the cold air. Since the short time she had been living in California, she had quickly grown accustomed to the beautiful weather. Anything less than sixty degrees was too cold and the bitter cold air whipping around Columbus reminded her that fall was ending. Her bohemian skirt and midriff shirt would not help, especially since she'd packed away her coat.

"I see you." She ran outside when she saw them pull up, rolling her suitcase next to her. She waved her arm frantically with her cell in her hand to catch their attention.

Derrick jumped out and quickly hugged her before urging her to get in the front seat. He lifted her suitcase into the trunk, along with theirs, before hurrying into the backseat.

Chelsea hugged Xavier in the driver's seat and then angled her body to see the rest of her family. Directly behind her sat Derrick and Onyx and in the last row, Phoenix attempted to stretch his legs out as much as possible.

Before she could greet them, they all looked at her and asked, "Where's your coat?"

"Hey to y'all, too." A round of heys and what ups were passed between them. Satisfied, she turned back to Xavier. "Okay then X. I see you out here living all luxurious. When did you get this?"

"Last week." Xavier, the owner of a lounge and multiple cigar shops spanning state lines, bobbed his head to the music playing lightly through the speakers.

"Congratulations."

"Thank you."

"You must be doing well, then."

"Business couldn't be better. I moved into a penthouse downtown, too."

"Are you serious?"

Onyx chimed in from the back, his eyes focused on the passing scenery. "He's dead serious."

"Okay then money bags. Let me hold something. You know I'm a teacher, I'm poor."

Phoenix responded first. "Xavier doesn't give anything away. Good luck with that."

Xavier allowed a short laugh to escape before glancing at Chelsea. "How much you need?"

"So you'll give her money, but not me? That's messed up," Phoenix said as the car erupted in laughter.

"You own your own gym, you ain't hurting for money," Xavier retorted.

As it calmed down, Onyx asked, "Do we have a game plan?"

"Leave it to the detective to ask if we have a plan," Derrick joked.

"It's a valid question," Xavier piped in. "What if Trey doesn't let us in?"

Chelsea smiled in her seat. "He'll let me in, I'm his baby sis."

"Your ass gets away with anything and everything." Derrick shook his head.

"It's because I'm the baby Dalton and I'm a woman." Chelsea rolled her hands around on her wrists like she was about to take a bow.

The GPS alerted them they were closing in on their destination, Trey's house. Onyx, the planner in the group, the one who stayed ten steps ahead of everything, was right. They needed a plan to get Trey back on track and if that meant Chelsea had to ambush Trey to get them all in the house, then that's what it would take.

Over the past week, each of them had held a conversation with Trey and they deduced, he was not okay. After their monthly Facetime they decided the best thing to do was to overload him with family love.

Chelsea had to admit that after Tristyn and Trey's blow-up, she thought they would make up, but now, she wasn't so sure, and she couldn't help feeling partially to blame.

Once in the driveway, Xavier cut the engine and turned around to face everyone. "How about this. Chelsea, since you're known to pop up on people, you show up at the door first to get Trey to let us in. If he sees us all he might not answer. Once we're inside, we'll see how he's doing and play it by ear. What's he like to do?" They all looked at Derrick.

"Basketball. It's his best stress reliever."

Onyx asked, "Is it a place we can play around here?"

"No idea," Derrick responded. "But I brought cards."

"And I brought cigars," Xavier patted his car's console.

"I brought liquor," Onyx smirked.

"I have a local massage therapist up here that I can call for him." Phoenix added like it was normal for him to have an on-call masseuse in another city. Everyone turned to look at him. "Mind your business," he responded to four pairs of questioning eyes.

"I brought sage, essential oils, and I can find some weed, if necessary." Chelsea unlocked her phone. "I think I still have dude's number."

Onyx shook his head and Xavier did the same. Movement from the corner caught Chelsea's eye and she saw Trey peek out the window from behind his curtain. "Busted. He knows we're here. I'll head to the door."

"What are you all doing here?" Trey asked from the doorframe. Everyone's movement stopped as they assessed Trey's appearance.

"Aww damn," Derrick's arm fell to his side. "This nigga done aged ten years on us."

Onyx scratched his nose. "I'm gonna get the bags."

Xavier shook his head. "I hope y'all brought enough clothes. Looks like we gonna be here a while."

"Clothes for what?" Trey asked. "Ain't no way all of you are about to stay here." Arms crossed over his chest, he looked nothing like he had when they last saw him.

Phoenix shut the door to the car. "I'm gonna get my clippers. I'm glad I keep them with me." He grabbed his overnight bag from the trunk and then mumbled to Onyx, "This dude ain't even had a haircut. Just how is he keeping his job looking like that?"

Derrick joined them. "I think he been working from home the whole time."

Chelsea gave them all the evil eye, warning them to stop talking bad about Trey. She turned to approach Trey, saying the first thing that came to mind even though it was a complete fabrication. "Don't tell me you forgot about the Gotdamn Dalton Crew Weekend."

Trey, with a face full of hair, a long Cleveland Cavaliers robe, and food-stained pajama pants, pulled his robe tighter against the cold air. "We lived together long enough for me to know when you're lying."

Chelsea bit the corner of her lip and shrugged. "We're just here to hang out. That cool?"

Trey observed her and the rest of the crew walking up his driveway with their luggage. He moved to the side to allow them to enter. "Seems as if I don't have a choice."

"You don't," Onyx patted Trey's shoulder as he walked in behind Chelsea. As the oldest and most responsible of the group, he'd entered college to receive a degree in criminal justice. Right after he turned twenty-one, he signed up for police academy. Now a detective, he didn't often wear his uniform, but with the long hours spent behind his desk and in the field, he regularly worked out with his twin, Phoenix, a personal trainer. "Your sister was driving us crazy because she was so worried about you."

Chelsea's mouth dropped open. "You're a hater."

"Someone had to say it, sis." Derrick walked in next and dropped his bags at the bottom of the stairs. He wrinkled his nose and looked at Trey. "Just like someone has to tell you that something in here stank. I don't know if it's you or your messy ass house."

Phoenix's eyes were drawn to the empty pizza boxes atop of the coffee table and torn open candy wrappers on the sofa cushions. He held up a fast-food bag. "Oh, hell no. Have you been eating this shit?" Trey didn't bother answering. Phoenix was the one in the crew just as concerned about what they put in their bodies as he was about what they put on their bodies. When with him, no one ate anything that wasn't organic, and he carried around a gallon jug that he refilled with berries and water to drink from daily. The crew often teased him about his glowing skin because his skin care regimen was equally important.

Finally, Xavier waltzed in with his eyes glued to his phone. At six-foot-four and two hundred thirty pounds of lean muscle, locs dyed blonde at the tips, and a Kool Aid smile that lit up his medium brown skin, he stood out wherever he went. But at thirty-one, the things he cared most about was minding the businesses that paid him and partaking in adventure. He stopped long enough for Trey to bump his fist, before he went straight to the chair and sat down to tap out an email.

"I'll clean it later." Trey shut his door and stepped over Derrick to head upstairs.

"Whoa, whoa, whoa," Onyx called out behind him. "Where are you going?"

Trey stopped in his tracks. "To take a nap."

"Aww, Trey, we just got here. Can you stay up a little longer? I know it's late but it's the weekend." Chelsea held out her arms for a hug. There was one thing Trey could never deny and it was her. She was sure that since they didn't grow up together, he often gave in to her requests because he was trying to make up for lost time. She didn't normally abuse that power, but she had a feeling she may need to lean into that heavily this weekend.

Trey moped back down the stairs. She held him tightly, trying to use her positive energy to clear his negative. People often slept on the power of hugs; she wasn't one of them. "I missed you," she whispered into his chest.

He released a deep breath. "I missed you, too."

"And just so you know, this doesn't count as getting me a flight. I fully expect you to still do that."

With his arm around her shoulders, they walked over to the sofa and sat down.

Derrick grabbed the remote and sat down on the empty cushion next to them, lifting his legs across their thighs. "Cavs game is on."

Phoenix sat on the loveseat while Onyx joined them after pulling up a chair from the dining room table. Conversations of playoffs dominated the air and before long, Trey loosened up enough for everyone to hear him laugh.

37

SUFFOCATE

CURRENT DAY
Around halftime of the west coast game, Onyx caught Phoenix with a goofy smile on his face that wasn't caused by the liquor that had been flowing for the past hour. "What you smiling about?"

Trey, finally feeling relaxed, stretched out his legs on the ottoman in front of him and rested his head on his arm behind his head. "Yeah, what has you smiling like that?"

Phoenix attempted to disguise his grin, but the result left him smiling even harder.

"It's a girl," Onyx confirmed. He and Phoenix were as identical as could be. The read each other's minds, performed the same movements even when they weren't around each other, and loved many of the same things. "What's her name?"

All eyes were on Phoenix when he confirmed he'd met someone. "Honestly, I don't even remember. But I do know we had a good time." Insinuation dripped off his statement.

"Aww, that's so cute." Chelsea rolled her eyes from her spot at the window. Trey had forced her to sit next to it to blow the weed smoke out his house.

Xavier rubbed his head. "When you say you had a good time, that means what we think it means?"

"I hate being the only woman," Chelsea took another hit of her blunt and faced the window.

Phoenix lightly scratched the area under his bottom lip. "A gentleman doesn't kiss and tell."

"Was it good?" Trey took a puff from his cigar and blew the smoke in the air, savoring the flavor.

"Hell yeah."

"She's single, right?" Onyx eyed Phoenix closer. "We know how you like to take married women home from the gym."

"I can't help who likes me." Phoenix confessed, as if that explained everything.

"I'll tell you like I told Derrick." Trey rested his cigar in the holder on the coffee table. "Leave the married women alone. That won't get you anything but heartache and a beat down."

Standing next to the window, Chelsea coughed. "You gotdamn Dalton men think you're God's gift. There's plenty of single, black women just waiting for men like you but y'all wanna go after married women. Lord," she looked at the ceiling, "make it make sense."

Derrick, who had too much to drink and was in and out of sleep on the floor, opened his mouth long enough to say, "Both of you can shut the fuck up." He laid his head back on top of his arms and closed his eyes.

"What Derrick said." Phoenix waved them all off. "What about you, Onyx, since you're in my business, who were you texting on our way down here?"

"It was work business."

Derrick piped in from the floor again. "Lies."

"I don't need to prove myself."

Chelsea put out her blunt and stepped closer to Onyx. "Shut up! Are you seeing someone at work?"

"No, that's against the rules, Chelsea. Plus, my department is filled with testosterone."

"It has something to do with your job though, doesn't it?" She surveyed his facial expressions and body movements. "What's her name?"

Onyx crossed his leg over the other. "You're not going to stop, are you?"

"No."

"You're about to be disappointed then because this story is extremely boring. The woman I saw has nothing to do with my job. I was a groomsman at a wedding not long ago and I saw a woman. Very attractive. Right as I was heading over to talk to her, someone tapped me on my shoulder. When I turned around, she was walking out the door. End of story."

"That's so sad," Chelsea fanned her eyes.

"Are you about to cry?" Phoenix watched her from the corner of his eye.

Trey responded for Chelsea, quoting what she'd repeatedly told him over the years. "She is having a healthy emotional response."

"Thank you, Trey."

Trey nodded and sat up with his cigar, looking at his feet. He looked around the room, at his family, and realized how much they cared about his well-being, just like Tristyn had. He took a deep breath. "I'm lost without her."

The crew connected gazes and Derrick opened his eyes. This was the moment they were waiting for.

"I don't know what to do. I feel powerless. She won't answer my calls or texts. I even sent a few social media messages and nothing. It's like she just wrote me off and never gave me another thought. And it sucks because now I know how it felt when I did that to her. Because of that, I wanna just sit here and not even try to get her back. I deserve this."

"Even if you deserve this, which you do, do you still wanna be with her?" Onyx asked.

"I always wanted to be with her. That's the one thing that's always been constant in my life, my love for her. Since the day I saw her in class I've only had eyes for her."

"That's beautiful," spoke Xavier. Although he stayed about his business, he looked forward to finding the love of his life.

"I just need her to hear me out. That's it. Then, if she still doesn't wanna be in a relationship, I'll deal. But to have it end like this, knowing she left based on something that isn't true, just hurts."

"What do you think you need to do to get her to listen to you?" Chelsea sat next to him.

"I don't know. She's so stubborn. And I've hurt her so many times I don't know if she'd listen to anything I said at this point."

"If we figured out how to get her to listen to you, could you take it from there?" Onyx crossed one leg over the other.

"Yeah."

"And you're sure you still wanna be with her?" Phoenix set his empty glass down.

"Without a doubt."

"Then I guess we're helping you get her to listen to you. Because you can't continue to live like this." Onyx surveyed the room.

Trey nodded slowly. "Y'all really think you can get her to hear me out?"

Onyx responded, "It's all about catering to why she hasn't listened to you yet. We figure out the why, we can figure out a way."

A smidge of hope bloomed in Trey's chest. "And then we can be together again."

"One struggle at a time," Chelsea patted Trey's knee.

"We got you, man. Between all of us, we'll figure it out and come up with a plan to get you two back together. You'd do anything to get Tristyn back?" Xavier confirmed.

"Anything."

"Like shower?" Derrick asked.

Chelsea threw a pillow at Derrick's head. "Too soon."

Derrick moved the pillow behind his head for additional support and closed his eyes again. "We were all thinking it."

"All right, then." Onyx stood up and stretched. In his line of work, there were nights where he got little to no sleep. He'd just come off an assignment and was exhausted. "Tomorrow we plan it out. For now, I'm heading to bed."

With them by his side, Trey felt like he had a shot. He just hoped they could pull off whatever plan they thought up. "Thank you, guys. I don't know what I'd do without our crew."

A variation of fist bumps, hugs, and shoulder squeezes ended their intervention until Trey's phone rang. "Tristyn."

Everyone stood there, staring him down, waiting for his next move. "You gonna answer it?" Chelsea asked.

Trey snapped out of it and picked it up. "Hey." His eyes went wide. "Yeah, I'd love to meet up and talk. You don't know how happy I am to hear you say that...Monday is good...See you then...Bye."

"Things are working out perfectly." Chelsea stood next to him, hands clasped underneath her chin.

"They are." He blew out a breath and looked into the faces of the family he'd forever be grateful for. "There's one more thing," Trey confessed.

The room went silent. Phoenix was the first to say something. "Spit it out. Between us all, we've seen or heard it all. Nothing you say will surprise us."

"I bought a ring."

Frozen in place, Xavier confirmed. "An engagement ring?"

"Yeah, I bought it before we split. I was waiting for the perfect time but this *may* be it."

Onyx's heavy hand on his shoulder relaxed Trey. "You wanna propose, too?"

"Yeah." Trey nodded his head, becoming more confident in his decision. He needed Tristyn to know that she was his all. "Yeah, I want to propose. I'm ready."

"Man," Derrick snickered and then flopped onto the couch. "How do you plan to propose when you don't even know if she'll take you back?"

Chelsea cut her eyes at Derrick. "Says the man who would propose to a married woman today, if he could."

Derrick closed his mouth and focused on the end of the game on TV.

Onyx checked his watch. "We have two days to get Trey ready and figure out a plan that assures Tristyn will get back with Trey *and* say yes. Everyone get some rest. The work starts tomorrow."

38

Let's Stay in Love

CURRENT DAY

Someone would feel her fury today. Tristyn didn't know whether it was the hormones or if everyone at her company had become an idiot over the weekend, but she was over it. And she was always hot. Georgia explained it was due to the excess blood volume but add in sore breasts, clumsiness, forgetfulness, and cravings, and she already couldn't wait to give birth. To top it off, Trey was meeting her for lunch, and she had to tell him she was pregnant. The thought of coparenting with a man she still loved, but hated just the same, worked her nerves.

And now she had to deal with this. She immediately walked back out of her office. Her hands landed with a thump on top of her secretary's desk. "Tell me why that woman is in my office."

The secretary, a young white man with small round glasses, a sweater vest, slacks, and hair gelled up and to the side, looked up from his phone. Andrew managed a smile, "She's your twelve-thirty."

Trey, not Chelsea, was supposed to be her twelve-thirty. To keep her blood pressure low, she mentally counted from one to five, then five to one. The thought of releasing her fury on Chelsea made her feel a little better.

When she marched back in her office, Chelsea held up her hands in a peace offering as soon as she saw Tristyn. "I know I'm the last person you wanna see but I have a gift for you."

Tristyn rested her weight on one leg and crossed her arms. "A gift? You think that I would want a gift from you?"

"Trust me, you want this gift." Chelsea handed Tristyn an envelope.

Tristyn debated walking it over to the shredder but curiosity was killing her. She snatched it from Chelsea's hands and tore open the thick, white envelope, eyes watering as she tried to make sense of the words. "This is a DNA test?" Chelsea nodded. "Between you and Trey?"

"Well, Derrick was also included but yes, it's a DNA test proving that there is a ninety-nine point seven percent chance that I am Trey and Derrick's half sibling. Trey was telling the truth. We all share the same father, David Dalton. When Daddy split with Trey and Derrick's mom, he met my mom and boom, I was born. Trey and Derrick didn't know our dad was alive until we were all much older."

Tristyn whispered, barely able to speak. "They thought he was dead."

"Yeah, unfortunately, that's what their mom told them. But Daddy got sick and wanted to make amends, so he asked me to reach out. I did and we were all able to reconnect before he died. All of this was going on while Trey was in college-his senior year."

Tristyn's hand flew to her mouth, and she gasped. "That's when things started going south between us."

Chelsea nodded, the memory of her father bringing her close to tears. "I can't speak for how or why he handled things the way he did, but he loves you so much and I know he regrets it."

Tristyn bit the inside of her cheek and nodded her understanding.

"It's really all an unfortunate series of events that led us here. And I'm really sorry we met in that manner but since Trey loves you so much, I know that you're a good person and I hope you can see that I'm a good person as well."

"I can see that now and I'm sorry, Chelsea. You caught me at a really vulnerable moment. I don't normally act like that." And pregnancy hormones were raging through her blood but that was neither here nor there. Right? Tristyn moved forward to give Chelsea a much needed hug.

"My brother is also a really good man who made some mistakes but I can tell you that after what happened, I doubt he'd ever make them again."

Chelsea offered a lighthearted chuckle that Tristyn returned. "I'd hope not."

"If it's all right, I'd like to build a relationship with you."

Tristyn thought for a moment, debating whether that would be feasible even if she weren't with Trey.

Chelsea added, "You don't know how hard it is being the only woman around all those Gotdamn Dalton men."

Tristyn released a laugh, finally able to genuinely smile. "Yes, I'd like that."

"I'm so happy to hear that." Chelsea wiped a tear from the corner of her eye before it dropped. "You know, you make my brother so happy. He's truly lost without you. I don't want you to feel ambushed or pressured, and it's up to you, but it would make my life so much easier if you made up. And if you don't wanna make up with him, it would make my day if you could just hear him out. He misses you."

The floor held Tristyn's attention but finally she confessed. "I miss him, too. God, I miss his arrogant ass. I'll hear him out. I actually called him over the weekend so we could set up a time to talk."

"I was hoping you'd say that."

Tristyn checked her watch. "He was supposed to be here already but I guess he's running late. No surprise there that he hasn't called."

The biggest grin spread across Chelsea's face. She grabbed Tristyn's hand. "Come with me."

Andrew met them at his desk. "Follow me, Tristyn."

Tristyn looked between Andrew and Chelsea in wonder. "What's going on?"

Chelsea couldn't keep the cheesy grin off her face. "Just follow Andrew. I'll see you in a little bit."

Tristyn did as told and followed Andrew to one of the executive conference rooms. When Andrew knocked on the door a voice she recognized responded. "Come in."

She fell into the room and practically burst into tears. Inside, the lengthy oak conference table was covered with an assortment of flowers and next to it, her mom and dad. She was so happy to see them that she ran into their arms. "What are you doing here? It's so good to see you." She hugged them again. "And why are all these flowers here? They're all so beautiful. You brought me flowers?"

Her father, a stocky man who held the same skin tone as her, rubbed her upper back. "Based on your reaction, I wish I could say we thought up this idea to surprise you with flowers, but it wasn't us." Tristyn's eyes were wide with confusion. "We got a call yesterday for a large order from your honey, Trey."

"We sure did," her mom, a practically identical version of her, but with darker skin, added. "That's a good man, Princess, as he calls you."

"Can't say I love that nickname," her dad snorted, "but it'll do. Where was I?"

"The call," her mom prompted.

"Right. Trey called us and asked us to bring down these bouquets. Each of these holds significance."

Tristyn looked at the table to try and figure it out but as far as she could see, they were just random bouquets. Beautiful, but random.

Tristyn's mom patted her dad's shirt pocket. "You wrote it down, get your note."

"Right." Her dad pulled a small piece of paper from his shirt. "These bouquets represent all the flowers Trey has bought you over the years." Her dad ran down the bouquets from left to right. "The red roses were the first flowers he ever bought you and he gave them to you on your first date. You were so surprised that you gave him a kiss on his cheek. The bouquet with the pink lilies is from the time when you agreed to be his girlfriend. The sunflowers were what he gave you when you two passed your English class. The other red roses are the bouquet he gave you when he met back up with you again. The calla lilies and white roses were what he brought when he visited after you visited him in Columbus."

Her dad squinted at the paper. "Can you read that honey?" Her mom shook her head, so he put the paper back into his pocket. "Well, there goes the explanation for the rest of them. But I do know that those other tulip and sunflower bouquets are there for a reason."

Tristyn laughed and shook her head. "That last bouquet holds one type of every flower we had on hand. That bouquet represents all the flowers that he sent you *just because* while you were together."

It was all so overwhelming. Trey had remembered every bouquet he ever gave her. She felt special and extremely blessed. Her mom handed her a tissue that she used to blot her eyes and blow her nose. On her other side, her dad said, "Me and Trey had a long talk and I'll tell you right now, I like him. I don't have any reason to doubt that his intentions with you are pure, but I'll tell you this. Stay with a man long enough and he'll prove to you that he's not a God, but a human. Humans make mistakes all the time. If you don't believe it just ask your mom how many I've made throughout the years. What matters is that I've righted those mistakes and Trey is willing to do that as well."

Tristyn nodded, dabbing her nose once more. Her mom took her hand. "I'm to escort you to the next room."

"There's more?"

"Sure is. How do you like this grand apology?"

"I'm blown away."

"Good," she patted the top of Tristyn's hand.

Her dad stopped them on the way out the door, lowering his voice. "Look, like I said, men are imperfect but if he hurts you like he did before, you let me know. I'm old now. Remind him of my rifle. I don't mind spending the last of my days in jail for you."

Her mom gently prodded him. "Honey, go back in the conference room."

Derrick met Tristyn at the door of the next conference room and pulled her into a big hug. She wanted to scream. "You're here, too? I missed you! How's it going with Georgia and the twins?"

"We'll talk about that later. For now, I'd like to introduce you to a few people." He opened the door and three large men stood up to welcome her. "These are my cousins, Onyx, Phoenix, and Xavier. Their dad is Uncle Wayne."

Each nodded as she stepped further into the room, waving. "It's so nice to meet you all. I love Uncle Wayne," she gushed. "He's such a character."

"She definitely met Pops." The three chuckled.

Derrick continued, "One more thing Trey regrets is not introducing the most important person in his life, you, to the rest of the most important people in his life, the Gotdamn Dalton Crew."

"Y'all need another name."

Derrick shook his head. "Not happening."

The deep voice speaking caught her attention, Onyx was looking directly at her. "It's nice to finally meet you." He pulled her into a hug.

Derrick continued, "From now on, there won't be anything that you can't ask Trey. No secrets. No nothing. What you see is what you get."

"And to be with him means you gotta take us as a package deal." Phoenix smiled from the side of his mouth before hugging her. "I hope you're ready to get to know us, and Chelsea, too."

"I can't wait." Tristyn laughed.

Xavier stepped forward with a medium sized box in his hand and gave her a big bear hug. He held out his hand. "A gift for you, from Trey."

After opening it, laughter bubbled up until she couldn't hold it in. Inside the box was an individual bottle of Mott's Apple Juice with a note. *I promise to share my family and my apple juice. ~Trey*

"That's how you know it's real." Derrick sat in an empty chair, crossing one leg over the other. "He don't share his apple juice with nobody."

*   *   *   *   *   *   *

One look at Trey and you could tell he was confident, suave, and at the top of his game. He was also sick to his stomach. There were two things he could not do right now, stop sweating and stop pacing. Today was the day he was asking for forgiveness and proposing to Tristyn. With the help of the Gotdamn Dalton Crew, the plan they set in motion was going perfectly even though it was all last minute.

Chelsea coordinated with Georgia to get Tristyn's final present delivered. Xavier had driven back to Cleveland to help Tristyn's parents bring down all the flowers. Phoenix had cut Trey's hair and given him the best line up he ever had, and had gotten his skin back up to par. Onyx coordinated with Bob to make sure they were allowed to take over their office building. And Derrick had purchased the perfect outfit for Trey.

He'd been sitting out of sight near Tristyn's office but was getting antsy. By his calculations, they should've made it back and he started to think that something in the plan went awry. Trey was about to sit but his breath caught when he turned around. He had to catch himself from running to her and holding her forever just to make sure she never left his side again. She remained the most important person in his life, and he couldn't see his life without her in it. He wanted it all. To live with and to love her, forever. He hadn't realized that he missed her so much until tears formed in the corner of his eyes. He quickly used his thumb to wipe them away and prayed for composure.

He stood in his tan slacks, debating removing his blue blazer, but with his nerves having activated his sweaty armpits, he didn't want to appear as disheveled as he felt.

Trey watched Bob lead Tristyn back to her office. The closer she got the more anxious he became to hold her, to know her again.

Tristyn had a signature walk, especially when she wore heels. It was one that shifted her weight from side to side right as her heel hit the ground. It was similar to a model on the runway except she allowed her hips to completely swing, utterly aware of watching eyes on her backside. Her thin waistline vibrated as her breasts jiggled under her top with each step.

Mid-sentence with Bob, she smoothed her hair out of her face and noticed Trey standing in front of her office door.

"I'll leave you two to talk." Bob bowed his head and stepped away.

"Hi, Trey," she stopped in front of him, her perfume permeating his nose.

"Hey, Tristyn, thanks for agreeing to meet me."

"Trey, this is beautiful and a hell of an apology."

"I have one more gift for you. Can we go in your office?"

"Of course." Tristyn led him inside and shut the door behind him.

Before he realized what she was doing she flung her arms around his neck. He savored her scent, the softness of her curves, the smooth skin under her clothes. He was all hers and she was all his. He was getting his happily ever after with the woman he'd always loved. His lips gently kissed her forehead and then he rested his against hers and whispered, "I missed you."

She melted into his embrace. "I missed you, too."

"I got my princess back?"

"I'm back, for good."

Trey yelped and picked her up, swinging her around, eliciting a round of giggles from Tristyn. "You don't know how good that makes me feel." He set her down. "I have one last present for you." He handed over a plain paper bag.

She playfully wiggled as she opened the gift. "Whenever we have our next fight you'll never be able to..." Tristyn gasped as she pulled out the white leather Prada bag she'd been dreaming about. Then she screamed and ran in place. "I can't believe you got me this bag. Did Georgia tell you I wanted it?" She spun around with closed eyes and when she stopped spinning, she noticed Trey on one knee. "Trey?"

"Open the bag, Tristyn." Watching her open the bag was the worst agony he'd ever experienced. Her hands trembled and he wished she'd hurry up so he could hear her answer. He was walking out on the highest limb known and although they were back together, there was no guarantee that she would say yes.

Her fingers trembled so badly he relieved her of the duty of opening up the blue Tiffany box. Inside, sat a brilliant round one and a half carat diamond. Their eyes connected and Trey prayed that she would say yes. The speech he practiced left his brain and all he managed to say was, "I was a mess without you. My work suffered. I didn't shower. It was then that I realized that I've been out of whack since I left you in college and I can't live that way anymore. I don't want to. You make everything make sense. Tristyn, will you marry me?"

Tristyn's features went from soft to confused to scared. "I need to tell you something first."

Trey's heart threatened to beat out of his chest. "Tristyn, what's wrong?"

"Get up, Trey, we need to talk." A light smile graced her face. She removed her jacket, placing it on the back of her desk chair. Her cheeks were flushed. "I, uh, woo," she fanned herself again.

"Everything all right?" Trey watched her closely.

"Yes, well no, well yes. The reason I reached out is because..." She fanned herself again. "I'm, uh, I'm pregnant."

"Come again?"

"With your baby. I'm pregnant with your baby."

Trey looked down at her stomach, looking for some sort of evidence that his seed was growing inside her belly. "Pregnant?"

"Yes," she nodded.

"And it's mine," he repeated more for him than for her.

"Yes."

"How far along?"

"I don't know yet."

Trey's mouth dropped open. "Well, I wasn't expecting this news. We were careful. Well maybe except the first couple times. Damn, the whole night I was in it without a condom. It didn't even cross my mind to put on a condom." Trey released an awkward chuckle. "But that was so long ago so that means you recently got pregnant? You weren't on birth control?"

"I was."

"And you're sure you're pregnant?"

"Four pregnancy tests from three different brands can't all be wrong."

"Wow." Trey dropped his head to the palms of his hands and blew out a breath. "This is unbelievable," he muttered. "The plot thickens."

"Tell me about it." Tears shone in her eyes. "I just felt like you should know before I said yes just in case that changed you wanting to marry me."

"You were going to say yes?"

"How could I ever say no to you?"

Trey's chest rose and fell more deeply. He had led them on many missions while dating, most fun, some mysterious, all meaningful. He led their relationship in all ways and now he was ready to lead them into marriage and parenthood. "Then I'm gonna ask you again." He dropped to one knee once more. "Tristyn Miller, will you walk by my side as my wife and the mother of my child? Will you marry me?"

Tristyn burst into tears. The words left her choked up so that all she could do was nod.

Trey sprung to his feet, lifting her off the ground. He wiped the tears from her cheeks, before wiping his. He moaned as soon as their lips touched. Tristyn pulled him in tighter. Their lips mashed together, moving in sync, her breasts pressed against his chest, Trey finally felt complete.

"Let's go tell everyone our good news." Outside her office, her coworkers, parents, and The Gotdamn Daltons had gathered and cheered as soon as they exited. When the applause died down, Trey took her hand in his and Tristyn announced that there would be a new addition to the Dalton Crew.

"Trey got that magic sperm. Got her pregnant already." Derrick was immediately elbowed in his side by Onyx. Phoenix and Xavier snickered.

Chelsea immediately ran over and hugged them both. "It feels so good to be a family."

EPILOGUE

PART II (ON THE RUN)

CURRENT DAY

"I'd like to make a toast to Mr. and Mrs. Trey Dalton." Xavier arose from the oversized booth and stepped to the side where he looked into the eyes of Derrick, Georgia, Aiyanna, Tristyn, Trey, Chelsea, and Phoenix. Onyx had called earlier in the day, apologizing for not making it after a new case was called in.

In full celebration mode, they had just left Tristyn and Trey's courthouse wedding, and were now enjoying a simple reception dinner in a private room at Xavier's lounge. Tomorrow, Tristyn and Trey were off to Zanzibar for a combination baby and honeymoon for two weeks.

Everyone raised their glasses while Tristyn raised a bottle of water. Now six months pregnant, she was proudly sporting a belly bump and each time she moved, Trey jumped to his feet to assist, much to Tristyn's chagrin.

Xavier continued, "This couple was destined to be together from the first time Trey saw Tristyn in their class. I think we can all agree that we're happy they're finally together. Now we don't have to listen to him groan about how much he misses her every year." Everyone nodded and then laughed, except Tristyn, who looked at Trey with questioning eyes.

"Congratulations to you two. You'll do great things together and baby Dalton is already blessed. I wish you..." Xavier paused midsentence when a woman walked into his lounge, catching his eye. They all turned to see what he was looking at, so he hurriedly finished. "Success and happiness! I wish you that. Cheers!" Meanwhile, Xavier watched as the woman made her way through the crowd, her full-bodied confidence leading the way.

"Cheers!" Phoenix initiated the clinking of glasses around the booth.

Trey leaned over, resting his palm on Tristyn's belly. "I'm the luckiest man in here tonight." His lips gently touched Tristyn's.

"Yes, you are." Tristyn smiled but then caught sight of Derrick's sad face. "I hope they work it out."

"They'll be fine," Trey assured her. "But let's not worry about Derrick and Georgia. This is our night. Our celebration."

"You sound so sure that they'll be okay."

"I know my brother."

Beside Tristyn, Aiyanna gasped. "It's him."

She looked to where Aiyanna's gaze had landed. "You know Onyx?"

"Onyx?" Aiyanna's face scrunched up. "I'm talking about the guy walking over here. That's the guy from the park."

Tristyn's mouth dropped open as she made the connection. "Are you kidding me? Aiyanna, that's Onyx, Trey's cousin."

Trey looked between the three. "What did I miss?"

Aiyanna smoothed her short hair down, hoping she didn't have any fly-aways. Inadvertently, she pulled the corner of her bottom lip into her mouth as she watched him approach.

When Onyx spotted Aiyanna, his walk slowed, processing the face of the woman in the booth. Ever so slowly, a smile lifted, exposing a dimple on his left cheek. When he reached the table, everyone greeted him, but his eyes never left Aiyanna's face.

Finally, Tristyn introduced the two, and then turned to Trey to explain the park situation.

Onyx stood at the end of the table, eyeing Aiyanna. "Nice to meet you, officially."

Aiyanna shook his hand. "Yes, it's nice to finally put a name to a face, Onyx."

WriteAndVibe
PUBLISHING

About Vibes: We are an independent publishing company that believes writers should only have to worry about writing. Meaning, you write your book, we'll do the rest.

To join our mailing list or to learn more about us, our authors, and their books, please visit us at

Writeandvibe.com | Fb & IG @writeandvibe

ABOUT THE AUTHOR

Chichima Cherry resides in Cleveland, Ohio, with her husband and kids, where she writes *real life with a scoop of spice.* Her passion for romance and writing was passed down through her late mother and grandmother, and she loves creating characters with true to life issues. In addition to writing fiction, she writes children's books under the pen name of Karen Mae, and runs writer's classes. In her free time she enjoys reading, baking, puzzling, and chilling.